Also by J. P. Smith

The Man from Marseille

Body and Soul

The Blue Hour

The Discovery of Light

Breathless

Airtight

THE DROWNING

A NOVEL

J. P. Smith

Published by Sourcebooks Landmark, an imprint of Sourcebooks, Inc.
P.O. Box 4410, Naperville, Illinois 60563-4410
(630) 961-3900
Fax: (630) 961-2168
sourcebooks.com

Library of Congress Cataloging-in-Publication Data

Names: Smith, J. P.
Title: The drowning / J. P. Smith.
Description: Naperville, Illinois : Sourcebooks Landmark, [2019]
Identifiers: LCCN 2017061738 | (softcover : acid-free paper)
Subjects: LCSH: Life change events--Fiction. | GSAFD: Suspense fiction.
Classification: LCC PS3569.M53744 D76 2019 | DDC 813/.54--dc23 LC record available at https://lccn.loc.gov/2017061738

Printed and bound in Canada.
MBP 10 9 8 7 6 5 4 3 2 1

For Sophie

You could see shapes against the firelight. They never sleep. They wander lost through their own narrative. They are night's children.

—Eoin McNamee, *Orchid Blue*

—

PICTURE THIS: A STILL, STARLIT AUGUST NIGHT, AS warm and clear as it had been all day and the day before and the same as it will be tomorrow. An open field, surrounded by pine woods so dense and dark that the seam between sky and earth has vanished. Soon, the campers will be packing their T-shirts and shorts, their tennis racquets and baseball gloves and bags full of dirty laundry, and heading home to New York, to Connecticut, to New Jersey and beyond.

Campfires light the faces of the boys as they sit in circles: the younger ones toward the center of the field, the older campers by the edge of it, nearer the woods. Dinner—hot dogs on sticks cooked over open flames, potatoes baked in foil among the coals, marshmallows blackening on twigs—is over. The fires move from glow into fade into cinders and, in just a few minutes, into ash as, pacing the perimeter of the circles, the counselors tell the same story they've recited from one year to the next, quietly and reverentially, as though it were a secret meant to be kept forever. A tale that was by now as woven into the camp's culture as the songs they sang in the social hall—odes to the outdoors, to teamwork, to Echo Lake and the hills beyond. The boys stare into the dying embers, watching the words come to life or keeping their eyes shut as though wishing camp were already over and they were home, where nothing bad could ever reach them.

"One night, every seven years since Camp Waukeelo was founded in 1937," one of the counselors begins, "long after lights out, a local man, John Otis, would sneak into the camp through the woods behind the bunks and take one of the younger boys." He falls silent, the better to let his words take root in the boys' minds. "Townsfolk said that John was someone who wouldn't stand out in a crowd, just a guy of average height and weight, but"—he pauses a moment—"with the eyes of a dead man. When you looked into them, you felt the temperature drop."

Another counselor is deeper into the story as he walks behind his circle of campers. "...because the seven- and eight- and nine-year-olds—you know who you are—are easy to grab. Easy to silence. Easy to make disappear..."

A third is saying, "...so the first to vanish was in July 1944, wartime, on a warm night just like this one." A few of the youngest campers try to stifle their crying. The counselor goes on. "The next to disappear was seven years later, in 1951—in fact, on this very date."

A fourth counselor says that John Otis was always watching from the hills behind the bunks, observing the boys line up for the morning flag-raising or jumping into the lake off the dock, deciding which one he would take next. "He might even be out there now, in the woods," the counselor said, and eight pairs of eyes looked up. "Watching. Thinking. Making his choice."

Apart from the counselors' quiet voices and the crackling of the campfires, there is nothing but silence. The campers are already wrapped in narrative, ensnared by words, at the mercy of their imaginations.

"He always goes for the loner," another counselor is saying, and some of the boys look around, wondering which of them that might be. "You know who I mean...the kid who doesn't really participate, who keeps to himself." A few of the campers look shyly down, because they know he's describing them.

The story always ends the next morning when the other campers in the boy's bunk notice his empty bed and wonder where he has gone, leaving no trace or clue behind. Had he been murdered, or was he with all the others who'd been taken by the man who lived high up in the hills in a place none of them had ever seen?

Over time, the legend of John Otis had gathered more details, and these, in turn, were passed along year after year to the campers. It was said that something very bad had happened to John late in the 1930s, when he was growing up in the house built by his father. His mother had disappeared soon after her only son was born, and there was talk of an older sister, though as there was no record of her birth, it was assumed she was delivered at home. And probably even died there.

One day John was at school, a withdrawn and uncooperative and sullen child, talking back to his teachers and picking fights, and the next he was absent, as he was the next day and the day after and then forever. Any attempts by law-enforcement personnel or school administrators to reach his house were met by a pair of watchdogs and, on more than a few occasions, John's father in the doorway, shotgun in hand.

It was felt in the community that what had befallen young

John was no longer of interest. He was either dead or being raised outside of society by his father, whose reputation for belligerence and outright violence was well known in the Berkshires. People steered clear of the old man on his rare appearances in the neighboring towns, where he'd buy slabs of meat and bottles of cheap whiskey, along with cases of baby food. After several years had passed, when his father must have been long dead and everyone presumed his son was also gone, John Otis drifted into a kind of malevolent afterlife, a rumor trapped among the hills surrounding the lake. Sometimes campers claimed to have seen him as an adult, in a rowboat in the middle of the lake at sunset, looking their way from the shadow beneath the brim of his hat. Or standing by the edge of the baseball field, among the trees, watching and smoking; vanishing when they turned to alert a counselor.

The sound of rustling in the woods behind the bunks was John Otis; the spark of fireflies was John's eyes. The very thought of him meant he was right behind you.

Within the fictions told and retold, embellished over the years at campfires and in bunks late at night, John Otis was even more vividly alive. If questioned by a camper who had heard the story the year before, counselors would only say that they had miscounted, that *this* was the seventh year.

The same names were repeated. There was Scott Gardner, the kid with the spiky black hair. Seven years before Scott disappeared, Jake Kaufman had been lifted from his bed in the middle of the night, and none of the others in his bunk saw or heard a thing, though in the morning, as the counselors savored in the telling, his bed had been made as neatly as he had left it the day before, except that an antique doll lay in his place, both its eyes gouged out. In early August of 1972, Billy Olsen had chased a ball into the heavily wooded area known as the Pines and never returned. Were they kept prisoner by the man? Tortured? Murdered? Were they there still, their cries unheard as John Otis descended the stairs to the dirt cellar of his ramshackle house?

Sometimes, the counselors would show the boys photos of the allegedly missing campers, in the dusty, leather-bound books kept on a shelf in the social hall, the name of the camp leafed in gold on the covers. There was the pale, blond seven-year-old Henry Cassidy, summer of '44, the faded one sitting in the front row, looking a bit lost. There was chubby, smiling Aaron Blume who vanished two days after the photo was taken in August 1958. And skinny nine-year-old Richard Ivory, all angles and sunken cheeks, who went missing in 1965.

Now it's time to go. The boys are silent as they follow the beams of their counselors' flashlights on the path through the woods back to their bunks. And when they do speak, it's quietly and with wonder, because fear has been given a name and a reality all its own.

"Do you believe any of that?" one of the eight-year-olds asks, and the boy walking beside him, Joey Proctor, says he thinks it might be true. The next night, Joey won't be there, and would never be seen again.

One day, many years later, a counselor would point to Joey Proctor's face in the camp photo and tell the boys about John Otis and how one day Joey was there, and the next he wasn't.

Joey had become part of a legend, and that was where he lived from the day he disappeared until the morning, twenty-one years later, when it seemed he had come back to life.

Part One

1

ON THE FIRST DAY OF CAMP IN THE SUMMER THAT would be his last, Joey Proctor's parents drove him up in his father's Mercedes, stopping for lunch just over the Massachusetts border at a diner called Little Dee's. The sign above the entrance must have been there for thirty or more years: a smiling young girl in a gingham apron carrying a tray heaped with food. For most of the ride, Joey had been trying to pay attention to a book he was reading in the back seat. Now that they were less than an hour away, his stomach tightened and his mouth went dry.

Camp was an abstract notion, like death or self or being grown-up: to Joey an unimaginable thing, without dimension, a word that meant nothing but a state of being he was about to embark upon. All he knew was that his parents had been fighting a lot lately, and they said they needed some time to work things out—which meant time without him. He was being cast adrift. Cut from the family equation. It had all happened very quickly.

He stared at the menu without really reading it. When the waitress came with her little pad and stubby pencil and great big painted smile, he dithered and then ordered a cheeseburger and fries and orange juice, as he wasn't allowed to have soda. He wasn't even hungry. His head ached, and what he'd begun to feel as they drove out of the city, this sense of unease and doubt, had deepened over the two-hour drive into a hollow ache of dread. While they waited for their food, his parents said nothing, as if they had never seen each other before, like people on the subway, looking anywhere but into the eyes of a stranger. Instead, they gazed out through the window or at the framed pictures on the walls: woodland scenes and waterfalls and a photo of Teddy Roosevelt in his Rough Rider hat, with his great big cowboy grin pointing at something.

His father went to the bathroom while his mother abruptly stood and, taking her cellphone from her bag, walked out to the parking lot. Joey watched as she gestured in the air, as though trying to stir it a little, and then touched her forehead, as if thinking hard about something. She put a fist on her hip and smiled in her crooked way, one side of her mouth higher than the other, and then slowly moved the toe of her shoe in the gravel, drawing an arc in the world, a memory from a career long since abandoned. Like his father, she was something of a mystery. They were two people so completely at odds with each other that, within the family, Joey had become an observer instead of a participant. A stranger in his own household. Someone suspended between two cliffs, always about to fall.

There was a man sitting at the next booth in a hat that said *John Deere*. He smiled at Joey and kept nodding, as if agreeing with a voice inside his head. He sipped his coffee and then got up and walked over until he was standing over Joey. He said, "All alone, little guy?"

"My mom's outside. My dad's—"

"Yeah, yeah, I get it." The man looked out the window,

then put his hands on the table and leaned in close. His hands were all knuckles, red and raw, and one of his nails had been hammered into black. "Bet you're going to that camp, right?"

Joey nodded.

"They all stop here. Little boys. Big boys. Fathers. Mothers. Sisters even, sometimes. That your mother out there?" Joey nodded again. "Frisky little thing, isn't she," he said. "How old are you, anyway?"

"Eight and a half."

The man stood upright and, looking down at Joey, just smiled as if he were considering a big meal made for him to devour with his grubby, wounded fingers. Joey's father returned to the table, and the man left without even looking back. Joey watched as the man paid his bill at the register, shared a few words with the woman who handed him his change, and walked outside. Passing Joey's mother, the man said something, she swung her head around, and then he got into his pickup truck and drove away with a smile on his face.

"What'd that guy want?" his father said.

Joey shrugged. "Nothing."

"Nobody wants nothing."

2

JOEY WOULD SEE THE MAN IN THE HAT A FEW TIMES at the camp, mowing the baseball field or picking up fallen branches after the big rainstorm in late July. He seemed to recognize Joey only once when, heading for his truck near the arts-and-crafts cabin, he'd stopped and smiled at him. He put two fingers beneath his eyes and then pointed them at Joey. The gesture meant nothing to Joey, and when he got back to his bunk and looked in the mirror in the bathroom, he tried it himself. Because it still didn't make any sense, he thought it might deal with something dark, occult, inevitably forbidden.

His father said, "Your mother on the phone again?"

"I guess." She was still outside, rubbing her head, no longer smiling. Like she was thinking hard about something, trying to squeeze out an idea or a word.

But his father smiled to himself as if he knew exactly who was on the other end. He shook his head and said to himself, "Man oh man," and then Joey's mother returned and their food arrived. His father said, "That couldn't wait?"

"You don't even know what it was about, who I was talking to."

"I can guess."

As always, they ate in silence, and when it was time to go

the silence didn't end, just like clocks kept running after you went to sleep.

Half an hour later, his father turned onto an unmarked road that seemed to go on forever. A dirt road leading off from it had a hand-painted sign hanging from a chain that read *KEEP AWAY!!! ENTRUDERS WILL BE SHOT!!!* They drove a bit more until the trees seemed to part and they could see the camp unfold before them, and then a woman's voice said, "You have reached your destination." There were lots of cars parked along the road and on the grass by the entrance, cars with New York and Connecticut and New Jersey plates, and an older boy came up to the Mercedes with a clipboard and checked off Joey's name. He said, "Bunk twelve," and he pointed in the direction of it. They could see the lake, deep blue beneath a bright summer sky, bluer than the sky in New York. Bluer than blue, deeper than deep.

As they walked to the bunk, his mother said, "Looks nice." She turned to Joey. "So what do you think?"

"It's okay."

"Just okay?"

"He hasn't been here two minutes, and you want him to form an opinion?" his father said, and Joey prayed they wouldn't begin arguing—not here, not now. When Joey once asked his mother why his father was always angry, all she said was that he'd been having a hard time lately, what with the economy the way it was, and besides, money was beginning to get a little tight. A few days earlier, Joey had heard his father on the phone with his lawyer, Leonard Rubicon, and he was arguing quietly, raising his fist in the air and then lowering it.

Raising it and lowering it. And then he shut the door to his study and raised his voice even more.

They lived on Ninetieth and Park, and his father drove the Mercedes and always dressed in suits. His mother had once been a ballet dancer who'd retired when she was twenty-seven after she'd been injured. There were a few framed photos of her on the walls of the apartment: his mother *en pointe*, as one swan among many in *Swan Lake*. She seemed to him completely different from the woman who lived with them: there, in the photos, she was a mystery. Her face was expressionless, her arms and legs long and slender, reaching, stretching, as though something unseen was pulling her away. When he looked at the photos, he sensed that people had a whole different life from the one he knew. That inside her, at this moment, was this other person, her arm aloft, balanced on the toes of one foot.

Now his mother restored furniture in a studio she rented in the East Village, though lately there had been fewer clients calling for appointments. His father said the economy was bad for everyone, even the multimillionaires with their Chippendale chairs and Regency whatevers. A few weeks after his father had the conversation with his lawyer and then his accountant, men with white gloves came and packed a few of the family's paintings into wooden containers. Joey's family no longer flew down to the islands during the Christmas break at school, and his father had had to begin taking commercial flights instead of corporate jets. Similar things had happened to others, his mother told him—they weren't alone in the world. When all the money ran out, Joey wondered, what would become of them?

Three of the kids in his bunk already knew one another,

and started roughhousing the moment they got together. They pushed each other around on the lawn in front of the cabin with its screens and front porch and the woods behind it. When they talked, it was almost in a secret code, and one of them called one of the others *You bitch*, though none of the parents noticed it. When the counselor, Steve, introduced him to the other boys, Joey knew he would never fit in. He wasn't like them. He was small and looked younger than eight, while they seemed more like the older kids at school with all their swagger and mayhem.

His mother had bought him a camp blanket with red and yellow stripes from a store in the Village near her studio. The other kids, Joey saw, had plain blankets, gray or blue, or fancier ones with logos of sports teams, and he was embarrassed that his stood out as something different. He was sure he saw one of the boys point at it and laugh. Unfolding it for the first time, Joey's mother made his bed for him, though Steve told him that beds in camp were called bunks, just like the building they were in was called a bunk, and that starting the next morning, it would be Joey's responsibility to make his own bunk, complete with hospital corners. *The next morning* sounded to him like a foreign country with its own language and customs. That he could survive that long in the camp seemed impossible.

Steve showed him the corners on his own bunk, and then pulled one corner out and made it all over again so Joey would know how to do it, though he'd never made a bed in his life. Their housekeeper, Daniela, always did it, just like she always cleaned the apartment, washed the dishes, did the grocery shopping, and made Joey a snack when he returned from school each day. She won't last either, he'd heard his father say only the week before, and, in fact, a week after Joey was dropped off at camp, she was let go.

The kid in the bunk next to Joey's had come with only his mother, and he looked like he'd been crying all the way up to camp. The boy's mother talked to Joey's mother, and Joey heard the other woman say that her husband, who had taught at Barnard, had died earlier that year of cancer. When he heard this, Joey looked at the kid's mother and could see it in her eyes: the sadness, the missing. The boy was named Greg, and he was from the other side of Central Park from Joey. Maybe they'd become friends. But, it turned out, Greg wouldn't last a week. He was too homesick to stay on past Thursday, tired of being picked on by the three boys who already knew each other, and his mother came to bring him home, after which the mattress on his bunk was folded over, as though instead of simply leaving camp, he had died where he had slept.

3

ON THE DAY JOEY PROCTOR DISAPPEARED, FIVE weeks after the opening day, Steve asked him how things were going as they walked back from the dining hall after lunch. He spoke quietly, the words belonging to them alone. Joey told him things were okay, and Steve reminded him that he'd done really well that summer: he'd put up with the problem with redheaded Ethan Daniels, who'd begun picking on him the day after camp started, but Joey knew that was thanks to Steve, who had had a long talk with Ethan and told him to leave Joey alone. Or else. It was the *Or else* that had secured Joey's trust in Steve.

It was twenty minutes or so before rest hour would begin, when the boys were able to read on their bunks or write letters home. Joey wanted to write every day, but had nothing new to say. He'd made a few friends, he enjoyed some of the activities, he liked his counselor, but his letters would also include lies, just to make his parents think he was having a good time, so they didn't have something else to fight about.

Alex, the swimming counselor, walked briskly by and said hi. Though Steve was smiling, he seemed pained when he saw Alex, as though he'd been stung by a wasp. As if Joey had been given a glimpse of another Steve. Steve asked Joey, "Do you like swimming?"

Joey put his hands in his pockets and looked up at Steve. "Sometimes."

"Do you like Alex?" He must have read Joey's expression. He laughed. He said, "Guess not."

"He's okay." Joey didn't know exactly why he didn't like Alex Mason, but he knew it was more about his fear of the water than anything more personal. He looked at Steve. "What do you do when you're not a counselor?"

Steve laughed again. "Mostly go to school. I'm studying to be a lawyer. At Columbia University."

Joey smiled. That meant they were both New Yorkers, and it lifted his mood: he had a counselor, but now he also had a friend. Joey told him where he lived, and Steve said that he lived in an apartment in Morningside Heights, near the university.

They walked past a group of kids playing Frisbee, and Joey paused a moment to watch a kid snatch it out of the air.

"Ever play Frisbee?"

Joey shrugged. "Sometimes. Just not at home."

"With the other kids in the bunk?" Steve said.

Joey shrugged again. "I guess."

The Frisbee drifted far beyond the kids waiting for it. Steve reached out and grabbed it, then told Joey to run back. He sent it aloft, and it landed gently in Joey's hand. Steve smiled, and Joey went to return it to the other boys.

"Looking forward to going home soon?" his counselor asked as they resumed their walk.

Joey's mood darkened all over again. "Yeah. Maybe."

And Joey started telling him things, how his parents fought all the time, and that it was really, really hard for him, and and

and, because the words just kept coming out, the things his parents said to each other, the heavy silences at mealtimes.

"Do you have a sister or brother you can talk to?"

Joey shook his head. "Just me." He was embarrassed to feel tears come to his eyes.

Steve considered this and nodded a little, a bit like the guy in the hat in the diner. He asked how that made him feel, being alone like that and having to hear his parents arguing, and Joey said it made him feel like he had no family, nothing to come home to. Exactly how he put it: *nothing to come home to.* Sometimes at home he felt as if he'd done something horribly wrong, something no one had warned him about or even mentioned to him, and that his parents were angry with him and not just each other for all the unhappiness they felt. Steve put his arm around Joey and gave him a kind of half hug, and then took his arm away and said that was tough, that he hoped it would get better, and just hearing Steve say that made Joey feel that things might just get better, that when camp was over in a week, when his stuff would be packed up and loaded on a bus that would take him back to New York, he'd discover that his parents were friends again, that they loved each other and were happy to see him and sorry to have left him there all that time. Now he was looking forward to going home, because there was a chance that everything would be just as it should be and not like it always had been. Sometimes you just had to believe in magic.

The night before this conversation was the night of the campfires, where everyone heard about John Otis, and Joey asked Steve if the story was true. Steve said it was just an old legend. And, besides, if John Otis was going to take anyone, and Steve lowered his voice and smiled, he would probably take Ethan Daniels, an answer that made Joey laugh out loud. Steve asked what activity was next for him after rest hour, and Joey said it was swimming.

Below, by the waterfront, Joey could see Alex in his blue bathing trunks diving into the deep water. He watched as Alex's arms lifted out of the lake, smoothly and effortlessly, and then he disappeared for several seconds until he bobbed up by the raft, his reddish-blond hair a contrast to the dark water. He hoisted himself up and sat there, looking up at the camp, at the boys playing Frisbee, and, more distantly, at Steve and Joey.

Like most of the counselors, Alex was a college student, and sometimes, instead of wearing a Camp Waukeelo T-shirt with its depiction of a boy paddling a canoe on the lake, as everyone there did, he wore a Sigma Alpha Epsilon shirt with its sleeves cut off, as he had been earlier that day when he was having lunch in the dining hall a few tables away from Joey's. His eyes had briefly met Joey's, and they'd registered nothing at all. Joey would always remember that look. Right up until the moment Alex swam for shore and left him to die.

4

IT WAS ALEX MASON'S FIRST YEAR WORKING AT THE camp, as it was Joey's as a camper, and it would be the last for both of them. Until that day, those who were already strong swimmers could go in the deep water, while the rest were restricted to the intermediate section with the security of their kickboards. But on that day, everything changed.

"Okay, camp's almost over, guys, and it's time to move into the big leagues," Alex said, and Joey noticed the big grin on redheaded Ethan's face, as if he knew what was about to happen.

"So line up along the dock. Right here, okay? You, too, Joey, come on."

Only twenty minutes earlier Joey had been writing a letter to his parents, saying how excited he was to come home, because after his conversation with Steve, he felt for the first time in a long time that everything was going to be okay. That he would be happy. That his parents would be happy to see him, and that they would all be happy together.

Joey wanted to ask Alex what was about to happen, but something inside him was already saying it. He felt suddenly very cold, even though the day was hotter than it had been all week. Joey looked into the water at the edge of the dock, and beneath the reflected ripple of sunlight saw nothing but darkness and depth and mystery. He'd never been in water that deep, never explored what lived there. He knew what was coming, what all his weeks at camp, swimming in water that didn't frighten him, where his feet could rest on the bottom, had been leading to. This was what Alex was expecting them to do. This was the moment of initiation; this was when all the boys would become swimmers in the deep water, the true test of Alex's skills as a counselor. For a moment Joey thought about turning and running and keeping on running until he ran past his bunk and into the woods, where they would find him in an hour or two, and he'd never have to go into the deep water. Not now, not ever.

"When I blow my whistle, I want you to jump in and swim to the raft and then back to the dock, okay? Touch the raft, then turn and swim back, and we're done for the day. Like I've always said to you, let instinct take over. Your arms and legs will do all the work for you, and you're going to be fine. You're going to become real swimmers. Everybody ready?"

But Joey wasn't ready and knew he never would be. He watched the other boys in the water as Alex turned to him. Gesturing wildly as if he were a character in a movie begging for his life, hands together, *please please please*, Joey told Alex that he couldn't swim, that he was afraid of the deep water, because it was true, and he had thought that by speaking the truth, people would understand him, and tears came to his eyes and his face seem to crumple, because he was only eight and had never confronted such a threat before in his life. Alex seemed to draw power from this face of a helpless child. Instead of arousing empathy, it stoked something fiery and lethal within him, something Joey could read instantly in the man's eyes. Losing patience, Alex picked Joey up and threw him in. There was no up or down, nothing to grab on to, no foothold or handle, nothing but the fluid uncertainty of his own death and a horrible rushing sound in his ears and the water flooding into his lungs.

Joey was drowning.

Alex jumped in beside him and tried to seize him as he thrashed and kicked. "Hey, relax, just let go. This is how you learn how to swim."

But Joey wasn't listening. He grabbed on to the chain around the counselor's neck with its silver whistle, twisting it hard to get a handhold until it snapped and broke off and sank to the bottom, and the look on Alex's face was of a man who had been crossed and challenged. Holding Joey tightly, he swam furiously away from the dock, from the camp, from safety and dry ground, and when they'd reached the little raft anchored to the lake bottom, he lifted Joey onto it.

Red-faced and furious, he told Joey he would sit there until he either died or swam back on his own. "You want to go back there? Want to see your friends and sleep in your bunk and eat dinner? Jump in and swim. I made a promise that every single one of my campers would be swimming by the end of the summer. And you're not going to ruin this for me. Now grow up and do the job."

Joey watched Alex swim back with long elegant strokes, his feet barely kicking, before he hoisted himself up onto the dock. He never looked back, not once. Joey closed his eyes, and the world vanished. There was no Alex Mason, no raft, no fear, no death. He opened them, and he was still on the raft as the last hours of the day ebbed away from him.

There was an especially beautiful sunset that evening, what some might characterize as mellow. The warm temperatures and gentle breezes lifted everyone's mood. The counselors had been given information sheets on how to get their campers prepared for leaving in another week, to make sure everything was packed and that the boys would be in the right bus at the right time, and everyone took a breath as "Taps" was played over the loudspeakers.

Steve pushed open the screen door to tell the boys it was lights out, and saw Joey Proctor's empty bunk with its striped blanket. He asked if anyone had seen Joey.

One of the kids said that Joey hadn't been at dinner.

"You're sure of that?"

The others agreed. He wasn't at their table. They thought he might have reported to the infirmary or something. Steve had also missed dinner, as he'd had an emergency dentist appointment in town to replace a lost filling. He walked to the bathroom at the back of the cabin. Across from a row of four sinks were two toilet stalls whose plywood doors were ajar. No one was there.

"Let's all settle down," he told his campers. "I'll be right back."

While he was gone, the other boys speculated as to what might have happened to Joey, and the name John Otis came up. They'd been told about this monster, and now one of their own was gone. One of the boys, Kevin Butcher, began whimpering and only stopped when Ethan called him a bitch-faced crybaby.

Four counselors, including Alex Mason, were sitting around a table in the staff room drinking coffee. College guys with time on their hands. Alex's sneakered foot was up on the table as if he didn't have a care in the world. Steve walked in and asked if anyone had seen Joey Proctor, and the counselors just looked at him. A few shrugs, mostly headshakes. Nothing more.

"He didn't make it to dinner, either."

Alex stood, scraping his chair over the rough wooden floor. He said, "I have to take a leak." Before he could get out the door, Steve said, "He had swimming with you at, what, four o'clock? Something like that?"

Alex nodded. "More like three thirty."

"He do okay?"

"Yeah. He did great."

Five minutes later, Alex was heading down to the lakefront, flashlight in hand, heart racing. Swimming at three thirty, and now it was eight thirty. Everything was going to be fine, he told himself. The kid probably fell asleep on the raft. He'd take a rowboat out and bring Joey back. Lesson learned. For both of them.

He switched on the light and aimed it at the empty raft as it gently bobbed in the water.

5

AT FIRST LIGHT, ON A DAY THAT BROKE GRAY AND misty, two police divers in wetsuits tipped into the lake off the dock, while a line of uniformed cops from the local police station, as well as officers from two neighboring towns, walked in formation through the thick grass at the edge of the big field before spreading out and entering the pine woods to search for evidence. Overhead, a state police helicopter flew low over the water, following the shoreline.

Dave Jensen, the camp owner, had asked the police not to mention anything to the press while he and his wife, Nancy, were still pondering how to handle the situation, the first he'd encountered in his three years at Waukeelo.

He stood with Alex, Steve, and a few other counselors as they waited for the divers to surface. Prematurely bald, Dave had compensated with a mustache and goatee, all salt and pepper, which he nervously stroked. Owning the camp wasn't his only responsibility. During the school year he was principal of a middle school thirty miles away. He and his family lived only four miles outside the camp. When Waukeelo came up for sale, it was an opportunity he couldn't pass up. As a principal, he had been praised for the work he did for his students and the community; running the camp in the summers would round off his efforts for an entire year.

"I called the parents at five this morning," he said. "I thought we'd find him during the night." He shook his head. "They're heading up here from New York. Jesus Christ, this is a real nightmare."

"What happens if they don't find him?" Steve said. "I mean, we're going to have tell the kids something. They'll see that Joey's not here."

"I thought maybe we'd have to cut the season short and send everyone home. But there's, what, five days left? They may still be searching for him a week from now. All those woods surrounding the lake." Dave shook his head and took off his gold-rimmed glasses and began to clean them with his shirt. Kids just don't wander away from a camp in an area they don't know. And the idea that someone might have driven up and taken him seemed ridiculous. Why Joey? Why not some other kid? Why not Dave's own son?

Steve turned to look back toward the bunks. A few boys on their way to an activity had been distracted by what was happening and stopped to stare, soon joined by more campers. "I'll deal with them," he said. "What should I say?"

"Anything but that we're looking for Joey Proctor. Maybe that we think one of the canoes was stolen. Just not the truth."

Steve walked off toward the kids.

Dave looked at Alex. "You're absolutely sure he got out of the water okay?"

"Yeah. Definitely. He did great."

"Did anyone remember him walking up from here?"

Alex said nothing.

"Anyone else? Nothing? No?"

Alex looked as if he'd just become aware of the man addressing him. "I don't know, Dave."

The divers emerged from the water and lifted off their masks. They shook their heads.

"Christ almighty," Dave said. "He's not anywhere."

6

JOEY'S PARENTS SAT ACROSS FROM DAVE, NANCY, and Steve in the owner's office in the cabin Dave and Nancy occupied during the camp season, separated from the bunkhouses, down the hill from the dining hall. Alan and Diane Proctor had arrived just before eleven and were briefed on the search effort and the plans for it to continue.

The phone call that morning had woken them both from a heavy sleep. They no longer shared a bed, especially now that Joey was in camp, and Diane had been content sleeping in her son's room for the six weeks he was away. She had continued seeing her therapist, and together they'd concluded the marriage couldn't be salvaged. Though she had no evidence of it, she suspected that her husband had been involved with some illegal activity that might ruin the family and send him to prison. There was a Russian businessman he sometimes dealt with who would call him at odd hours from Moscow, from London, from wherever. All those phone calls. All those closed doors. But all she had been worrying about was Joey and how he would deal with an impending separation and eventual divorce.

"Before you go off and speak to a lawyer, think about the good times you had with your husband," her therapist had told her.

"Why should I do that?"

"I'm just looking for something, anything, that might hold even a little of this relationship together. For your son's sake. Especially if you divorce. Because right now, Joey's the only person both of you should be thinking about. And he needs to know that he has parents who can be civil to each other."

There had been good times, the best being when Joey was born. And then everything quickly went sour. She'd suffered from postpartum depression, and her husband had no patience for her, especially when he began to bleed clients as the economy tanked.

She looked at her therapist. "After we were married, we went to Europe."

"Honeymoon?"

"For three weeks."

"And that was good?"

"It was wonderful. I'd retired from the ballet company, my back had begun to heal after the accident, and I thought it was time to start a family."

"And your husband was okay with this?"

"He was very excited. Joey was conceived in Paris."

So all of the happy moments she could recall had to do with Joey. The plans. The pregnancy. The baby. And now that he was missing, now that she was sitting in this cabin, hearing how no one knew where he might be, it was as if her whole life was worth nothing. She wanted to go back and burn down their apartment, dismantle her business, do herself great harm.

"All the local authorities have been alerted," Dave Jensen told them. "Police departments in Lenox, Lee, Pittsfield, and Stockbridge are coordinating their efforts. Roadblocks have been set up on all of the primary and secondary—"

"We saw a few on the way here," Joey's father said. Then he ran his hands hard over his thinning hair and just kept them there as he stared at the floor.

"I want to know how my son was feeling," Diane said, turning to Steve. "You're his counselor. Was he happy, was he being picked on, was he worried or depressed or..." And running out of words, she opened her hands. There had to have been a reason why her son would just get up and walk out of camp. She thought of how nervous Joey had seemed in the diner, his tension becoming contagious. She'd decided to make a call and walked outside, because hearing that voice would calm and reassure her. She'd become friends with the man who rented the studio below hers, Eli Fuller. He was a successful sculptor, with pieces in museums both here and abroad, and they'd often run into each other in the café on the ground floor. They began to talk. They showed each other their work. He bought two of her chairs. And then one day she put a hand to his face and kissed him. He was her anchor, she thought. Her stability.

When she had spoken to Eli on the phone outside the diner that first day of camp, some creepy guy had walked past her and said something, she wasn't sure what, but when he drove off in his truck, he seemed to leer at her, as if he knew exactly to whom she was speaking at that moment, just as her husband knew.

"Well, I guess now we're even," Alan had said on their way back home after dropping Joey off.

"Meaning?"

"What, you haven't guessed? You don't think I have some-one else?"

"I'm sure you do."

"You want to hear about her?"

"Why, you want me to tell you about mine, who is half your age and ten times more successful?"

She watched her husband bunch his hand into a fist, and she shifted even closer to the door. "If you lay a hand on me, I'll get a restraining order. You'll be out of that apartment so fast you won't know what hit you."

"My apartment. *My* apartment, let me remind you."

"So divorce me."

"No," he said. He put his hand back on the wheel. They were crossing into New York, and the day was almost done.

"Why do you even bother staying with me, then?"

"Because if we go through a divorce, you'll suck me so dry I'll have exactly nothing left. And what you'll end up with will be a hell of a lot less than you expected. Everything I've achieved is going down the hole, or haven't you noticed yet? This car's the next to go; I've already got a buyer for it."

"I don't care about stuff. I'll have Joey."

"We'll see about that."

But she knew Joey feared his father, and she also knew that if she stayed with him much longer she would begin to feel that way as well.

"Mrs. Proctor?"

She looked at Steve. They were still in the Jensens' cabin, in the owner's office. Once again, on the drive back to the city, she went over it, as if looking for a clue, a hint, a way in to the disappearance of her son.

His counselor said, "I was saying that new kids usually go

through a rough first week, like they do in any new situation. But Joey and I got to know one another pretty well. We talked a lot, and he'd come a long way since he first got here. He was doing great, really. I was proud of him, and told him so."

She smiled slightly, with only the corners of her mouth. "He's small for his age," she said. "It can be hard."

"He loves school," Joey's father said, and it was true, Joey did like school, which was only a block away from their apartment. He had a few good friends there, with one living just around the corner, and he was always talking about his teachers as if, after only a few hours home each day, he already missed them. That, too, with its exorbitant tuition, would have to come to an end.

Dave asked if Joey had written them frequently from camp.

"Well, it was kind of strange. We thought kids here might be allowed to phone home now and again—"

"I thought that was made clear in the information packet we sent all the parents. Some camps do allow it, but this is a more traditional camp, almost old-fashioned. So many of our campers come from cities, and the thinking was always that they should have new and different experiences here."

"He wrote a lot in the beginning, then less. We hadn't heard anything from him in the past few weeks."

There was a knock on the cabin door. Nancy went to see who it was. When she returned a few moments later, one of the local police officers trailed behind her. He said, "Are you the, uh, parents of the boy?"

Joey's father nodded and rose to his feet, as if preparing for the worst news in the world.

"I just wanted to say that we are doing as comprehensive a job as we can right now. This is our priority, and it will remain so until we find your son safe and sound." The officer shifted his weight from one foot to the other. "The state police helicopter has several more square miles to cover, and our teams are combing both the camp itself and all adjacent woods and neighborhoods. Fortunately, the nights have been warm, and if he is lost, he's probably okay." He turned to Dave. "You say he was last seen around four o'clock yesterday?"

Dave nodded. "Approximately, yes."

"Has he ever tried to run away from home before?"

"Who does that anymore?" Joey's father asked.

The cop said, "You'd be surprised."

The officer had seen it all before: the kid runs away, and it's like opening a suitcase full of snakes. All the truth comes slithering out—the abuse, the screaming, the punishment, the beating. He turned cold eyes upon Joey's father and asked again if his son had ever run away.

Joey's mother said that had never happened, but the officer kept looking at her husband as if he could read the man's true nature.

The cabin door opened, and everyone turned. For a half second, Diane thought it was Joey who'd just walked in. The boy stopped dead when he saw the policeman and Joey's parents.

"Everything okay?" his mother said to him. "This is my son," she said to the others.

He came over to whisper in her ear.

"I know," she said. "That's why we're here." The boy

smiled shyly, revealing a large gap between his front teeth. She put her arm around him and led him out of the room. A year younger, he was even smaller than Joey.

Joey's mother said, "You said he was last seen around four. What was going on then? What was his, whatever, his activity?"

"Swimming," Dave said.

She looked at Steve. "Are you the swimming counselor?"

"No. That would be Alex Mason."

"We want to talk to him," she said.

Steve volunteered to get Alex. When he walked out and crossed the campus, only the sound of a police helicopter in the distance could be heard. The day had remained leaden and drizzly, and the campers had been corralled in the social hall for games. Steve went into the staff room. Alex was there, as were three other counselors, standing at the coffee urn.

"They want to speak to you," Steve said quietly, trying not to draw attention.

Alex looked at him blankly.

"Joey Proctor's parents."

"They're here?"

Steve nodded.

"How are they doing?"

"How the fuck do you think they're doing, Alex? Their kid's gone missing."

7

ALEX SAT ACROSS FROM MR. AND MRS. PROCTOR. He'd brought in his mug of coffee, which Nancy quickly took from the table. It seemed to her indecent that he should be enjoying his beverage while these two people were agonizing over their son's whereabouts.

Joey's mother asked about what had happened during the swimming activity the day before.

Alex shifted uncomfortably in his chair. He said, "The usual. You know, Joey was really making progress, and everything was good. Great. Really great kid."

His face reddened, but no one noticed.

"What do you mean by 'good'? My son can't swim. He's afraid of deep water."

"We were in the intermediate section. His head's always above water there."

"But what do you mean by 'good'?"

"Just that he, you know, was doing fine."

"Doing what?"

"Working on treading water. Stuff like that."

She looked at her husband, who seemed more than willing to leave this line of questioning up to her.

"And you definitely saw him leave the waterfront?"

Alex nodded. He shrugged a little, as if he'd been talking about just another day in his life.

"Did he walk up with you?"

"I think he was behind me."

"You think."

"I'm sure."

"And this was what time?" her husband asked.

"Around four," Alex said. "Yeah. Definitely at four."

Joey's father checked his watch. "That's twenty hours he's been gone." He looked around, as if an answer might be right in front of his eyes.

Diane Proctor leaned in. "You checked the lake."

"Yes," said Dave. "It's… We found nothing. No one."

"And the woods."

"The search there is still continuing. It's pretty dense out there, but they're looking."

Joey's mother sat back and looked intently, curiously, at Alex, as though trying to read the young man's subtext. Just as ballet had its own geometry, so did the world. There was one particular point on a plane where you achieved just the right distance to see the truth, where everything that had come before could be judged for what it was, and everything that was about to be could be discerned. One of her teachers at the City Ballet, a German woman who had begun her career with George Balanchine, had said that long ago, but only now in her retirement had Diane begun to comprehend it.

She said, "There's something else, isn't there?"

Alex said, "I told you everything." He shrugged.

"I just need to know that you were aware that my son couldn't swim, that he was afraid of the water."

"I knew that, Mrs. Proctor. I knew that the first day we had swimming. He told me." His voice began to rise. "I mean, that's my job here, to make sure each and every camper ends up being as strong a swimmer as he can be." He smiled a little discordantly. "I pride myself on that. I'm a trained instructor, I've done all my lifesaving courses with the Red Cross, and—"

"Alex is the best swimming teacher I've ever worked with," Dave said, placing his hands flat on the table.

"Well, I think," Joey's father said, "if my son doesn't turn up, this all goes to a whole other level."

"What are you saying?" Dave asked, his eyebrows shooting up.

Twenty-four hours later, at noon the next day, the search of the camp property was called off. Joey could not be found.

Part Two

21 YEARS LATER

8

ALEX HAD FORGOTTEN HOW LONG IT TOOK HIM TO drive from the house to the girls' school, Long Hill Country Day, so he was running almost an hour late that day. Usually Ashley would drive them, but her Mercedes was in for service. He didn't mind taking Becca and Lyndsey to school on these rare occasions; it was a pleasant drive along the perimeter of the Rockefeller estate, and the ride from there to work gave him a chance to think through his day. Meetings. Money. Phone calls, many of which were conducted on the way into the city. People needed to be placated or praised; appointments had to be confirmed or delayed; deals needed to be concluded; problems required solving.

When he'd first started out in business, before they had kids, he'd walk down the station road and ride the train into the city each day, but that was when they lived in a condo near the river. Now they had a spacious home with five bedrooms and an equal number of bathrooms, located on just over six acres of land, enough of it wooded to provide them with the degree of privacy they had always desired. When he'd first hired an architect to help design the house, he'd also contracted with a landscape designer. Many of the trees had been cleared, and some of the property bulldozed and leveled for a swimming pool and tennis court. They were so isolated from their neighbors that when the girls were on sleepovers, Alex and Ashley would sometimes swim naked in their pool, witnessed only by the moon and the stars.

When he walked into his office, his secretary said, "Don't forget you have a call with Milt Golub this morning regarding the Brooklyn property."

"Right, right."

She looked at her computer screen. "That was supposed to be ten minutes ago, Alex."

"I'll talk to him now, Carol."

"And then there's the full-team meeting at eleven thirty. After which you're lunching with Jake Levitt from the mayor's office."

"Where?"

"Olive Garden, Times Square."

"Jesus, he's cheap as hell, isn't he?"

She smiled. "Civil servants aren't millionaires, you know."

"Why not just a dollar-slice place on Eighth Avenue? What time is this for?"

"One thirty."

"Okay. Make sure the car's here."

"It's all arranged. Oh, and Pete Kellerman wants to talk to you about the Mason House."

"Send him in after I speak to Golub. And I need coffee."

"In the thermos on your desk, as usual."

Unlike other property developers in the city, Alex prided himself on selling quality and comfort, not just personality, and when he turned a location into a first-class hotel, his name was always above the entrance: *A Mason House Property*.

On the office walls were framed magazine covers featuring his photo: *Forbes*, *Time, Inc.*, and *Fortune*. He'd worked on his smile over the years, trying to lose the self-satisfied smirk of his frat boy years and finding a gentler, more benign look that suited his age well and his brand even better. There were photos of Alex with two different mayors of New York, the current governor, both New York senators, and two former presidents, as well as several celebrities from the worlds of entertainment, dining, and fashion. There was a photo of him and some old college friends from the Wharton School of Business at a reunion a few years earlier—the other men not quite as successful or wealthy as Alex—as well as a selection of framed certificates: honors, degrees, things that mattered only to him, but which might well impress another.

On his desk stood a large silver-framed photo of Alex, Ashley, and their two daughters. Becca had just turned thirteen; Lyndsey was eight. The photo had been taken the summer before when they were on Nantucket and had been sailing on a friend's forty-footer. Ashley had her arms around a smiling Alex, her blond hair caught in the wind, while the girls leaned into the shot on either side of them.

Picture perfect: that's what people said about the Mason family. Ready-made for *People* magazine, each of them seemingly cut from the same cloth: something in a pale gold, made of only the finest silk to flatter one's form. Of course, shadows had been cast over the years, especially on Alex's business. There was some question regarding his tax returns for a three-year period, and when he'd become involved with another woman, enough people knew where to look, what to look for, and how to put it into words and images for the *National Enquirer.*

Nothing had really stuck, and he'd since vowed to keep both his life and his business clean. His hotels were all four-star establishments, his restaurants within them always well-reviewed, and his private life had calmed down enough that no one was paying much attention. His reputation as a real-estate developer rested on what had made his fortune: buying up derelict properties and turning them into top-rated boutique hotels, the result of which was the elimination of an eyesore and improvement of the neighborhood. Doing well and doing good: another tagline for the Mason brand. He had a lot to protect, and an equal amount to lose.

Alex sipped his coffee as he stood at the window, taking in the view all the way down to Battery Park and, beyond it, the Statue of Liberty, talking via speakerphone to Milt Golub, who owned a property in Red Hook Alex had been eyeing. The district had been slowly improving over the years, and Milt's building was either going to be sold or taken down. No one had lived in it for well over a decade. No one would ever want to live there. Neighborhood activists routinely stormed Golub's office complaining about the vacancy, and some had even taken to picketing his house in Scarsdale. But Alex knew exactly what he could do with the derelict building. With its small footprint, he envisioned a ninety-five-room hotel with a first-class bar and a ground-floor restaurant. Small, but not too small; *intimate* was the word to be used in all its advertising. Could the people who lived in the neighborhood afford his rates? Probably not. But one day they might, once their property values had skyrocketed.

At first, Alex had known Milt Golub only by reputation as a man who'd inherited several locations in Manhattan, as well as the outer boroughs, where property had become increasingly more desirable. He'd heard rumors that Milt was considering divesting himself of his buildings before retiring, and Alex had invited him to lunch a few years earlier. Since then, they'd talked regularly and had developed a good relationship based on anticipation and profit.

"So how do you want to handle this, Alex?"

"Arrange to have the key left for me, and I'll swing by first thing on Monday and have a look that same morning, okay?"

"Not today?"

"Not happening, Milt. Friday's always hell. You know that."

Golub laughed. "Tell me about it. In a few months I'll be out in Palm Springs, where every day is Saturday and I'll be teeing up first thing in the morning. You should try it sometime."

"Not my sport, as you know. I like being in the water. And retirement is, well, a long way off. So, tell me… Can you wait until Monday?"

"Whatever, sure."

"Just do me the favor of not entertaining any bids till you hear mine. Can you do that?"

"Of course," Golub said, hanging up without saying goodbye. Alex pressed another button on his phone. "I can see Pete when he's ready."

"He's waiting here with me," Carol said.

Pete Kellerman had already begun making a name for himself after only a month with Mason House Properties. He was eager, worked late hours, looked sharp, and had a genuinely sincere smile. Alex could see him rising through the ranks and becoming a real force in the company. He'd been charged with covering an issue that week at the Mason House Hotel, Alex's flagship operation located on Madison Avenue. The fire alarm system had become unstable and had gone off several times while guests were asleep, forcing them to get out of bed and stand outside in the middle of the night. It was as much a public relations matter as a technical one.

Pete walked into Alex's office with the slightly manic bounce of the overly caffeinated. "I stopped in before I came to work this morning," he told Alex. "The problem was fixed last night."

"How many guests did we lose?"

"None. It went off twice—false alarms, of course, once at one forty-five, the next at just after three thirty. Everyone here at the company was sent a text with the info. People were pissed, but I thought if we comped them for their breakfasts, we'd make up for it. I told Chris Harper to run off flyers and make sure they were slipped under every guest's door before dawn." Chris was the manager Alex had hired just before the hotel was officially opened.

"Jesus, what time did you get there?"

"Around quarter past five."

Alex was impressed. The kid really was on the ball.

"That was smart," he said. "Great work, Pete."

"Sorry I didn't check in with you beforehand about the breakfast thing, but I thought we had to do something right away."

Alex prided himself on his hires. Most who were on his staff had remained there, moving up in the ranks, taking on greater responsibility over time. He had a separate department that dealt with his international properties, and a legal team to review all the paperwork and contracts, but when someone new was being interviewed, the final decision was always his. He remembered meeting Pete Kellerman that first morning. He seemed younger than the usual recruits, but his background was impeccable, and in an odd way, he reminded Alex of himself when he was that age. He decided then and there to bring Pete onto the staff. Get him up to speed. Most of all, keep him close. The kid was ambitious, and Alex knew that sometimes, in the beginning, ambition had to be kept in check.

At just past seven thirty that evening, Alex pulled up his driveway, followed the curve around to the portico, and locked the Bentley. When he opened the door, Ashley was sitting on the stairs, dressed in her best, flimsiest lingerie: lace bra and panties, both in black. The foyer was aglow with all the candles she'd set out. She sipped from a champagne flute and crossed her long legs and leaned back. He could never quite believe he was married to someone so extraordinarily beautiful. When they went on vacation, every man would turn to watch her in her white two-piece as she strolled by the pool, drink in hand, to sit beside him.

"Wow," Alex said. "How long have you been planning this?"

"Since yesterday. I thought we deserved some serious us time."

"Where are the girls?"

"Not here, obviously."

"Sold them, did you? Hope you got a good price."

She laughed. "They're both doing sleepovers." She held out her hand and led him up to the bedroom. "Let's grant the lobsters an extra hour of life."

Sometime after twelve, long after dinner, they wished each other a good night and turned over, each facing a different direction. Ashley always wore a satin sleep mask, while Alex was perfectly happy having the sun rouse him every morning.

"Did you arm the system?"

"Of course," he said, then tried to remember when he'd actually done it. He slipped out of bed, and Ashley laughed a little.

"We're getting old," she said.

He put on a robe and went down to the panel by the front door. The light showing the alarm system was up and running was gently flashing. He went back to bed and fell into a deep sleep.

He woke abruptly from his dream at just before eight the next morning, gasping for breath as if he'd been underwater and unable to surface for air. He had no idea what he'd been dreaming about, but it had left him shaken. It was a sensation he'd had occasionally over the years since college—coming out of a dream he couldn't remember into an oppressive sensation of fear and suffocation. As if he had emerged from sleep only to find himself in some kind of trap. As if someone were holding him down.

He put his hands on his chest and took slow, deep breaths, letting his eyes take in the room, rebuilding his universe one element at a time. He was a man who was always more comfortable in a world of structure, of ceilings and walls, foundations and roofs. The more abstract things of the world—emotions, fantasies, beliefs and feelings—seemed to elude him. It was Ashley who could deal with the worries of their daughters, as if she had the affinity to their hearts, their souls, that he somehow lacked. He turned on his side and faced the sunlit window. A bird flew close to it, nearly colliding with the glass, then darted away, beak open, eyes full of alarm. He watched the leaves on the oak tree rustle in the wind and then abruptly go still. A milky sky was beginning to shatter into pieces of blue.

He heard the shower turn off. The girls would be back before eleven, Ashley had said, which gave them a few more hours of each other. He felt himself getting aroused at the thought of it, and when Ashley opened the bathroom wearing only a towel, he threw off the duvet. She smiled and said, "Hello, boys." She dropped her towel and started to come to him, to take his outstretched hand, to straddle his body and let him settle inside her, when she glanced out the window. And because they lived so far from their neighbors, Alex was the only person to hear her scream.

9

THEY STARED AT THE POOL, NOT QUITE BELIEVING what they were seeing, while the two detectives, Lieutenant Carver and Detective Ettinger, went over their notes.

"I don't understand how this can happen," Ashley said. "I mean, someone dyed the water red, and we heard nothing?"

The lieutenant, who seemed to Alex a little young to have achieved such a rank, looked toward the house. "You said you were both at home last night. It seems strange that you weren't even aware of it."

"The whole thing seems impossible," Ashley said.

"Have either of you been threatened lately? Or felt threatened? Had you seen any strangers near the property?"

Alex shook his head.

"Mrs. Mason?"

"Everything has been just like usual. Quiet."

"How about regarding your business, Mr. Mason?"

"What are you asking?"

"Everything like usual?"

"Of course. Everything's under control. Just like always." He thought of the fire alarms going off at the Mason House Hotel and shrugged it off. If someone wanted to get at him in some way because of his business, that would be a pretty feeble way of doing it.

The detective shut his notebook. "I'd put it down to someone's idea of a prank. At least no one was hurt. And, you know—? Maybe your insurance company will cover some of the costs."

Alex had already called the pool service, and even though it was a Saturday—a busy one for the company—they said they'd be able to send someone over in a few hours to drain, clean, and refill the pool.

The detectives turned when they heard a car pulling up the driveway. "That's Becca, our older daughter."

"Driving?"

"It's her friend's father. Sleepover," Ashley said in explanation.

She went up to meet the car. The last thing she wanted was for her daughters to see the pool like this.

Becca had already begun the descent into the abyss of adolescence, honing her attitude like an ax on a sharpening stone. Questions and comments barely reached her before she'd cut them down. Alex suspected that his wife had been like that when she was thirteen: blond, strikingly pretty, full of snot and insolence, so he left Ashley to deal with their daughter at times of crisis. Becca would do fine, Alex knew. With her looks and her manner, she'd always succeed. After all, she was her father's daughter.

Lyndsey was another matter. Shy, unsure of herself even at the best of times, she seemed almost to be defying Alex and his brassy confidence in the way she kept her head down and peered up through her bangs. She was an average student, never as consistent as her sister, and Alex, who viewed her as a challenge, was intent on turning her into as much of a success as he was.

The detectives drove away, and Alex and Ashley went up to the house just as Lyndsey's ride pulled up. When they were inside, Ashley began making lunch for all of them, but Becca wasn't hungry and Lyndsey didn't feel well. Ashley put a hand on her daughter's forehead. "You're not running a fever."

"We didn't sleep a lot."

"I remember not sleeping much when I had sleepovers."

"And I threw up."

"Like always," Ashley said. "Too much junk food, too much excitement."

"You ever have a sleepover, Dad?" Becca wanted to know, and she offered him a very sly, grown-up look, almost begging to embarrass the man.

"Yeah, plenty of times. But I'm not going to tell you about them."

Ashley and Becca both laughed. They knew exactly what he was talking about. Before Ashley, there had been a string of girlfriends and at least one fiancée, leaving a trail of broken hearts and simmering resentments. Ashley was the prize, though. In his life, everything was a prize.

Alex said, "The pool guy's here. I'm going down to talk to him."

The pool guy—who looked nothing like the standard-issue buffed pool guy of Malibu and more like an overworked, drain-hardened Roto-Rooter man—shook his head as he looked at the red water.

"What is this?"

"Someone's idea of a stupid prank," Alex said.

The guy just stared at him. He said, "Because of this red stuff, this whatever, you'll probably need to have the filter replaced, along with everything else I'll have to do. You'll definitely need a new lining."

"Just do whatever's needed."

As the man began to drain the pool, Alex watched the level of the red water drop, inch by inch, revealing the pale blue of the pool walls and the ladder at the deep end. It was only when there were six or seven inches left of it that he headed back up to the house.

"Sir?"

Alex turned back.

"You'd better have a look at this."

As the last of the water ran down the drain with a loud gurgle, they could see what was crudely chiseled into the floor of the pool.

Remember Me

10

LIEUTENANT CARVER COUNTED UP THE NAMES ALEX had written: forty-seven of them. He said, "These are all the people who might be holding a grudge against you?"

Alex had been sitting with the man for nearly an hour, filling out a report and watching as the police photographer took shots of the words carved into the pool.

"I can't remember the names of all the rest."

"There are more?"

"When you're as successful in business as I am, you build up a whole list of people who got shouldered aside in a deal, or who just can't let things go. They don't think I'm entitled to the rewards of my labors. I suspect that because I have no time for them, they're a little pissed off. I'm sure there are people you've arrested who would love to get back at you."

"Yeah, well, that goes along with my line of work as well."

Alex shook his head. "The thing is, I don't know that anyone on that list would stoop to this kind of stunt."

The lieutenant sat back, tossed his pencil on the table, and looked at him. "Why not?"

"It takes planning, right? And then, what—getting into the pool and carving the words with a chisel or whatever? I can't see any of these people doing such a thing. They'd get nothing out of it."

"Except the satisfaction of turning your morning into several hours of misery. You'd be surprised at what turns some people on." The lieutenant stood and stretched. "All right, Mr. Mason. I have a feeling you'll think of someone more likely to do this than the people on this list. Just let me know when it comes to you."

Alex shrugged. "I will."

The detective put on his jacket. His partner closed his folder and got ready to go. "'Remember me,'" the lieutenant said. "That mean anything to you?"

Alex thought for a moment. No one came to mind. "Not really, no."

"Think hard, Mr. Mason. Who have you forgotten lately?"

11

WHEN ALEX ARRIVED AT WORK EARLY ON Monday, before even his secretary was expected in, the door to his office was ajar. Pete Kellerman was standing behind his desk, rifling through a drawer. He looked up and smiled. "Morning, Alex."

Alex stared at him. "Is there a problem?"

"Why do you ask?"

"Because you're in my office looking through my desk."

"Easy explanation. The L train was shut down for track repairs. So I grabbed an Uber and got here"—he checked his watch—"half an hour ago, maybe? Milt Golub phoned just after I got in to confirm you'd be at the site this morning. You weren't here, so the call transferred to the main number and I picked up."

Alex set down his case. "And you're in my office why?"

"I thought I'd do a little background on the Red Hook property. I went through all our online folders and couldn't find the history on it, only the current reports. I'm looking for all the background Sandy Merritt had done."

Alex opened his hands. "It's not your project. That's why you couldn't find anything. It's a locked file, for my eyes only. And there's no paper backup. No one outside these four walls is even supposed to know about it until it's a done deal. I have an agreement with Golub. Radio silence until I've put in my bid."

Pete slid the drawer shut. "Sorry, Alex. I was just trying to be helpful."

"Look, it's no big deal. You're still learning how things work around here. I've got a lot of faith in you, Pete. I'll let you know when I need you in on a project. Just don't jump the gun, okay?" Alex looked at his watch again. "I have to leave in ten minutes to look at the place."

Pete wished him luck and walked out just as Carol arrived.

Alex said, "When you left on Friday, did you make sure my office was locked?"

She gestured to the outer door opening to her space. "I usually just lock this one. It's always been enough."

"Except for last Friday when you forgot."

"Oh Jesus. I don't know what I was thinking."

"From now on, just be sure both doors are locked if we're out, okay? Even if it's only for lunch."

"Absolutely, of course."

Carol had been with him for almost ten years. Before then, she'd been working for a New York-based publisher, reading through slush piles and, having wearied of it, was looking for something different. Also something that paid somewhat more. When he interviewed her for the job, he asked what made her think she'd be qualified to be the executive secretary for one of the most successful property development companies in the city.

She said, "The truth? Because I've spent the last three years sifting out the crap and trying to come up with the gold."

He laughed. "And did you?"

"Once. It was a first novel, and it was on the *New York Times* bestseller list for eighteen weeks."

He hired her on the spot.

He said, "Did Milt say where I could pick up the key?"

She took an envelope from her desk drawer. "It arrived by messenger just after you left on Friday. And your ride's waiting outside," she said. Alex had an account with an executive service that provided Lincoln Town Cars with tinted windows.

"I should be back before lunchtime."

The building was just as the photos had shown: its exterior tagged with spray paint, all of its windows boarded up. The outside vestibule was littered with empty coffee cups, an old sweater, a crushed beer can, several cigarette butts. People had slept, smoked, and drunk there and, from the smell, also used it as a public toilet. Before unlocking the front door and letting himself in, Alex walked farther down the block to get a feel for the neighborhood. Empty storefronts, a warehouse, a vacant lot beside it, and then, just a block or two away, things started to improve. At the other end of the long street was a decent-looking sushi restaurant, the chefs already busy at this time of the morning. As he crossed over and headed back to Golub's building, Alex saw a brightly lit upmarket home-furnishing shop, a funky little vintage jewelry place, a wine store, and a coffee-and-pastry shop called Take the Cannoli, filled with hipsters on their laptops or smartphones.

As in so much of Brooklyn these days, there was potential here. Like too many of those in his line of business, Alex was Manhattan-centric, realizing almost too late how much money could be made in Brooklyn and Queens. It was another reason why he'd hired Pete Kellerman. He lived in Brooklyn, knew the neighborhoods, and had a feel for the culture.

Alex remembered how Williamsburg had come roaring back until it had become unaffordable save for the wealthiest of New Yorkers, and he could visualize run-down spaces such as Golub's being snatched up in the next eighteen months and turned into restaurants and shops. He walked back to Milt's building feeling more optimistic. He unlocked the front door and took a small Maglite from his pocket, piercing the gloom with its bright, focused beam. Most of the furniture in the small lobby had been removed or stolen. There was a pair of elevators, the doors pried open. The door to the office behind the front desk had fallen off its hinges and lay on the floor.

Inside the empty office, Alex's light picked out a wall calendar from August 1987. Copies of old Brooklyn and Manhattan yellow pages were stacked on a shelf, covered with a thick layer of dust. He found the stairwell and, testing each step for soundness, cautiously climbed to the second floor. There was more graffiti on the walls, and in one of the rooms he found an LP cover from Michael Jackson's *Thriller*, its corners chewed by rodents.

In another room, empty, dust-covered Pabst Blue Ribbon bottles lay on the floor, a used condom, shriveled and dry, beside them. In the corner was a *Hustler* magazine from 1984. Alex was bending down to pick it up when a cluster of baby mice scurried out from under it and a door slammed inside the building, from what sounded like the floor above him.

He returned to the hallway. The noise had startled him, and he took a moment to recover his bearings. He called out,

"Yes? Is someone there?" but there was no response. Again: "Hello? Anyone else here?"

Alex heard the footsteps above him, slowly creaking down the length of the corridor, and he looked up at the ceiling. When the steps stopped just over his head, he held his breath. There was definitely someone else in this building with no electricity, running water, or heat. A homeless person? He heard what sounded like a piece of furniture being dragged above him, before it came to a stop with a startlingly loud bang.

Alex had never been a coward, and wasn't about to become one. He returned to the stairwell and moved slowly upward, avoiding a solitary sneaker on one of the steps. When he reached the top, his flashlight revealed nothing but an empty corridor.

"Anyone there?"

He walked slowly past all the open rooms, aiming his light in each, until he came to the only one whose door was closed. He tried the knob, pushed once, twice, and it gave way only after a firm third push.

Alex passed his light over the space until he saw a freshly lit cigarette standing on its end on the windowsill, a spiral of smoke rising from it. Someone had just been in the room. Someone knew he was there.

Someone was watching him.

He stepped out into the hallway. "I know you're there," he said, raising his voice. "I'm not going to get you into trouble. Just step out and show your face."

Nothing. Not a footstep. He moved slowly down the corridor, passing his flashlight beam from one side to the other. All the other rooms were open and just as empty as the one he'd just been in.

He stopped when he heard it again: someone walking, again on the floor above him.

"Milt?" It was conceivable that Golub could have come earlier and was checking on the state of things, except that now someone was running down the hall above Alex. He returned to the room with the lit cigarette and shut the door firmly behind him. He'd broken into a sweat and felt his shirt sticking to his skin. He turned the Maglite on the face of his watch: he had been in the building for less than fifteen minutes.

Now it was quiet. No footsteps, no chairs being moved. It was time to go, and Alex whispered it to himself, *Time to go*. He wanted to walk away from whoever was in the building, find his driver, go back to the office, wash away the filth of the place. He went to open the door, but this time it wouldn't budge. He banged hard on it, rattled the doorknob, tried to get the door unstuck. He waited a moment to catch his breath. Sweat dripped off his chin onto the floor. He put his ear to the door and listened, and once again there were footsteps, this time outside in the corridor. Stealthy footsteps.

The footsteps stopped on the other side of the door. He could hear someone breathing. And then it was flung open, almost throwing him off balance, while a bright light aimed at his eyes nearly blinded him.

"We had a call that someone had broken into this place."

A female police officer averted the flashlight from his face and shone it over his body. Checking for a weapon?

"The owner gave me the key," Alex explained. "I'm

thinking about buying the building. But there's someone else here. I'm sure of it. A homeless person, maybe. I don't know."

The cop looked past his shoulder and held her light shoulder-high. "Joey?" she said.

"What?"

She nodded toward the wall, and Alex spun around. Above the lit cigarette, the name *Joey* had been painted in big red letters from one edge of the wall to the other, too large to be seen anywhere but from the across the room, as crudely as if done by a child. And the paint was so fresh, like blood from a slaughtered animal, that it was dripping onto the floor.

12

HE WAS IN THE DEPTHS, GENTLY KICKING HIS LEGS, his arms pulling him through the shadows, long tendrils grazing his body in the hush and eventide of water. Rippling threads of the last light of day pierced the murk, shivering and fading with the passing of a cloud. Suddenly, it rose up before him, the body of a young boy trapped in the tall grasses, arms spread wide, eyelids open to reveal empty sockets. Alex wanted to swim away, but he was trapped, unable to rise out of this depth, this water, and only when the boy grabbed hold of Alex's throat and wouldn't let go did he wake in a cold sweat.

Alex sat up gasping for breath. *Just a dream*, he told himself. He looked at the clock on the dashboard; only a minute or two had passed. He switched off the engine and tried to regain his composure. Seeing that name painted on the wall brought it back to him after all these years of not allowing himself to remember: Joey, the raft, the emptiness five hours later. How Joey had let him down by never trying to overcome his fears. It was a memory that had faded over time, subsumed by his years at college and grad school, the fraternity parties, the drinking, the affairs, his marriage to Ashley, when thoughts of Joey were replaced by dreams of success. And money. And then of what he had achieved, and what remained to be done.

He recalled the words roughly etched into the bottom of the pool.

Remember Me

And now he did.

But it was impossible that Joey could still be alive—or if he was, if he'd somehow managed to escape the raft, that he could have known Alex would be at that hotel at that time. It was beyond imagining. He'd left the boy on the raft, and hours later he was gone. After they'd been through the camp and the lake that day and the next, and the police had extended their search for a full week beyond that to a ten-mile radius, they had come up with nothing: neither an item of clothing nor a single person who had seen him or who would have admitted to having witnessed what had taken place. Dave Jensen had assembled all the campers and members of the staff in the social hall the day before the season was to end. He told them in only the vaguest terms what had happened, assuring them that Joey would be found.

It was a quiet, unsettled few hours the next morning as everyone waited for the buses to arrive to take the campers home. The younger boys were subdued, many of them saying they would never come back to camp. A few spoke of John Otis, as if the monster of the campfire story were flesh and blood, a predator living in a big house high above the lake who at that moment had Joey Proctor locked away. They imagined a little boy calling for his parents, and a man coming slowly down the cellar stairs. Joey would have already spent several nights there, some of the campers must have thought, their imaginations filling the empty hours with all the terrors of a horror film. Joey chained to the wall. Joey screaming for his mother. Joey slowly dying.

After the last bus pulled away, a somber Dave Jensen, along with his wife, met with the staff in the dining hall. The Jensens' son remained in their cabin, too upset to emerge. Dave looked around at the faces of his counselors, clasped his hands before him and began. "I just want to say how grateful I am for all you've done during this time. Our campers were understandably shaken by this, and it's thanks to you that this past week went as smoothly as it did, considering the circumstances. It's a tragic thing, and of course we all feel for Mr. and Mrs. Proctor back in New York. They believe Joey is out there somewhere. Maybe he just walked away, like some kids run away from home. In all confidentiality, I can say that Nancy and I became aware that his parents were not on the best of terms, and this may be one possible explanation for what has occurred."

The counselors avoided looking at one another. Steve Fenton nodded a little in agreement. On the first day of camp it was something he'd sensed immediately as the kids and their parents were about to separate for six weeks. He'd seen it in Joey's eyes, the lost, unfocused look of someone who had no idea what the future would bring him as his parents barely acknowledged each other.

Dave went on: "Kids, well, sometimes they do things for attention, other times because they're afraid. But"—he waved his fingers through the air—"I really shouldn't be speculating. Basically, we have five lost hours during which time Joey disappeared. Between his swimming activity and lights out, he was gone. No strangers were reported seen on the camp property, and none of Joey's counselors or bunkmates noticed anything different about the boy. It was just another day. That's what they said. Another day."

Steve Fenton said, "If he walked off on his own, he would have left during the daylight hours. Which means before, what, seven thirty or so?"

An eight-year-old probably wouldn't have risked leaving after sunset. The point didn't have to be debated or discussed. There were no clues to go on, nothing that could lead them in any definite direction. Dave lifted his hands slightly, as if to weigh the air between him and his staff. But like everything else in this story, it merely ran through his fingers. Because of his relationship with Joey, because the boy had told him so much about his life at home, his fears, his worries, Steve only wanted to find him in a safe place. And then take him back to New York to his apartment in Manhattan. He wanted to protect him. And all he had now were Joey's name and an empty bunk bed.

"I know most of you will be leaving later today or tomorrow," Dave said. "A few have asked about working here next summer, and frankly, I don't know what lies ahead for Camp Waukeelo. I've spoken to our attorney, and we're looking into the various permutations of this, all the fallout that might occur, should Joey not be found."

Sitting toward the back of the dining hall, Alex looked up at the ceiling and closed his eyes, trying to think ahead—a week, a month, anytime but the present—as though mapping out a future that would erase the whole incident. When he opened his eyes, he saw Steve staring at him. And then Steve turned away.

Alex had never really liked Steve. Now, all these years later, he thought he understood why. He'd disliked Steve because he was unlike Alex. Steve seemed too calm, too deliberate. Watchful to a fault. A man of thought, not action. As though he were waiting for Alex to slip up and betray himself. Had he seen him leave Joey on the raft? Or had someone else seen him and spoken to Steve?

"Does that mean we may have to testify?" another counselor asked.

"It's a possibility. And, of course, if any of you remember even the slightest detail that might lead the police to where Joey is, his parents would obviously be very grateful. In the meantime, I'm going to ask all of you to leave me your contact information at college or at home, so that if something does come up, if someone has reported a sighting of Joey, you would be available to fill in the details of his last day here."

The counselors agreed with a nod or a word.

"For those of you not leaving today, you're of course invited to spend one last night in your assigned bunk. I understand"—he glanced at a sheet of paper—"that so far nine of you will be here. Nancy and I will host a cookout, and yes, alcoholic beverages will be served." He smiled and added, "That may up the numbers a bit," and everyone laughed.

Alex remembered—it came back to him now as he sat in his Bentley, such a tiny detail after twenty-one years—that as he'd walked back from the waterfront, he'd passed one of the younger boys standing alone and watching him approach. Alex didn't even know the kid's name. He could barely remember what he looked like.

And now this, twenty-one years later. The pool. The name

on the wall. Someone knew, someone remembered, someone was coming after him. He blinked his eyes and looked around him as Ashley came to the car. She said, "I heard you pull in, like, five minutes ago. Are you okay?"

Long day. Hard day. Bad day.

Joey. On the wall, in letters so big that you had to stand all the way across the room to see it.

It took him a few seconds to get out of the plushness of the Bentley. "I must have dozed off for a moment or two."

"You look like you just lost your best friend." They stepped inside, and she shut the door.

They went into the kitchen, and she put some ice into a glass for his drink. He took the bottle from the counter and poured a double Johnnie Black. "Lousy day," he said.

"Bad enough for a big gulp?"

He took a long sip and laughed a little. "Guess so."

"Well, ready for some more bad news? That detective who spoke to us—?"

"Carver?"

"He said there was nothing to investigate about the pool. Probably a prank, he said. Kids." She shrugged. "You know."

Alex sat on one of the stools by the counter. "C'mon, it's trespassing on private property."

"There's no evidence linking it to anyone. He said it was probably the same kids who tore up the eighteenth green at the golf course the other night."

"I don't understand how someone could've gotten into the water and done all that damage on the bottom. And then, what, add food coloring?"

"That's the thing," Ashley said. "It wasn't food coloring. It was blood."

Alex looked at her.

She said, "The pool company had a sample of it tested. They said it's standard practice when this kind of thing happens, so they know how to deal with the job. They called this morning. It turned out to be animal's blood mixed with the water. From cows or pigs. The girls don't know this, so let's keep it that way." She put a hand on his. "Anyway, they're coming tomorrow to repair the floor, sanitize all the surfaces, and flush the filtration system before they refill it. It's an all-day job that may run into another day. They think we have a valid insurance claim, just like the cop said."

"In the end, it's still going to cost us something."

She put an arm around him. "Hey. It's our pool, babe. Let's make it good again and just move on, okay?"

He remembered that next Monday he had a team meeting scheduled for six thirty in the evening, keeping everyone a little late. Normally, he'd treat the staff to drinks afterward, but as it was early in the week, he figured everyone would just want to go home. He said, "On Monday, I think I'll just stay in town. Sleep at the hotel apartment for the night."

"Okay. Whatever."

"So if anything else comes up with the pool, you can deal with it, if that's okay."

"Something's bothering you, isn't it."

"It's nothing," he said.

"No, I can see it in your face. Do you want to talk about it?"

He put on a smile for her. "I'm fine."

"There's no one else in your life, is there? Because if there is, I want to know now, not by reading the gossip columns."

She was really going to start on that now: a brief affair—no, the word is *fling*—he'd had almost four years earlier with a divorced woman he'd known from the business, Karen Cain. They'd met at a conference at the Grand Hyatt, wandered off afterward for what they thought would be a cocktail and some shoptalk, and ended up spending four hours drinking and drifting off to have dinner, and when they parted, there was the kiss. The relationship lasted for all of three weeks, ending when Ashley found out while Alex was in the shower and his cell phone rang. He'd taken a day off so he could accompany his wife to parent-teacher conferences at the girls' school. Karen's name came on the screen, and Ashley had taken the liberty of answering it.

When he came out of the shower, she said, "Your girlfriend called."

"What are you talking about?"

"Karen. I just spoke to her."

He took a step back. For once in his life, he couldn't find the words.

"She thought I was your secretary. She said something about making reservations for dinner for the two of you for Thursday."

On Ashley's prodding, and after the story was leaked to the media—out of spite, he suspected, by Karen—they went to couples counseling. No number of apologies could sway Ashley. She was humiliated by the press coverage, the embarrassing photos, the smarmy claims of the woman in question. Only time would let the details, imagined or otherwise, fade from her mind. Or, it seemed, maybe not.

"There's no one else," he said. "You're the only woman in my life. Everything else is in the past."

But nothing was ever over. Karen Cain may have been history, but it seemed Joey was never going away.

13

ASHLEY FELL ASLEEP JUST AFTER SHE TURNED OFF her light and put her head on the pillow. Day was done; the light had faded; voices had fallen silent.

But Alex was still awake at two, then two thirty, his mind still not at ease, and at three he quietly slid out from under the duvet, picked up his robe, and walked down the stairs. The door to the basement was just off the kitchen, and before opening it, he disarmed the alarm system, set to go off should any of the downstairs doors or windows be opened. He paused for a moment before descending; it was like crossing a line, he thought. You open the door and have no idea what might be waiting within. He could ignore what had happened: the swimming pool, the room at the Brooklyn property. Or else he could admit that whatever it was out there had already come inside. It seemed so insignificant: a simple slip of the mind, a moment of forgetfulness more than twenty years ago, so why should this boy—now this man—be back in his life? Alex shut the door behind him and went into the basement, a place of discard and memory, where they stored the girls' once-treasured playthings and the gifts he and Ashley had received and rejected, from which they somehow couldn't part.

There were the children's old toys, dollhouses, and board

games, stuffed animals that had been cast away, no longer loved. A dartboard hung crookedly on one wall. A set of golf clubs his father-in-law had given Alex when he and Ashley married, assuming that all property developers were eager players, leaned still unused in a corner.

Alex pulled a cardboard box from a shelf and set it on the ping-pong table beneath the overhead light. He lifted out his old high-school yearbooks, set aside a few of Ashley's, then at the bottom found a large folder with the logo of the canoeist and the name *Camp Waukeelo* printed on it. He hadn't looked at it since the day it was handed to him at the closing dinner at camp that summer, when awards were bestowed. Afterward, everyone had walked down to the lakefront and watched the year go up in flames, the numbers constructed from tree branches and twigs mounted on a raft and doused with gasoline, a Viking funeral for another memorable summer. He had stood there apart from the other counselors, watching as it floated slowly behind the raft where he'd left Joey Proctor, the flames crackling in the evening quiet. As though seeing the year turn to smoke and ash would make everything bad disappear. Some of the boys wept quietly for a summer that would never return, while others thought of Joey Proctor, somewhere out there but no longer among them. Now Joey lived only in their imaginations, in scenarios that bordered on nightmare and horror. The flaming makeshift raft tilted, tipped, and when it sizzled into the water, there was a round of cheers and the singing of the camp anthem. The flag was taken down and folded, and everyone walked back to their bunks. Alex turned once to look back at the lake. The surface was as still as it always had been. Whatever had happened there had vanished like the summer itself, into its depths.

And if Joey should return? Would he be utterly changed? No longer a child, and not quite a monster? The idea lingered in the back of Alex's mind.

Inside the folder was a ten-by-fourteen photo of the entire camp—counselors and kids, the owner and his wife. Alex remembered when it was taken, barely two weeks after the camp season had begun. He slid his finger along one row, then the next, from the youngest campers to the oldest. Then he stopped.

"Joey," he whispered to himself.

Joey must have moved the moment the shutter opened. Because his face, out of all the others, was slightly blurred. As if he were already existing in another time, midway between life and death. Alex looked closely at it. Then he switched off the light.

14

It was just after the first fall of snow—seven years after Joey Proctor disappeared—that two hunters, father and son, were out on the first day of deer season high above Echo Lake. Though by dawn others like them were usually out in their orange vests and jackets, Ben and Nick Wheeler saw no one else. It was so quiet, so still that morning, the snow pristine, the wind calm, that it seemed almost sacrilegious to break the silence with the crack of gunshot and the heavy fall of a graceful beast. They'd hunted together ever since Nick was a boy, and now he was engaged to be married, and two weeks from then, on the day after Christmas, he would be moving to be with his fiancée in Santa Barbara and take a position as a lecturer at the university. Ben didn't like to think about it too often, but he knew that this part of his life would soon come to an end. It would be their last hunt together.

Things end, and endings were what growing old had come to mean to him. People die; doors close; you became invisible to others, a ghost before your time. He'd lost a wife, and now he was losing a son. All that was left was himself—the worst, most forlorn company he could ever imagine. He could get a dog, something friends his own age had often suggested, but then he'd die and the dog would grieve. A terrible thought. He reminded himself to get rid of all the mirrors in the house: his face was the last thing he wanted to see greeting him each morning.

He knuckled away a stray tear, hoping Nick hadn't seen it. Again he took in the landscape: he'd lived in this area all of his life, met Helen here, married her in a Lenox church, buried his parents in a Lenox cemetery beside his forebears going back to the earliest years of the eighteenth century. He'd buried Helen there as well.

For sixteen years he had worked preseason at the camp down below as a carpenter, repairing the buildings after the usual hard winters, replacing torn screens in the bunkhouses, buttressing the dock, should there be any damage. He enjoyed the work and did his best to ignore the others from town who were hired to work there, rough men who could barely wait to return to the bars after they clocked out. He didn't kill whole evenings drinking, didn't idle away afternoons like some did over a bottomless cup of coffee at Little Dee's, always preferring to come home to Helen and young Nick and get a fire going on those cool early spring nights, when the more sultry evenings of summers past were just fading memories, like snapshots left too long in the sun.

With the campers and staff gone for the season in late August, he would sometimes walk down to the lake at the end of the day, sit on the dock, and watch the sun set. Then, a little stiff from the labors of his day, he'd get in his truck and head home, one more day behind him. Sometimes when he was working on a bunkhouse he'd find things the boys had left behind: tennis balls and socks, and once even a half-eaten hamburger under one of the beds, teeming with maggots.

When the Waukeelo sign at the entrance to the camp needed to be repaired, he replaced it with a new hand-carved one and hung it a week before the season began. It depicted a boy, his back to the viewer, paddling a canoe into the same sunset he now savored in the solitude of a day gone by, as though the boy were heading off to something more everlasting. By then, Ben had started his own carpentry business and, until he sold it, had three young craftsmen working under him at the shop behind his house.

"Hell of a morning, isn't it," he said, almost under his breath.

"I'd forgotten how pretty it is up here," Nick said.

Ben smiled. "You just realize that? We've been coming up here since you were nine years old. That's twenty years by my counting."

"Maybe I'm old enough now to appreciate it."

"You'll miss it, won't you?"

Nick smiled. "Yeah, maybe. While you're hunting deer, I'll be surfing."

"Yeah. Maybe." They shared a quiet laugh.

Ben knew that Nick's heart was no longer in this annual ritual of theirs. Stalking a deer, aiming for a clean shot—it belonged to another time, an earlier age.

Nick elbowed him, but Ben had heard it, too, what sounded like a footstep, or an animal's hoof against the fallen leaves beneath the few inches of snow. They scanned the woods ahead of them until Nick stopped and pointed up at the branches of a tree. His father didn't see what it was at first, but Nick went ahead and cracked the crust of the night's fall of snow, making enough noise to scare away a whole herd of deer, stepping until he stood beneath a birch and looked straight up.

Hanging from a length of rope was a boy with a noose around his neck. The boy was naked, and where his genitals were meant to be was a gaping hole, bloodred around the ragged edges. And the footprints beyond it were those of a man, not a deer.

15

THE MEETING BEGAN AT SIX THIRTY IN THE CONference room down the hall from Alex's office. He took his seat at the end of the table. He said, "Everyone's here but Pete Kellerman?"

"He's on his way," Sandy said. She folded her hands on top of the leather folder before her. "Can I start?"

Sandy Merritt was chief business development officer at Alex's company. He appreciated her ambition to branch out to other regions, new markets, and although he didn't always agree with her choices, he considered them all seriously and sometimes, against his better nature, circled back to revisit and often cut deals in those areas she felt most passionately about. She was also one of the top-level African-American executives in the business, having been hired by Alex just out of NYU's Stern School of Business. As always with Alex Mason, the optics were impeccable.

"Please do," Alex said.

"I know we've been looking into branching out of Manhattan into the outer boroughs—"

"Don't even think about saying Queens, Staten Island, or the Bronx," Rob Lawrence said, and everyone laughed.

"Queens is the next to start looking like Brooklyn," Sandy

said. "Just saying. But since we've been exploring other regions, other possibilities outside the Northeast and the West where we're already established, I still think, whatever the decision is on the Brooklyn location, that the Detroit property we researched is worth looking at."

"Your old hometown," Alex said, smiling widely.

"Back-of-my-hand territory." And she laughed.

"What is that called...'flyover country'?" Rob said. He mostly handled the Seattle, San Francisco, Palm Desert, and Los Angeles properties and would say anything to make his usual case against any potential ones in the Midwest, due to a bad experience at a college there which remained part of his personal arcana and not, as he always had to remind his more waggish colleagues, his arrest record. "I see no growth potential there," he said. "I mean, look at Harvey Laughlin, with his hotel in Indianapolis. Only fills it if there's a convention in town, and even then it's tough to beat the rates of the chains."

Sandy disagreed, as Alex knew she would. "I know the place has been going through some really rough times, but I'm also seeing indications that Detroit's going to be the comeback city."

"You hope," Rob said. He didn't have to remind them about their venture into Vegas real estate years earlier before the economy tanked, a hotel a little too far from the Strip. Fortunately, Alex had been able to sell the property to another, more established hotelier who, he last heard, was barely breaking even.

"I really do think we're going to see a lot of very positive changes in Detroit," Sandy said. "And they're starting to see an influx of young professionals who can't afford San Francisco or New York or Boston."

"So we've definitely ruled out the New Orleans project?" Alex said.

"Too much risk," Rob said. "And the insurance would kill us, Alex. Another Katrina, and we'd lose big time."

Alex pulled out another document. "What's happening with the Sturges?"

Rob said that it was still available, and there was every evidence that the price on it would continue to rise. "It's between Seventh and Eighth in a neighborhood that's been somewhat stagnant in the past, but the rollout from the whole Times Square thing has helped, and with some of the Garment Center zoning restrictions being relaxed, and the development of Hudson Yards, I'm thinking this could be a tremendous success. I would put it up there with the Mason House."

"That's pretty damned tremendous," Alex said, and everyone laughed. "What would be the cost of conversion? And—this is important—what's the licensing situation?"

"Still working on the conversion estimates. And from everything they've told me, licensing shouldn't be a problem. There's another hotel going through a renovation a block up, on West Thirty-Eighth, and everyone sees it as a plus."

"It's close enough to the theater district," Sandy said. "That's going to be a marketing point for us."

"All right, look. Rob, Sandy, why don't you run with this. Put in the bid we discussed. We'll wrap up the Sturges when I get back from Florida."

Ellen Siegel, who had been appointed as CFO not long after Sandy joined the company, asked about the Brooklyn property.

The one Alex had just visited. *That* one. Now he hated even thinking about it, as though it had been tainted for him forever.

He said, "I'm still thinking it over. It's not a bad location. Even if we tore it down and started over, it could be something."

"I mean, what's the issue, Alex?" Rob said. "Brooklyn's about as hot as it can get. If we don't do this, someone else will jump in and turn a ruin into millions of dollars."

"I know, but...just walking through it, you know, looking it over... There was something about the place that bothered me."

They waited for clarification.

"It just rubbed me the wrong way, you know?"

How did Joey know he was even interested in the building? Had he been watching Alex all these years since the incident on the raft?

"So, what, you don't think it's worth salvaging?"

Alex shook his head. "I'm just not sure. The only issue is in putting my name on a property that's going to end up nowhere. As always, of course, the brand comes first."

He'd thought that what had happened that afternoon with the raft was long buried in his past. People make mistakes, take wrong turns, choose the wrong paths in life, but now what had happened was coming back to haunt him. But he was a practical man, a man who lived in the real world, who dealt with things of substance—and memories, to him, were like movies viewed and forgotten. You remembered the titles, sometimes, and maybe one or two scenes and characters, and then they were gone. Forever.

Sandy said that sooner or later the neighborhood was going

to heat up, as Williamsburg had. The way things were going, it was inevitable.

Pete walked in and took a seat. "Sorry about that. I was on the phone with Chris at the Mason House."

"Please don't tell me the alarm system is misfiring again."

"He just called to say that there've been no problems since the last time. It's booked solid for Thanksgiving, Christmas Eve through New Year's Day, and before I forget, the weekend of the marathon is also sold out."

Alex grinned. "Can't beat that news, right?"

"And they know you'll be spending tonight there. So all's good."

"What's happening with the restaurant?"

"That's the really big news. Word's out that a review in the *Times* may be forthcoming."

"Chef's on the ball, then?" Alex said.

"Well, standing over the stove, anyway," Pete said, laughing.

"We're discussing the Brooklyn property. Any thoughts on that?"

"I think a high-end boutique hotel would fit right in," Pete said. "Unlike, say, a big modern high-rise, which would just look ridiculous on that block."

"And which would also make us a lot of enemies," Ellen said. "Have you seen those towers in Williamsburg? I mean really, right?"

Sandy said, "I agree. Keep it small…maybe a hundred and fifty rooms at the most."

"How the hell are we going to get full occupancy?" Alex said. "Red Hook is definitely not a primo location."

"But it will be soon enough, and then we'll lose out to other developers. So if we jump in now, we can make it primo. Great restaurant, nice neighborhood bar, not too flashy, maybe a little funky. Turn it into a location. Make it an anchor for everyone else." She shrugged. "I think it's a no-brainer."

"You agree, Pete?"

"The only issue I see is parking."

"There's a parking garage two blocks from there," Ellen said. "Maybe we can cut a deal to give hotel guests a discount. There's also a subway station within walking distance, and a water taxi from Manhattan to Red Hook."

"Well, I could use a second opinion," Alex said. "This seems to be something you're interested in, Pete. Why don't you take a look for yourself first thing tomorrow? I'll tell Golub that I want an extra day or two before I come up with an answer. I'll have him send over a key for you."

Pete brightened. "Great, yeah. I'd love to have a look."

They discussed four other projects, then Alex put his hands flat on the table and nodded. "All right. We're all tired. So go home, enjoy your evening. I need to do a little more work here. And don't forget—Ashley and I are looking forward to seeing all of you the Sunday after Memorial Day. Bring your swimsuits and an appetite."

It was something they did every year, giving the staff—the team, as Alex referred to his people—a chance for the new hires to meet Ashley and the girls, to unwind a little and talk about anything but real estate.

An hour later, the office deserted, Alex locked up and walked down the hall to the elevators. One of them had just risen to his floor. He slipped in as the doors were about to close. He pressed the button for the ground floor, and as the elevator began to descend, it stopped dead.

The lights went out.

"What the hell—?"

He took out his phone and turned on the flashlight. He pressed the ground-floor button again, but the elevator remained stuck. Nothing happened when he hit the alarm button. He pressed it again: still silence. It was nearly eight, and he knew the building must be empty by now. He went to call 911, but there was no cell signal.

He tried to pry open the doors, but they were firmly shut. He resorted to banging on them and shouting for help. There was no response. He pressed more buttons on the panel, until suddenly the elevator began to plummet, hurling him to the floor.

And then it abruptly stopped, bobbing a little at the end of the cable. Alex felt the hair on his arms rise up as he heard the voice of a child distantly echoing in the elevator shaft: "Help me… Please, someone help me…"

He stood and pressed his ear to the door. "Hello? Is someone there? I need help," he shouted. "I need you to call the police."

He listened more carefully and could hear the sound of a child quietly sobbing. "I can't… I can't swim… Please. Someone. Please…"

Alex banged hard on the door. "Is someone there? Can you hear me at all?"

"I'm drowning," the child said. "I'm drowning…"

Alex was backing away from the door, breathing hard, sweating heavily, when the elevator's lights flickered back on.

The doors slid open, and there was Pete Kellerman with his laptop bag, ready to go home.

"Alex. You okay?"

"Do you have any idea what just happened?"

"I finished work and was just on my way out."

"Did you hear anything? Some kid, maybe, crying for help?"

"I didn't hear a thing. Just your voice in the elevator. I figured you needed help."

Alex looked up at the elevator panel. "Wait a moment. This isn't even our floor."

"I know. My elevator also got stuck, but I managed to pry open the doors." He smiled. "Weird, isn't it."

16

On that day in the woods seven years after Joey's disappearance, the police homed in on Ben Wheeler's cell signal and met up with him and Nick some twenty minutes later. Ben imagined that the wildlife, now safely burrowed and sheltered, were watching this with amusement. The first day of hunting? Forget about it.

The officer looked up, stopped dead in his tracks, and said, "What the hell is that?"

Nick said, "It's not a real kid. It's, I don't know, a dummy of some sort?"

The cop looked at him. "And you called us for that?"

"It looks real, doesn't it? Even the bloodstain."

The cop scratched the side of his face. "Maybe so." He got on his radio and asked someone back at the station to bring a ladder. "This could take a little while," he told Nick and Ben.

That was the end of their hunting morning, all because some jerk decided it would be fun to hang a dummy from a tree. Ben looked up again. It must have been fifteen feet off the ground, swaying a little in the cold breeze that had risen up in the past hour, cutting across the frozen lake below.

"Do we need to stick around?"

"Not unless you can add anything to this."

"The footprints," Nick said, and when the cop seemed confused, Nick pointed at the tracks in the snow. The cop went over, got down on his haunches for a better look, then followed them for some forty yards.

"Weirdest thing," he said as he rejoined them. "I'm guessing a man's size twelve, like mine, but then the tracks just end, right before the woods clear."

"That's impossible," Nick said.

"You'd think so, wouldn't you?"

But the officer was right; the tracks came to a dead stop. The snow beyond them was smooth and untroubled.

When an officer with a ladder backed his vehicle up to the woods and hiked over, the first thing he noticed after looking up was that there was no sign of a ladder having been recently set up there. "It's a fall of fresh snow. There are the footprints, but nothing else. I'm going to guess that that thing was put there before yesterday afternoon's snow."

"And the prints?"

"Someone heard you out here this morning, and he's screwing with you. That's what I think. Or maybe it was just another hunter who wanted to leave you be." He leaned the ladder against the tree and climbed up until he was even with the body. He said, "It's a real noose, like in the old days, with the coils and all." He took out his knife and sawed away at the rope until he could get hold of the body and lower it onto a tarp. It looked as though someone had gone to the trouble of cutting out sections of pink cotton and sewing them together before stuffing them with rags. The face—the mouth in a big toothy smile—had been drawn on with marking pens, and details had been added to the torso: nipples created by some clever stitchery, a suggestion of a navel, everything cut and stuffed to look anatomically correct. The space where the genitals would have been was ripped and splashed with red paint. It was as if someone had made a model of something seen in reality: a child who had been mutilated.

The police took photos of it before wrapping it up and carrying it back to their SUV. Nothing about it would yield up any clues as to its origin.

The cops joined Nick and Ben. "Sorry about your hunting being ruined for the day. I'd chalk this up to a dumb prank." He pulled on a pair of gloves. He said, "They expect some frigid temperatures to set in later this afternoon. Get home, stay warm. Hope you have better luck tomorrow."

But this was the last day they'd be hunting together. Nick would be packing and preparing for his new life in California, and Ben would spend what would turn out to be the longest, most brutal winter in a hundred years in the solitude of his house in Becket. Six weeks later, Nick's calls to him from Santa Barbara would go unanswered, and when finally Nick called the police to check on his father, Ben had been dead for nearly a month: sitting in his chair before a cold fire, the day's newspaper on the floor beside him. Pipes in the house had burst, leaving his feet encased in ice. At least they would have a date to put on his gravestone.

They all headed out of the woods. None of them saw what had been drawn on one of the trees: a small, red stick figure spread-eagled on white birch bark, its face twisted with pain. And hammered into each of the eyes was an antique iron nail, two inches long.

Part Three

17

THE MASON HOUSE ON MADISON WAS THE JEWEL in the company crown, like the firstborn child, something to be treasured, coddled, and showered with the best money could buy. It stood in place of an office building that had suffered a gas explosion in the ground-floor deli and couldn't be salvaged. Three people had been killed, every unit was declared uninhabitable, and there was no way the owners were going to rebuild. Nor were they willing to spend the money to clean up the site. Alex had sat down with them, their management company, attorneys for both sides, and made a lowball offer. After a few hours of negotiation, a number a few million less than the asking price was agreed to. The location was perfect for a hotel. During the time when it was being built, a Starbucks opened on one side of it and a satellite of the Metropolitan Museum shop on the other. Alex had chosen the decor himself, from the front desk to the chairs in the lobby, evoking both the great New York hotels of the past as well as the contemporary, hip ones of his more ambitious competitors.

It was a warm, somewhat balmy evening, and Alex would have liked to walk for a bit, just a block or two, but it was difficult for him to go anywhere in the city without being recognized. Some wanted to shake his hand; others, bitter castoffs from the real estate business who had been reduced, in their estimation, to living lesser lives, to curse him out. And the paparazzi were always at hand, looking for that single unflattering moment to record forever. Alex had been through it before, mostly during the time of his very public affair. Photos in the *New York Post* and the *Daily News* always flattered the woman, never him. The caption *Beauty and the Beast?* was used one too many times. Seeing him arrive, the manager stepped out of his office and greeted him with a handshake.

"Good to see you again, Alex. Your suite is all ready for you."

"I hear there are no more problems with the alarm system."

The man smiled. "None whatsoever."

"Good. And thanks for being on the ball with this, Chris. We all appreciate it."

"Especially the guests," he said, and Alex laughed.

On this typically slow Monday night, Alex was pleased to see the bar so busy. On his way to the hotel, he had begun to think about branching out more to other countries. A second hotel in Britain, perhaps in Edinburgh, and the idea of relocating, to London, maybe, with the family for a year or two came to mind. He hadn't been to England since his senior year in college, when he did a semester at the London School of Economics and mostly majored in pub life and women. He knew he was talking himself into something that was just an excuse for an escape. Too many things had been happening here. The swimming pool, which had left him feeling that the house had been somehow corrupted. The name on the wall in the Brooklyn property. The elevator with the crying child. *I'm drowning…*

And now, as he sat at the bar and sipped his drink, he remembered Joey. Not his features, not his voice—those were as much a blur as the face in the camp photo. What came back to him was the moment he returned to the lakefront after dark, turned on the flashlight, and saw the boy was gone. He remembered how the wind had risen and ruffled the surface of the lake, making the raft bob and dip a little in the water. Where was Joey at that moment? Underwater? Alex slept little that night in the camp, thinking that by dawn the body would be washed up on the shore. Except there was no body. Not then, not ever. Joey Proctor had ceased being a child and had become an absence.

What had been simply a moment of carelessness—leaving behind a numbing sensation that Alex hadn't shaken off until a few weeks later when he returned to college with all its distractions and one too many nights of hard drinking—had left him with the memory of sitting across from Joey's parents. The quiet in the Dave Jensen's cabin. The agony on their faces. He thought of how much grief his action had caused them. They were reduced to two despairing people with nothing left but each other, caught in the bind of mutual resentment. How do you face that? How can one live like that?

He never heard from Dave Jensen about the camp's future, and busy with the beginning of his sophomore year at Penn and his active social life, Alex had let it slip from his memory.

Except now it seemed that Joey knew where Alex could be found: where he lived and where he worked. And he was getting his revenge. Alex's phone vibrated, and he answered it in his usual manner: "Go."

It was Rob. The owners of the Sturges had been looking

at more bids, even though Alex had specifically requested his be considered before any others. Alex pressed his lips together, thanked Rob for updating him, and clicked off. *Fuck that*, he thought. *Just—*

"Nice place."

He looked around until he saw the woman two stools away from him. She smiled with eyes brighter and bluer than Ashley's.

"Thanks, yeah."

"Yours?"

He nodded. "Actually, I own it."

"Just like that?"

"More or less," and they both laughed.

She held out a hand. "Jennifer Ammons." Her accent was patrician southern, all mint julep and magnolia blossom, easy on the ear.

"Alex Mason."

She held his hand a half second longer than most would, and out of habit his eyes instantly went to her left hand. No ring. An evening out all alone.

"And you come all the way down and drink with the proletariat? Gotta tell you, but I feel mighty honored, Mr. Mason."

"Yeah, well, it can get a little dull up with the gods," he said, and she laughed. "It's nice to meet you, Jennifer Ammons."

The bartender set a bowl before Alex, who in turn held it out to Jennifer. "Nuts?"

"Oh, maybe just a little crazy now and then." This time they both laughed. This was the dangerous moment, when one small act shifts the balance, and with just a gentle nudge, life tips into catastrophe.

She moved to the stool next to his, and when Alex turned to look at her, he didn't notice the person sitting behind them, midroom in a booth, alone with his drink, watching them.

"And I must say that when you sat down just now, you looked like the saddest man in the whole wide world."

"I was just distracted, I guess."

"Rough day?"

He smiled a little. "You might say that."

"I had my ups and downs today as well."

"I just bet you did," he said, and she laughed and briefly touched him just above his knee.

He'd never felt uncomfortable talking with a woman. It was as if he was always looking for a way in, a fresh bed, a new body, a voice he'd never heard before. It was a bad habit that had very nearly cost him his marriage, his reputation, and his brand, and try as he did to restrain himself, there was that part of him that could always fall for a pretty face and an inviting smile. Everything was a deal to be concluded; everything was a potential win.

"So what do you do, Jennifer Ammons?"

She shook the ice in her glass. "Mostly I'm in the process of going through a very complicated and difficult divorce from a very wealthy man."

"Here in New York?"

"So you might think. I moved up here after we separated. My husband is not only rich but also very dangerous. You should see my bruises after three rounds with the bastard." She touched her rib cage, a fresh memory. "Putting miles between us was the smartest thing I've ever done."

She said she was from Charleston. "Born and bred South Carolinian. And you are...?"

"New Yorker. Raised here in Manhattan."

"And hotels are your business, I presume?"

"They are. How are the ones in Charleston?"

"Charming, of course, just like the city. None of these flashy gold-and-glittery high-rise places you see here. Yours excepted, of course."

"I try to keep it tasteful," he said.

She finished her drink, and Alex offered her another. "Hmm, I don't know if I should. I may not make it home in one piece."

"Home being where these days?"

"Where I hang my dress, Alex Mason," and when they both laughed, she touched his wrist. She was making a bad day turn very pleasant indeed.

"I can have my concierge call you a taxi."

"And stumble and stagger all the way up to my apartment?"

"Why not take a room here. I'll be more than happy to comp you a night."

She looked him straight in the eyes. "You are one amazing man, you know that, Mr. Mason? But I am not going to take advantage of your better nature, as we say where I come from. Though"—she lifted her fresh drink—"I must say, your better nature is really quite exceptional."

She was making herself irresistible through a script of seemingly endless clichés, and though he was finding himself dangerously attracted to her, the last thing he needed was to stray again. Before his affair with Karen Cain, he'd slept with a few other women, most of them one-night stands when he was out of town visiting his hotels, though one relationship, with a part-time bartender at the Tahoe location, had lasted three very interesting nights. And every time he woke up the morning after, he regretted it, the regret sometimes feeling as warm and satisfying as the sex the night before. As though sometime in the night he had bought something valuable and knew that he'd never let it go. But since then, he'd kept his word to Ashley. This time, he knew, were he to succumb, he would lose her forever. He finished his drink and smiled.

"Jennifer, I must say good night."

"Oh, so soon. No, not really?"

"I'm going to have dinner sent up to my room and get to sleep. The day's catching up with me a little too quickly. If you'll stop at the concierge's desk, I'll be sure they'll call the car service we often use here. We'll be more than happy to cover the cost. And thanks for a pleasant twenty minutes. You made my day."

She held out her hand and he took hers, and when the man who had been watching them got up and walked out of the bar, neither of them noticed.

18

WHO IS SHE?"

He'd barely gotten out of the Bentley when, waiting for him on the outside steps, Ashley held up her phone and displayed a photo of a smiling Jennifer Ammons with her hand on Alex's thigh.

"What are you talking about?"

The next shot was of Jennifer with her hand on his arm. Then the same woman with her hand on his shoulder. One more: his hand on her stockinged knee.

"We can either talk out here or go upstairs," Ashley said. "I don't want the girls to hear this. And don't even think about raising your voice to me."

They went up to the bedroom and she shut the door. She said, "You told me you weren't going to do this again."

"Where did you get these?"

"Who the hell is she?"

"How did you get this stuff?"

"They were messaged to me an hour ago."

Alex scratched hard at his scalp. "Who sent them?"

"The number was blocked." She crossed her arms and just looked at him. "So who is it now, Alex?"

"Look. She was at the bar at the hotel. She just started talking to me. I'd never seen her before in my life."

"And you put your hand on her knee? And let her squeeze your thigh? This is pretty intimate for just another customer at the bar, you know that?"

"Will you listen to me for just two minutes? I'd had a really rough day. This crazy thing happened with the elevator and really spooked me. The thing went out of control, and I thought I was going to die. So, yeah, I had a few drinks, she was at the next stool, and we began talking, then I went upstairs. Alone, I promise you. I had dinner sent to the room, and I went to sleep. Again alone. Ask anyone at the hotel."

"I'll tell you what happened," she said. "So maybe you had a bad day. I know what you're like after a few drinks. You get a little happy, you get a little goofy and playful, and all of a sudden you're the life of the party. A pretty woman sits down next to you, and you're sucked right into it all over again. Just like the last time. I bet she laughed at everything you told her."

"Nothing happened, Ashley."

"Swear on my life? How about our kids' lives?"

"Come on, do we really have to go there?"

"Just say it."

"Absolutely. I swear on the girls' lives."

"I'm not finished," she said, scrolling to the next screen showing a nude Jennifer Ammons having sex with someone whose face was out of the frame. Then to the next: a different angle. And the next, and the next, and the last one, Jennifer Ammons lying on a bed, wearing nothing but a smile.

"That's not me with her."

"There's a straight line between you at the bar and you in bed with this woman. They're even time-stamped. It all took place in just under an hour from when the first shot was taken in the bar."

"I'm not even in those photos."

"I find it hard to believe it isn't you, though." Ashley put the phone into her pocket and stared at him.

"Wait a minute," Alex said. "These were sent to your phone. How did someone get your number?" He sat on the end of the bed, and when he reached for her hand she stepped back. "Look… Look, someone's trying to set me up. I talked to her for no more than fifteen minutes, tops. I finished my drink, ordered dinner sent to the room, went upstairs, turned on the TV, and waited for them to deliver. I ate, I showered, I went to sleep. That is the honest-to-god truth, Ash."

She put her hand on the doorknob. The conversation was over.

But he knew the incident would always be there, unvoiced, unexplained, and once again a splinter of doubt had entered their marriage. She left the room and shut the door.

He took out his phone and called the hotel. "Is Eric working the bar again tonight? Patch me through, will you, Chris?"

When the bartender answered, Alex could hear that the bar was busy.

"Eric, it's Alex Mason. Just quickly… Last night at the bar, did you see anyone taking photos of me? Anyone, say, with a phone pointed in my direction?"

"I really didn't notice, Alex."

"No one looking suspicious, at all?"

"I'm sorry, I just don't remember."

"The woman sitting next to me... Had you ever seen her before?"

"No. And I have a good memory for my customers. She was new. I'm pretty sure of that."

Alex asked to be reconnected with the front desk, inquired if there had been a guest at the hotel named Jennifer Ammons, and learned there was no record of anyone by that name. "Did a woman stop by to have you call for a car service? I'd asked to have it comped if she did."

But there was no one. She'd come from nowhere, and walked right back out into the great big nothing.

19

Mike Farrelli had been with the local police force ever since he was twenty-two, just another cop in a uniform stopping speeders, handling the occasional booze-fueled domestic incident, and dealing with the usual break-ins and robberies of vacation homes supposedly locked and secured for the off-season. When the tourists arrived, mostly for Tanglewood, came also the drunk drivers, tipsy on prosecco or eight-dollar chardonnay consumed on the lawn during a Mahler concert. And then, with the deep autumn and the cold nights came the peace. The campers had gone home, and the population had been reduced to its normal manageable proportions. Cops knew the usual troublemakers: the teenaged boys in their oversexed cars, the inebriates, the crazy men who shouted at trees and, in the case of the late, deeply disappointed and endlessly aspiring Howard Shrug, took to depositing with impressive regularity his prolific bowel movements in the aisles of the fiction stacks in the public library.

Two weeks after Joey's disappearance, on a quiet, rainy afternoon at the station, Farrelli had been looking over the reports compiled during the initial investigation. Something about them didn't seem right. Few people simply vanished into thin air, not to mention that, according to police records, there had only been one missing-persons case in their jurisdiction, some twenty years earlier, involving a local boy, months after the camp season was over, who'd gone missing and was never found.

A boy at a camp—with its strict supervision and daily timetable that allowed for little idle time—wouldn't just wander away. Not an eight-year-old. But this Proctor kid had just disappeared. He wasn't in the lake and, unless he'd been buried, certainly wasn't anywhere on the campgrounds or in the area surrounding it. Everything had been checked twice, there had been no sightings of any fresh diggings, and now the investigation was slipping quickly into cold-case mode. Yet Farrelli knew that above the lake and stretching for long distances was woodland, some of it barely penetrable. Not every inch could be adequately searched. Acres could be overlooked. Unless some evidence materialized, the case would never be solved.

The human factor: it always came down to that. Not clothing fibers or strands of hair, but someone stepping forward who might have seen something, or someone who might have heard something, or someone who might one day feel the need to confess. Time was never on their side in cases such as these. Windows of opportunity closed rapidly, shutting out daylight, obscuring the truth. A cold case was just another mystery lying dormant, waiting until someone or something might come along to give it warmth, to bring it back to life.

Then he remembered hearing the name John Otis mentioned by one of the officers. He went back twenty years in the online police files and found nothing. He wandered off to another room at the station where Jeff Hooper, a detective who'd been there a few years longer than Mike, was reading the sports pages and sipping coffee. Farrelli tapped on the open door.

"Have a moment?"

"Maybe in ten minutes. I'm on my break."

"Just spare me thirty seconds, okay? Anything seem strange to you about the Proctor thing?"

"Anything? Yeah, like ten thousand anythings. Like no one's contacted the family about a ransom payment. And we're way past the usual forty-eight-hour limit."

"Because he wasn't kidnapped for money."

"And you know this how, Mike?"

"I don't, at least not for sure. But we have to consider he may have been taken for the gratification of the abductor. There's something else I'm wondering about. Who or what is John Otis?"

"You know about that, too?"

"There's nothing in our records. And nothing in the census that shows a John Otis living anywhere near here."

Hooper had heard the legend from one of the kids in Joey's bunk. The boy was scared shitless that this Otis had taken his friend.

"So I asked one of the counselors about it—" Jeff began.

Mike checked the papers he was holding. "Alex Mason, the swimming guy?"

"No, the counselor in Joey's bunk."

Mike turned to another page. "That would be, who...Steve Fenton?"

"That's the one. He said it's this bullshit story they tell the campers about this crazy guy Otis who comes down from the hills and steals one of the boys every seven years."

Farrelli smiled. "Seven years. Well, that's kind of random."

"You know what they say, Mike. Add a weird little detail, and it makes it all the more believable."

Mike ambled back down to the break room. He glanced up at the clock on the wall: nearly two. He took his lunch from the fridge and returned to his office. It was possible, he thought, that there really was a John Otis living far enough off the grid that no census would note his existence. And with no police record, there was no way of locating him.

But there was nothing in the case records showing that campers had been disappearing regularly every seven years.

He wrapped up the other half of his sandwich and put it back in the fridge. He walked up the stairs of the town hall and asked the clerk to check on the owners of the camp, current and previous, going back, say, thirty years.

There had been three camp owners in the past three decades: Frank Parent, who had been associated with Waukeelo for twenty-four years and was now deceased; afterward a Dr. and Mrs. Leonard Kelvin; and finally the people who currently held that position, David and Nancy Jensen. The Kelvins had owned the camp for twelve years, and when Dr. Kelvin died, his wife put the place up for sale. Her whereabouts were unknown to the town clerk, nor was there a forwarding address listed for her.

Joey Proctor remained a mystery. But it was one Detective Mike Farrelli couldn't get out of his mind.

20

On the last Friday in August, the Masons' Gulfstream, which one particular New York tabloid was fond of calling the Frequent Flyer, was fueled up and ready to take off at Westchester County Airport. It was a dark morning, heavy with clouds, and rain had begun to fall as they climbed out of the Bentley while their luggage was taken from the trunk and carted over to the plane. The flight would take just over four hours, transporting them from this miserable weather to the sun and sea and warmth of the Gulf Coast. Though they owned a summer home in Amagansett, it was being renovated and wouldn't be habitable until the following spring.

Alex was looking forward to a change of scenery and a chance for the two of them to be intimate once again. Since the day she'd received the photos of Jennifer Ammons, Ashley had said little to him. She spent the nights in the guest room at the end of the hallway, slipping out early each morning so the girls wouldn't be aware of it. He knew it wouldn't take much to lose her for good. He would see other men looking at her with those familiar hungry eyes, and he'd sometimes catch her gazing at some guy across a restaurant or at a party. He thought that if they could survive this as a couple, he would never even appear to stray again, a deal he made with himself. The same one he'd made the last time. After all, he was one of the great dealmakers.

First the pool, then the room at the Brooklyn building, now this. Bad luck always comes in threes, his grandmother used to say. She was a woman who never wanted for anything, and who had left Alex's father enough money to launch his own son in his successful career as a property developer. What came with his fortune and his name was an unhealthy interest in his private life, thanks to gossip columnists and the usual suspects of the internet. He wondered if one of them had been responsible for the photos of him on Ashley's phone. Had he been set up? And why? Marital discord, a matter better suited to bedrooms and arguments over a bottle of Scotch, was hardly going to put a dent in his business. And who was this Jennifer Ammons? Probably no one at all. And now she was gone, undoubtedly forever.

But then again, he'd always thought, so was Joey.

The morning of their departure, Ashley at least smiled at him and put a hand on his arm as they were leaving the house. And he knew that the villa they were renting at the resort only had two bedrooms, so they would have to sleep in the same bed. If he tried too hard to win her with favors, she would believe he was guilty of having taken this woman to bed. He had to play it properly, just as he always did in his day-to-day business, step by step, one thought ahead of everyone else. You admit no weakness and never, ever go on the defensive. But he would do his level best: for the sake of their kids, for the sake of their marriage.

They arrived at the resort in Captiva just over an hour after landing at Fort Myers, and after their luggage was brought up to their room, they had lunch on the terrace at the Pointe and went down to the pool. While the girls sat on the side with their feet in the water, Alex and Ashley lay back on adjoining loungers. She was wearing one of her white two-pieces, always a favorite of his and, it seemed, everyone else's.

"Becca's turned out to be a pretty strong swimmer," Ashley said.

As the pool wasn't crowded, Becca started doing laps, just as Alex had taught her, with focus and strength. Lyndsey stayed by the side of the pool near the deep end, dangling her feet in the water. Becca was the prettier of the two, and Lyndsey envied how the boys in the pool kept staring at her sister. Nobody paid any attention to her, with her baby fat and chubby legs.

Alex watched her for a few moments. "Lyndsey, not so much, though."

"She's a little nervous in the water. Give it time."

He set down his Bloody Mary and headed for his younger daughter. "Hey, Lynds? I want to try a little something with you."

He squatted down next to her. "Hop in."

She gaped at him. She couldn't believe her ears. "What?"

"Jump in the pool. You'll see, you'll start to swim."

"No, I'm scared, Daddy." She even shivered a little.

He put a hand on her arm. "Hey. I'm right here. I won't let anything happen to you."

"But it's deep, and I'm scared. I'm really, really scared." There were tears in her eyes, which made him even more eager to get her off her perch. Leave a fear unchallenged, and it'll always be with you, like a mangy, flea-ridden dog, panting and limping in your shadow. No one deserved to live like that. He certainly didn't.

Quietly, he said, "Do it for me. For Mom. I promise it's going to be okay."

Ashley set down her drink. Something was happening, something was about to happen, and she couldn't read it, she couldn't see what was impending. All she could see was the back of her daughter as she seemed to shrink in the presence of her father.

"Just do it," Alex said. "It's so simple. Try it at least? For me? For Mom? She's watching, you know, and she'll be so proud if you just go ahead and jump in. Soon you'll be just like your sister. See how she's swimming laps?"

But Becca wasn't swimming laps, for now she was treading water next to a boy her age with an absurdly uncool fauxhawk and a fake diamond in one earlobe.

"Try it," Alex said, this time loud enough to attract attention.

Ashley got off her lounger and watched the scene unfold. "Alex? What's going on?"

"I won't let anything hurt you, Lynds, I promise. Just try it. Try it, for Christ's sake!"

He should have seen it coming—the tears, the incoherence—her response to so many things. Now everyone by the pool was witnessing it.

Ashley said, "Leave her alone, will you?" and as if a plug had been pulled, he just stopped.

He said, "You're right. You're right. I don't know what I was thinking. I'm sorry, Lyndsey. I really am."

He put his arm around her, but he felt he was already slipping out of her life, becoming just another stranger. The kind of person your parents warned you about. Like John Otis, Alex might have thought, had his mind been clearer.

Ashley stood over them. "Just leave her be, Alex." She spoke quietly and reasonably, so as not to be heard by anyone but him.

He was about to turn his face to her, to tell her exactly how he felt, when instead he slipped down into the water and swam slowly toward the opposite end. He hoisted himself up and looked back at Lyndsey.

But it wasn't his daughter he was seeing. It was little Joey Proctor. He watched the boy as he stared back at him, not even blinking. Just sitting there, staring. Waiting. Alex dropped back into the water and began swimming furiously toward Joey. The closer he got, the more distant Joey seemed, as if he were still on the raft, bobbing gently in Echo Lake twenty-one years earlier.

When he reached the end, Joey wasn't there. The sky had clouded over and there was distant thunder; rain was imminent. There was no one else around. Not a soul.

21

BY NINE O'CLOCK, SEVERAL COCKTAILS INTO THE evening after the storm, and with the girls in their bedroom eating room service and watching a movie on TV, what had happened by the side of the pool Alex had been pretty much forgotten. All that remained with him was Joey Proctor's face. This time it wasn't the sniveling little boy who had begged Alex not to make him go in the deep water, but someone who had come back to face him down.

Alex and Ashley found seats by a fire pit. There were others there who kept to themselves, quietly chatting, laughing, drinking, and ordering small plates from the attentive waitresses who cruised the area.

Ashley rested her head against Alex's shoulder. She said, "That whole thing with Lyndsey really scared her, you know."

"I know. I just, I don't know… I guess I just lost it. I'm sorry, babe. I really am."

She took her head away. "I know all about your temper, Alex. I've had to put up with it for too many years."

He put an arm around her. "Hey. That's history now, and you know it."

"Do I?"

"That wasn't my temper today. I just wanted to get her in the water."

"Against her will. Is that how you treat an eight-year-old? Really? She'll come to it eventually, Alex. Just let her live by her own clock." Ashley glanced at her watch. "I'll be right back. I'm going to check on how the girls are doing."

The waitress brought them margaritas. He was about to sip his when he heard a voice.

"I know you."

He looked up to find a man around his own age, a Scotch in his fist. "I'm sorry?"

"Yeah, definitely, I know you really well. Alex Mason, right?"

"Yeah, that's right." Alex turned away. He had no interest in this man with his belly stretching the overpriced Captiva T-shirt he'd bought at the resort shop.

The man said, "Remember that building on the West Side you were looking at a few weeks ago?"

Alex sighed and turned back to him. "I look at a lot of buildings. Which one are you talking about, and why is it any business of yours?"

"The Sturges. Between Seventh and Eighth on Thirty-Seventh?"

Now he recognized him. They'd crossed paths before, at conferences and a few cocktail parties. "You're Pearson, right? Mark Pearson with the Goodman Group?"

The man nodded.

"Well, I thought the place would make a nice hotel," Alex said. "With about a thirty-million-dollar makeover. Anyway, my bid's in, it'll almost definitely be accepted, and we'll sign next week. Why don't you sit down instead of standing over me, okay, Mark? Let me get your drink topped up."

Alex reached up to take the glass from him, and Pearson took a step back.

"I think I'll just stand over you a little more, if you don't mind. I like to see you at your true stature. You've bullied your way to the top, which makes you a very, very small man with a very big mouth."

Alex set his drink down. "You know something? I don't like to lose. And I'm sorry you don't approve of my attitude or my methods, which have always been aboveboard. And they work. Really well."

"Maybe I like to win just a little more than you do."

Alex got to his feet. He had a few inches on Pearson and lifted his chin to accentuate it. "What the hell are you talking about?"

"The Sturges is my building now, Mason. I closed on it yesterday afternoon. And I've got my eyes on a lot more of them. Just watch your back from now on. Because my company is about to overtake yours."

Alex jabbed a finger in Mark's chest as the others at the fire pit stopped to watch. One of them said, "Take it somewhere else, okay, guys?"

It was Ashley who put an end to it. She was coming toward him, looking grim, holding up the phone he'd expressly left in the hotel room so as not to be bothered. "Alex—?"

"What's happened?"

"You need to fly back first thing tomorrow."

22

Mike Farrelli was never comfortable in the woods. He'd been raised in Hartford, where he'd spent a good many years of his life, and had only moved up to the Berkshires for the work. Eleanor took to the place immediately, proving what she'd always said, that she was a country girl at heart, even though she was from Washington, DC, a location more feral than pastoral.

Mike wasn't at ease there because he couldn't read his surroundings, not like some who'd been born and bred there, who had the skills needed for negotiating life, as he saw it, in the middle of nowhere: the edgelands, as he thought of it, the place where weird things happen. But over the years he'd found a middle way that allowed him some comfort. He'd made friends in the area, although not as many as his wife had, his mostly drawn from his own police station and departments at neighboring towns and villages, and he had come to like the people who lived around them. And now, when they went to New York City for a weekend, or once traveled back to Hartford to bury his 102-year-old aunt, he tried hard to hide the fact that he missed home.

Now, seven years after Joey Proctor went missing, on the verge of retirement, Mike had been asked to take another look at the case. A couple of hunters had been out a week earlier and had seen some peculiar things—or at least one peculiar thing. The drawing on the birch tree was only spotted afterward, by Mike himself, as he stood in the snow and touched one of the nails with the tip of his finger.

A hanging of a replica of a mutilated child; a drawing of a boy with nails driven into his eyes. This was what was meant when locals who knew their way around the woods spoke of knowing where and how to look. You could spot a deer or another hunter, or the things that simply didn't belong.

Mike looked up at the tree where the dummy had been hanging. Some of the rope remained, and he could see that whoever did it had spent good money. It wasn't just some clothesline rope; it really was what hangmen used back before they decided it was more humane to inject a cocktail of questionable chemicals into the condemned.

He thought of the legend of John Otis and knew in his heart that up here in the woods you could find any manner of person—from a homeless guy to a madman to a college professor taking a stroll. Looking carefully up and around, he followed a path of his own devising between the trees. He stopped and looked back to where he had entered the woods, memorizing the view to recognize it when he returned to go home. It hadn't snowed for over a week, and with the deep cold of the past few nights, what was left of the snow had crusted over. Unable to see what lay beneath, he stepped carefully, taking his time. His phone rang, and he stopped to answer it.

Eleanor said, "You weren't at the station."

"I'm up above the lake. Just having a look around."

"If you break your leg, you'll be in trouble."

"You think?"

"Just be careful, okay?"

"I should be home within the hour."

He took another step and immediately sank in up to his knee. He winced as he extricated his foot from what must have been soft ground.

When he took it out, he saw that he had stepped into a hole. He switched on his flashlight, and when he caught a glimpse of what looked like a rib cage, he phoned the station.

He wouldn't be home within the hour. It would be late into the night when he finally walked through the door.

—

The sun was hovering just over the horizon when everyone arrived, two officers from Farrelli's department plus the van from Pittsfield with the forensics team. They would have to work quickly, as the light would soon be fading. It took them almost forty minutes to excavate what had turned into a pit, working slowly and deliberately, clearing the sides of it to leave what lay there intact—like archeologists, Mike remembered from a TV documentary, on their knees with their brushes and fine tools. A police photographer captured the scene from all angles: a human skeleton with bits of leathered skin still attached, its wrists and ankles bound to each other with copper wire. A tangle of faded red hair remained on what was left of the skin on the skull. It was in a crouching position, as if the person had been ordered to kneel, as though in prayer, as if whatever had taken place was in service to some dark ritual.

"This person must have struggled for a long time," one of the cops said. "See the bone on the wrist? That wire dug right into it. Cut a groove, it looks like."

The forensics expert they'd brought in from Pittsfield squatted beside the remains, hands on his knees. "First of all, it's a female."

"You're sure of that?"

"See the pelvis? It belongs to a woman of childbearing age, I would guess between fifteen and maybe twenty-five at the time of death." He got

back onto his feet and shook his head. "I'm thinking she may have been buried alive after she'd been tortured."

Jesus, Mike thought, never usually one for prayer or invocation.

"It's been here a while."

"Too hard to say anything more definite than from as few as ten to as many as fifty years." The forensics expert looked closer. "I can be more definite once we get it under the lights." He rubbed the ache out of his thighs. "What were you thinking, that it was that little boy who disappeared all those years ago?" As he peeled off the gloves, he said, "Up where we are, folks think that the boy will never be found."

Farrelli looked at him. "Why do you say that?"

"We've tossed around all kinds of crazy ideas, but the one no one's really looking at is that the whole thing might have been a hoax. He's alive, he's somewhere, but this skeleton...?" He shook his head. "It's not him."

Mike thought about this as he drove back to the station. He wondered if it would be worth his while to call the boy's parents, just to see what was what. A hoax? Perpetrated by whom?

And what would be the point? People didn't just abduct children for ransom money; they also took them to use them, to make them their playthings, and then, when they were done, when they'd gotten what they wanted, they discarded them. Unless something had moved whatever remained of the abductors' hearts, and they ended up keeping the child as a kind of penance, nurturing it, watching it grow. Up here, where few people lived in the hills, anything could happen.

He decided calling the Proctors wasn't worth the grief he'd cause them, reminding them of everything they'd lost seven years earlier. And what would be the point in reviving a case that had gone cold? In a few months he'd be off the force, and he'd promised Eleanor they could celebrate by going somewhere warm for a few weeks. Florida, maybe. Anywhere but here.

23

ALEX ARRIVED OUTSIDE THE MASON HOUSE HOTEL in the early afternoon, having landed in Westchester County Airport at just past one o'clock. Ashley had insisted they all go back together, a decision that left Becca in a sour mood and Lyndsey perfectly content. Returning home meant no more flare-ups from her father. Ashley promised that on the next school vacation they would return to Florida for a longer stay.

Ellen and Rob were already outside waiting for him. It was a warm September day, and Rob held his jacket over his shoulder, his shirtsleeves rolled to the elbows. He looked somber.

"How bad is it?" Alex said.

"You'll see for yourself. The inspector should be here any moment."

"I don't see why we can't start without him."

No one noticed the man standing in the doorway of the Citibank branch across the street, looking right at them, smiling a little to himself.

The lobby was deserted. Chris stepped out from behind the desk, looking like he hadn't slept in days.

"Guests are all gone," he said.

"How did that go?"

"About as well as you might expect. Most said they'd never

stay in a Mason hotel ever again. First the alarms, now this. Not a lot of happy campers."

This was the first time anything like this had ever happened in any of Alex's properties. He had heard an overview of the situation on the phone the night before, and after that, he stayed in the room at the resort, trying to work things out.

"Just give me the whole deal before the health inspector comes."

"I think you'd better see yourself. We'll start with one of the guest rooms."

Alex put a hand on his arm before they entered the elevator. "How many are there?"

"So far thirty-four rooms. Which means there'll almost definitely be more." As Chris opened the door to room 237, an overfed rat waddled under the bed. He said, "We counted at least ten in this room alone." The carpet was littered with droppings, and there was a rancid smell in the air.

Alex aimed his flashlight at a corner, where three of the creatures huddled together and stared them down, like gangsters with too much fuck-you in their souls. "If you go into the bathroom, you'll see more in the shower stall. Now you need to see the kitchen."

It looked as spotless as it always had. The hotel's star chef, London-born Reg Dwyer, had that week earned a rave three-star review from Pete Wells in the *Times*, and reservations were booking two months ahead. Until now.

"Where is he?"

"Reg? Meeting with his lawyers. It's your hotel but it's his brand, and he has to protect it. Possibly even sue Mason

House Properties for negligence. The shit hit the fan when the inspector flew in on a surprise visit to check out the kitchen, like he does every year. This was before the guests started calling the desk. He found a ton of mouse droppings. And then this." He opened one of the oven doors to reveal a dead mouse lying in it. "This place is cleaned every night. It's the chef's most profitable venue. More than London, more than Vegas."

"It's always had an A rating from the city," Ellen reminded them.

"The odd thing is that—see that mouse in the oven?—there are no droppings. Which means it was placed in there after it died. Someone's behind this, Alex."

"You've checked the names of the hotel guests?"

"They'll have to be questioned, and that could take a week or two, maybe more when we've tracked them all down. If they're willing to talk to us. And who says the person responsible is going to admit to it? I'd say it's someone who's trying to sabotage you. Whether they did it through a hotel guest or on their own doesn't matter. That damage is done."

Immediately, the name Mark Pearson came to mind. But as despicable as the man was, Alex knew he was also lazy, and to do this, to wreak this kind of havoc in Alex's signature hotel, involved too much time and effort. That left all the other developers in the city as potential suspects. He shook his head a little as they left the kitchen.

"They're everywhere," Chris went on. "In the rooms, in the service areas… We're assuming the entire hotel is infested."

"The dining room?"

"And the bar."

One of the employees pushed open the kitchen door. "Inspector's here, Chris."

"Thanks, Miguel."

The health inspector was waiting for them in the lobby, as grim-faced as he always was, even when he was the bearer of good news. "You have one of two choices. Shut the place down, have the exterminators in, have it cleaned, top to bottom, and then we'll revisit."

"That could take a week or two," Alex said. "I'd lose a lot of business."

"Your other choice is to have your building flat-out condemned, which would seriously damage your brand, Mr. Mason. Are all the guests gone?"

"That's what I've been told."

The inspector fished a document from his briefcase. "Sign that, keep the second page, and close everything down by six o'clock today at the latest. That's an hour and a half from now."

—

Stalled in traffic, Alex began pounding the steering wheel and screaming at the top of his lungs, getting louder and louder each time, "Fuck fuck *fuck fuck fuck!*" until he realized his window was open and other drivers were staring at him. This is what his life had become, he thought. Out of control, cheap and profane.

He pulled up to the house just after seven that evening. He was already beyond rage and a layer deeper into the thing, trying to work out exactly who might be behind this. Other names of competitors came to mind, and he omitted them one by one from his list of suspects. For another property developer to get caught would ruin his brand forever. Nothing like this was ever worth such a risk. He switched off the engine and saw Ashley sitting outside on the step by the portico, two glasses of Scotch beside her.

"Your face is red." She handed him his drink. "You okay?"

"Yeah, well, you know. It's been hell all day long. Then the traffic, and the fucking accident on the Saw Mill, and the—"

"How bad is it?" she interrupted.

"The place has always been spotless. At up to eight hundred bucks a night, it had better be. It looks like the mice and rats had been brought into the hotel from outside, which means someone's trying to get at me. There's a pattern. First the thing with the pool. Then those photos from the bar. Now this. And—I didn't tell you—something happened when I looked at the Brooklyn property. I still can't make any sense of it. Let's go in."

"Talk to me here."

The vivid sunset was a view wasted on them now.

Ashley set down her drink. "Just tell me the whole thing."

He sat beside her. "Someone's trying to bring my business down. Trying to ruin me."

"Someone."

"I don't know who it is."

"How many enemies could you have made over the years? I mean, you've always run a clean operation. You've never broken any laws or threatened anyone."

He said nothing.

"Have you?" she added.

Once again, he saw himself swimming from the raft, leaving

a small boy stranded on it. *Swim or die*, he'd told the kid, and now he was gone. Except he wasn't.

"It's impossible," he said. "It can't be."

"What? Just tell me."

"Look. This is so crazy. I mean, a long time ago—like over twenty years ago—I was hired to teach swimming at this summer camp in the Berkshires. There was this eight-year-old, Joey Proctor, who was afraid of the water and couldn't swim to save his life. I carried him out to this raft and left him there. Told him he would have to swim back on his own."

"Even though he was afraid of the water? And couldn't swim? Eight years old… That's Lyndsey's age. Would you just abandon her like that?"

Alex paused. "Probably not."

"But you might?" Ashley's voice rose.

"It's how you learn, Ash. You dive in the deep end, and you just do it. That's how I learned when my father did it to me at our country club, and I ended up captain of my high school swim team." He shook his head, as if to dislodge the shred of a bad memory. "Look. When I was a counselor, I was just a dumb teenager. I made a big mistake. And I thought it was behind me."

"It sounds stupid, not fatal, for god's sake, Alex. Why would you think that had anything to do with what's happening now?"

He jiggled the ice a little in his glass and stared into it. "That's the thing. I forgot about him."

"You *forgot*?"

"I thought he'd try to make it back on his own."

"Even though he couldn't swim." Ashley shook her head and looked away from him. "So what happened?"

Alex dropped his head into his hands, barely able to get the words out. "They never found him. He wasn't in the water. He wasn't in the camp. He was just nowhere." He took a breath. "And now he's come back."

Ashley looked at him as if he'd become a total stranger.

"I didn't make him disappear," he said.

"No, you only made it possible for him to go missing. When did they find him?"

"That's the thing. They never did. The campers thought this legendary crazy guy must've taken him." His shoulders sagged. "It was a long time ago."

"And you just walked away and moved on with this behind you. And blamed it on, what, some insane person?"

"The kid vanished, Ash. He was gone. That had nothing to do with me."

Angrier with himself than with her, he clenched and unclenched his fists. She stood and backed up against one of the columns of the portico. Only once before had he actually struck her, following an argument after too many drinks. He'd apologized at once, swore it would never happen again, and within a few months, he was having an affair. Though she would have walked out on him at the time, she was glad they were able to reconcile. Since then, he'd had better control over his emotions, though what had happened with Lyndsey on Captiva Island showed his temper was always smoldering in the background.

"So maybe this kid is all grown up and has come back," she

said. "Maybe he's been in your life this whole time. For all you know, maybe he even works for you."

"That's crazy, Ash."

"Anything's possible. Just remember… You started it by leaving him on a raft. That's not something anyone would easily forget."

He reached for her hand as she headed for the door and slipped away from him. "Don't be mad at me, Ash. It was a lifetime ago."

But it was too late. Because now it was out in the open between them. Now this thing was in both of their lives.

Now it had a name.

Part Four

24

In the end, Mike Farrelli and his wife went to St. Petersburg, when after an hour of online research Eleanor found a hotel not far from the beach with a decent rate and—always a plus—a bar. All she asked was that he not talk about work during their entire time away. No cops, no murder, no theories. No more investigations. No more bodies. This was a vacation; life as a detective was behind him. He promised he wouldn't give any of it a second thought. But Joey Proctor was still within him, tapping on the wall of his skull, begging for release from his mystery.

That first night Mike and Eleanor went out to a local restaurant that turned out to be pretty good: a decent martini, some excellent fish, and a bottle of wine, after which he tucked away the splurge purchase of a single malt. It was only in the middle of that night, around three thirty, that something came to him.

He slipped quietly out of bed, stepped out to the balcony and just sat in the balm of the early morning, tapping his fingertips together and thinking. It was only one possibility out of many, but now he was wondering if a counselor had been behind the boy's disappearance, if possibly a fatal accident had occurred out of sight of other campers and counselors, and the person responsible had buried the body outside the camp.

As he understood it from talking to the officers and detectives originally assigned to the case, counselors usually had cars and, on their nights off, would go into town for a hamburger and a beer, or to catch a movie. If a counselor was headed out on his own, it would be easy enough to take a detour, dispose of the body, and let the cops scratch their heads until it all went cold. He remembered reading through the interviews conducted with the staff that summer and learning that Joey's own counselor, Steve something, had driven into town to see a dentist. That's what had woken him. While Steve was away, Joey had gone missing.

To investigate this meant a detective would have to question all of the counselors who'd worked at Waukeelo that summer. It was seven years after the boy had disappeared, and now there was nothing Mike could personally do about it. But he knew how he thought about things, that this idea would be followed by another, and another, and before long there would be a full deck of possible solutions no one had ever considered before.

Seven years since the Proctor boy's disappearance, and by now the counselors would have been out of college and well into their new lives and careers, which meant that over the years memory would fade, and all guilt, if there had ever been any, would have turned to dust.

Or maybe not. Sometimes people forget themselves: a few drinks into a Saturday night, and it all comes out—how the kid had drowned or fallen, and how in a panic the counselor had dealt with the body and said nothing about it. Otherwise there would have been implications that might have affected the man's life for years to come. A stellar university student, for example, on the fast track to a dazzling career: the last thing he'd want would to be held accountable for the accidental death as well as for hiding the remains, which could result in decades in prison.

And still sitting there, as the breeze rose up from the gulf, another possibility occurred to Mike. What if it hadn't been an accident? What if the counselor had a bad temper and had lost control and hurt the boy so badly that he killed him?

Mike got up and returned to bed. He didn't sleep for the rest of the night.

25

IT WAS A GOOD TURNOUT AT THE MASONS' PARTY, especially since, as had often happened in the past, people were away on vacation or busy hauling their kids off to college. But this year, the entire top ranks of the Mason House Properties team in New York had been able to attend, along with the secretaries.

A bartender served wine and beer by the pool, while caterers laid out platters of food on long tables. Music played quietly through speakers. A few members of the staff were already in the water, and Becca and Lyndsey chatted with Pete Kellerman, the only one not dressed for swimming. Alex watched him out of the corner of his eye: the guy had an easy way with young people, as though reluctant to shed himself of his youth. Ashley joined Alex and took his hand. She was wearing jeans and a crisp, white blouse tied at the midriff, her hair pulled back into a loose ponytail, her sunglasses propped up on her head.

"It's a nice crowd," she said. She followed Alex's gaze to Pete. "What?"

"What do you think of him?"

"Becca and Lyndsey obviously think he's pretty cool."

What was it Ashley had suggested? Maybe all of these things—the pool, the room in Brooklyn, the elevator, possibly even the infestation at the Mason House—were due to someone who worked for him. He looked more closely at Pete, the newest member of his company.

Joey, he recalled, had been on the small side, and Pete stood maybe five seven, tops. He was also the right age, about twenty years older than Joey had been when he disappeared. Pete could potentially make Alex's life very difficult. Yet if he really were Joey Proctor, then obviously no crime had been committed. Joey wasn't dead, and Alex hadn't done anything more than forget about the kid for a few hours.

Which meant that his career would remain intact. Unless Pete—if he were really Joey—wanted something in return for his silence. An accusation of negligence wouldn't hurt for more than a week or two, not for a man in Alex's position, not for something that had happened twenty-one years earlier. Yet if the incident at camp had somehow affected the boy, changed his life in all the wrong ways, then Alex would have to be held responsible.

Maybe Pete wanted money. Maybe he wanted influence. Alex couldn't see what else would be demanded of him.

The bartender came over and whispered something in Alex's ear. He said to the man, "Sure, no problem. Open another case." He said to Ashley, "The prosecco's going fast."

"It's a hot day. And people are taking it slow. That's good."

Now Pete was smiling at Alex in an unsettlingly peculiar way. She looked at Alex. "You think he's the one who could be the kid from the raft?"

"I'll be right back," he said to her.

"You're not going to confront him here, are you?"

"I'm only going to sound him out a little. Don't worry. I

won't lose it." He hated it when she talked to him like that. As if he had no control over his emotions.

He and Pete shook hands. "Having a good time?" Alex said.

"Definitely. Your daughters are great, by the way."

"They come from good stock." Alex stood back and took him in. "Not swimming?"

"I don't swim, actually," Pete said, and the comment stopped Alex dead. "Never have, really."

"That's…that's unusual these days."

"I've always had a problem with deep water." Pete laughed. "I mean, you're not going to make me, are you?"

Alex also laughed, though a little too loudly. "Why would I do that?"

"Someone did when I was a kid."

"Scared you?"

"Enough to keep me out of the water."

Alex's gaze lingered on him. Though he'd only had two beers, he could feel himself tipping into a dangerous and unpredictable zone. He took a breath. Smiled. *Calm down*, he thought. *Be cool.*

"Stuff like that, it can really affect you, can't it?"

"I like to keep my feet on dry ground these days," Pete said.

A few other team members passed by. Alex's secretary, Carol, waved to him from the edge of the shallow end of the pool, where she was sitting with her husband. Alex smiled and offered a cursory wave before turning his attention back to Pete.

"Listen, I hate to talk business on a day like this, but now that Pearson's cut a deal for the Sturges, I want you to spend all of next week working solely on that Brooklyn building, the one in Red Hook. I've spoken to Milt Golub, and he's willing to wait for a bid."

"You've already had a look at it, right?" Pete said.

Alex had tried hard to forget that someone had been in the building with him, someone who might have painted Joey's name on a wall. He wouldn't return there until negotiations were completed and contracts signed, as though the legalities and paperwork were a form of exorcism.

"We've cut deals together before, and Milt's agreed to put all the other bidders on hold. Call our usual people, all the contractors we deal with. Have them check the place out. I need to know if the bones of the thing are sound. Any sign of water damage or issues with the roof or the foundation, that's something we need to think about. And go over there with them, okay? It'll keep you out of the office, but this is important."

Pete seemed genuinely surprised. "Yeah, well, I'd love to, Alex. I like the property a lot, as you know. It has some amazing potential."

Alex tried to find Joey's face in Pete's, but too much time had passed, and in his memory, the boy's face was merely a blur, as it was in the camp photo. Yet it was how Pete looked at Alex that struck him; as though he recognized in his boss the same man who'd left him on the raft.

"I've been impressed with how you do things, Pete. And I like your attitude. Make this work. And keep me updated. Every day, okay?"

"Thanks for having faith in me, Alex. I really appreciate it."

"And don't worry about not swimming. You can be the designated drinker. Get yourself another beer."

He watched Pete as he went to the drinks table. Ashley whispered in her husband's ear. "Is it him?"

It's him, Alex thought.

26

AT A QUARTER TO TWO THE NEXT MORNING, while Ashley and the girls were sleeping, Alex sat in his home office, the glow of the computer screen on his face. He clicked on Google and typed in *Joey Proctor.* Among unrelated items about other people with that name was a link to an archived news item from twenty-one years earlier in the *Berkshire Eagle* about a missing camper. There were no further mentions of the incident, which obviously meant that his body hadn't been found.

Alex went to Facebook, typed in *Pete Kellerman*, and found him fourteenth on a long list of Pete Kellermans, some in England, another in Belfast, one in Sydney, the rest in the States. But this was Pete. This was the man who couldn't swim.

The usual photos: Pete and friends tailgating at a football game. Pete and a pretty blond woman. A plate of spaghetti in a restaurant. A photo of a dog. Pete and a friend waiting to see a Springsteen concert, holding up their tickets. Pete at a friend's bachelor party. Alex shook his head: there was nothing there that offered even a hint of the guy's childhood.

Before heading back to bed, he tried one more thing. Back in Google, he typed *John Otis.* He remembered that this was a big story the counselors told the boys, about some guy who kidnapped a Waukeelo camper every so many years. Just a legend, just another horror story.

One item popped up. Someone had written and directed an episode on Otis for a cable documentary series titled *Dark Murmurs: Legends Rural and Urban*. Alex wrote down the writer and director's name: Marty Pollock. And then he shut down the computer.

When the man outside saw the light in the office switch off, he sat on the grass and waited for Alex to go back to sleep.

27

Think about it, Mike Farrelli said to himself as he lay in bed that night in Florida: the boy might have been sacrificed to satisfy some angry god. Or some hungry devil.

He backed away from the idea with a smile. It was the kind of thing you said to your colleagues in the department and they just laughed at you, because in that tight little world, in that particular Western Massachusetts jurisdiction, the closest you got to stuff like that was busting a guy hallucinating on LSD, or taking into custody an old codger who claimed he was Satan and was going to turn you into a goat. But now that he had retired, Farrelli could let his imagination run wild. As long as he didn't share any of his thoughts with Eleanor.

The next day, while Eleanor was out for a walk, he called a detective who'd been on the original case the day the boy disappeared, and pitched his idea about Steve Fenton. The detective, Paul Casey, was a step ahead of him.

"We thought of that, too."

"So you spoke to him?"

"We contacted the dentist Fenton had visited. The counselor was there for forty-five minutes. The drive there and back was half an hour each way, so that was close to two hours that he was gone. There wasn't a lot of leeway for burying a little boy."

"Still, it's a possibility."

"Won't do you any good, Mike. Steven Fenton's dead."

It took Farrelli a moment to let it settle in. "Meaning...?"

Paul laughed a little. "I don't know how to make it any more clear, Mike."

"I mean, how did he die?"

"He was murdered. In New York, near where he lived. Down by Riverside Park. Looks like he was mugged, fought back, and ended up being stabbed to death."

"Did they catch the perpetrator?"

"I have no idea."

"This was when?"

"A few months after camp was over. The same year the kid disappeared."

Mike realized he was finding too many dots to connect. "Was there any other counselor whose statement seemed a little off to you?"

Paul laughed a little. "Mike, they could have all been lying. Does it matter anymore at this point?"

Farrelli thought if it had been his son, yes, it would have mattered a hell of a lot. "I guess not," he said. They made a little small talk about how Mike was handling his retirement, and the call came to an end.

He kept coming back to the case from different angles, the most outlandish to the mundane. And then he found a whole new way to get into it. The next day, Eleanor needed to buy a new suitcase at the giant twenty-four-hour Walmart a few blocks from their hotel. While she was in the store browsing, he lingered in the entrance area, gazing up at a wall of photos of children, forty or fifty of them, that had vanished. Some had been gone for years; Photoshopped portraits of how they might appear now were displayed beside the ones taken around the time of their disappearance. Many had probably been abducted by an estranged parent, others by sex predators: the pretty blond girls with their weirdly knowing eyes, the cute little boys with their smooth skin and innocent affect. As for the rest, some must have run away; some may have sunk into the underground of a distant city, selling their bodies, feeding their habits. They'd come from everywhere: the Midwest, the Plains, but mostly from the southern states, as though slipping out of the world was a kind of regional pandemic.

When Eleanor finally came out, wheeling her new red, thirty-seven-dollar suitcase, she read her husband's face. "What?"

"It just occurred to me," he said. "Joey Proctor—"

She grabbed his arm. "I'm driving, mister. You're in no state to pay attention to anything but some cold case that everyone else has forgotten."

She was right. It was over, though he thought that maybe years from then there'd be a lead, there'd be the child's remains, with no one left to mourn him. Or out of the mists of the future a Joey Proctor would stagger from nowhere, wounded, broken, scarred, wondering if he still had a place in the world.

The human factor, Mike reminded himself. He remembered having read an anecdotal report from the first police interviews that took place at the camp that noted how the Proctors were obviously hostile to each other. And because even a retired detective has to look at every angle, even the outrageous ones, this led to him thinking that they may have wanted the child out of their lives. An eight-year-old becomes a nine-year-old becomes a sixteen-year-old, and then the lid comes off. So wrapped up they might have been in their own troubles that their son had become nothing but what Eleanor had gone into Walmart to replace: a piece of broken luggage.

28

CLICK—AND YOUR WORLD TURNS FROM BLACK TO sickly green: the house, the immaculate lawns, the tasteful plantings, the pool, the tennis court. A grainy, shimmering universe where everything is possible. His watch in the moonlight displayed three twenty-two. It was a little cooler than the past few nights, and because the air was dry and crisp, he knew that sounds would travel more easily. One wrong step, the crack of a twig, and he could be heard, a daughter would be roused, or maybe the master of the house himself would open his eyes and leave his bed, while his wife lay in her presumably pharmaceutical doze.

He suspected, but couldn't be sure, that Alex Mason kept a gun in the house, possibly even in his nightstand drawer. But he also sensed that Alex Mason was a coward, a man who lived in a world of anticipated moments and predictable outcomes. What was about to happen would shatter that illusion forever, just as the incident of the blood in the swimming pool had taken the air out of Alex's life for a handful of days. And the thing in the Brooklyn building? Pure spookcraft straight out of a midnight screening at the local Cineplex.

All he could hear was the sound of his own breathing, in and out, in and out. He'd entered the estate not by way of the locked front gate, with its security camera and intercom, but through a gap in the perimeter fence, deep in the scrub beyond the swimming pool and tennis court. He moved cautiously toward the front door, approaching from the side to avoid being seen from the windows, sidestepping the ground triggers he knew were embedded outside the windows and entrances. Under the portico he was out of everyone's view.

The Masons subscribed to one of the more expensive security companies, whose devices and panels he knew well. Picking the front door lock, a high-end, coded Schlage dead bolt, would take no more than forty seconds, as long as he used the key override, which would allow him 120 seconds before the alarm would go off both in the house and at the local police station. Once he'd slid the picks into the lock, it was a matter of feeling them snap into place. He tried twice more, and the bolt was free. Fourteen seconds in all.

The panel was where he expected it would be, just inside to his left. He took a small mechanism from his pocket and held it a few inches away from the display as it ticked off the seconds before it did its job. He wanted to laugh: millionaire Alex Mason had chosen the most obvious code, his wife's birthday, something a quick internet search had turned up. Click, fizz, it was off. The house was his. And he would luxuriate in it as if it all belonged to him.

The living room was filled with treasures for the taking: a Warhol on one wall, a Morandi over the mantelpiece, a few antiquities probably plundered from looted museums and the sepulchers of the rich and powerful in Europe and beyond. But he wasn't there for the art, nor for the framed photos on a table of their own: the Mason family in ski gear, probably in Aspen; the Mason family on a sailboat, probably off the Hamptons; the Mason girls at a water park.

The kitchen, the home office, an entertainment room with nice comfortable chairs and a giant screen for watching movies or TV shows, as well as a popcorn cart—all empty. Alex Mason was asleep. His pretty wife was asleep. His little girls were asleep. And now it was time to pay them all a visit.

29

THE DOORS TO THE DAUGHTERS' ROOMS WERE ajar, as he'd hoped they would be. He stepped quietly into the first one on the right, paused a moment to be sure the girl hadn't been roused, and peered at the youngest, the eight-year-old. Had she awoken, she would have looked up to find a giant insect, his eyes at the end of two stems peering down at her, tubes emerging from his mouth, and she would have screamed and screamed and screamed, and by the time Daddy had lumbered out of his room, he would have been halfway across the lawn, damage done. But that wasn't going to happen. He was only there to make a little home movie, this being the first act. *Here's Lyndsey with her stuffed animals and her dolls, and now let's go down the hall and here's Becca. Pretty Becca, saucy little girl who will soon be a tarty little teenager, please have a look, world. She also has a stuffed animal, a one-eyed bear.* "Hello, little half-blind bear," he wanted to say, because it was staring right back at him like some malign thing from a horror flick.

He walked back into the hallway. There's the girls' shared bathroom with the comforting glow of its little night-light. Here are some more photos—*god, so many photos*, he thought—lining the hallway, as though they might one day forget who they were, what they once looked like. And the thought made him smile. After all, a photo is only a mirror of what you'd once been. Of what you might have lost. Of what you may never see again.

And look—the door to the master bedroom is also ajar, lucky day. Let's push it carefully open. And there they are, sprawled out on their giant bed. Alex is snoring, of course, a hibernating beast tightly wound in his sheet and duvet, a big, pink pig awaiting slaughter. All he can see is the top of the man's head, and he forms his hand into a pistol and aims it at Mason's head, mentally blowing his brains out with silent intent.

On the floor next to Mason is a puddle of something white that turns out to be a robe. Ashley is flat on her back, her eyes hidden behind satin eyeshades, and the covers have made their way down below her bare breasts. A 34C, he guesses, speaking from experience.

He comes in close to film her breasts, first the left one, then the right one, with the little birthmark next to the tan unerect nipple, its shape suggesting Australia. Pretty breasts, unenhanced, with a natural fall, just as they should be. He passes his gloved hand an inch or so above them. And then he films the smile on her face. What, he wonders, is she dreaming about? Alex Mason? Not with that kind of smile. He's sure she has as many secrets as he possesses. And one day he might be privileged enough to learn one of them.

It was time to go. He'd seen enough. He'd done enough. Though after this, there's no going back. Not for Ashley Mason. Not for her husband.

And definitely not for him.

30

IT WAS STILL DARK WHEN THE MAN IN THE LIVING room began singing so loudly that his voice filled the entire house, rousing Alex from a sound sleep. He was halfway down the stairs, struggling to pull on his robe, when he picked up on the words, something about sitting on a dock and watching the tide go away, or something like that. He was half-asleep, and nothing was making any sense to him.

Realizing what was going on, Alex switched off the CD player. The time display registered 4:08 a.m. He could hear the girls padding around the hallway upstairs, and Ashley came down, her robe tied tightly around her. Alex continued to stare at the stereo system. Then he shook his head and ejected the disk.

"Who the hell thought this was a good idea?" He switched on a lamp and looked at it. "Wait a minute… This CD isn't even ours."

Halfway down the stairs, Lyndsey seemed to be in shock. "Mommy?" she said.

"It's okay, sweetie," Ashley said. "Go back to bed."

"I'm scared."

"It's okay. Go back up." She looked at Alex as he stared at the disk. "Did you do this?"

"Are you out of your mind? I just told you, we don't even own this CD."

She took it from him. “Are you sure?”

“I’m positive.”

“Why is the front door wide open?” Becca asked as she stood at the top of the stairs.

31

WHILE TWO UNIFORMED OFFICERS, HAVING already checked the areas closest to the house, walked the perimeter of the property, Lieutenant Carver and Detective Ettinger stood talking to the Masons in the living room. Ashley sat on the sofa, her hands trembling, a tissue gripped in one of them. Alex hadn't even taken a few minutes to shower. His hair still tousled from sleep, he wore his old college sweatshirt, a pair of workout pants, Gucci loafers. The pool was one thing—what he considered no more than a prank, something to shrug off and forget. But what had happened last night was different. Someone had gained entry, turned off the alarm system, and put a CD in the player. It meant that Alex's home was no longer the fortress he'd always thought it was. It had been breached, and his family could be at risk. Lyndsey had taken it hardest. She'd gone back to her room and was still there, hours after they'd first heard the music, too scared to come out.

Carver stepped outside for a moment, spoke to one of the cops, and came back in. "Our officers can't find any evidence that someone tried to break in, or that there's been an intruder anywhere on the property."

"That's impossible."

"Let me put it this way, Mr. Mason. It doesn't appear that

someone had been on the property or in your house. Your front gate has a camera and a bolt that opens and closes with, what, a remote in your car—?"

"And in the house," Ashley said. "If someone's there, we can call down on the intercom. It's in the kitchen. And there's a monitor that displays whoever's at the gate."

"Does it record at all?"

"It's just a monitor," Alex said. "The gate's usually open during the day when we're home. It's only at night or if we're away that it's locked."

The same uniformed cop leaned in through the front door. "The gate is secure. No signs of tampering there, either. No one could have gotten in that way."

Carver acknowledged his words with a nod, and the officer headed out to his patrol car. "If that's the case, it means that someone managed to get onto your property and gain entry into your house without setting off your alarm system. Except"—he turned to look at the panel on the wall—"you have a top-of-the-line security system. I know that electronic things sometimes fail. We've all had it happen. When's the last time the system was inspected?"

Alex looked at Ashley. She said, "Maybe a month and a half ago?"

"And I'm guessing you armed it before going to bed last night."

"Of course I did," Alex said. "I just can't understand how this could have happened."

Carver held the CD by the edges in his gloved hand: *The Very Best of Otis Redding*. "You know his stuff?"

"Before my time," Alex said.

"I like him. 'Try a Little Tenderness,' 'Respect.' Aretha also recorded that one. Too bad he died so young. I'm just sorry you took it out of the player, Mr. Mason. It probably had his fingerprints on it. Now yours will have smudged them, so this is useless to us as evidence. You're sure this disk isn't yours?"

"Absolutely not."

"You know," Carver said, "sometimes we buy music and forget about it, and then years later, *boom*, there it is."

"Like that Nickelback album I bought when I was a little buzzed," Ettinger said with an embarrassed smile. "C'mon, I was only seventeen."

"I don't even know the song that was playing," Alex said.

"So you're saying you didn't do this," Carver said.

"To what end, Lieutenant?"

The detective looked again at the disk. "'The Dock of the Bay.' The title mean anything to you?" Carver couldn't help but notice the look on Ashley's face. "Okay. Look, as far as we're concerned, this is your CD and someone in the house put it on. Which doesn't constitute a crime in and of itself. There's no evidence of forced entry or tampering. No evidence, even, of any wrongdoing."

"Except that someone left the door open."

"Again, it could have been any of you."

"And the security system was disabled."

"You know the code?"

"We all do," Alex said.

"You and Mrs. Mason both?"

"And the girls know it, of course," Ashley said.

Carver turned to her. "So I need to ask you: Did you do this?"

"Why would I do such a thing?"

"That may be a question only you can answer," the lieutenant said.

"No," she said. "It's ridiculous even to think that."

Carver smiled a little. "Case closed, then, Mr. Mason. Unless, of course, you tell me that something was taken from the house. Jewelry, a TV, computers…? I didn't ask that at first because I figured you'd have already told me."

Alex rubbed his brow. "My wife and I looked over every room. Everything's where it should be."

"You're sure of that? You get so used to where things are, what they look like, that if one day they're gone, you still see them there."

He noticed Alex's slightly bewildered look.

"Forget I even said that," he said.

Ashley said, "We've checked everything, every room."

"Anyone in your family sleepwalk, maybe?" Carver said.

"Come on," Alex said. "After what happened with the pool, and now this? I mean, look, obviously something's going on."

Carver leaned against the doorframe. "You think they're connected?"

"I mean, what else could it be?"

"In the first incident, someone put animal blood into your pool," Carver said.

"And etched words into the bottom of it."

"And this time—if it really did happen this way—someone walked into your house and put a CD in the player. Why would someone do that without stealing all this nice artwork?

What's the kick in it? What's the link to the pool?" Carver glanced at his watch. "I mean, is there one? Do you have any domestic workers in your employ?"

Ashley told them they had a housekeeper who came twice a week. "But she wouldn't do something like this. She's worked for us since the kids were little."

"How about gardeners? Pool guys?"

"Why would they go to the trouble to put blood in the pool and walk in here in the middle of the night to play music? It makes no sense."

"Something will come to mind, I'm sure. In the meantime I suggest you upgrade your security system." He tapped the wall with a knuckle by the security panel. "Have it checked out, overhauled if needed, and definitely program in new codes."

"I've already spoken to them. They'll be here this afternoon."

"Give us a call if anything like this happens again."

Alex watched from the doorway as the patrol cars pulled away, Carver and Ettinger following them in their Crown Victoria.

He shut the door and went into the kitchen. Having been up for hours without anything to eat, he was suddenly famished. Ashley was in the kitchen, making a fresh pot of coffee. He took a stool at the counter and picked at a bowl of blueberries. She sat across from him and folded her hands around a coffee mug.

"Let's get away for the weekend. What happened this morning really spooked the kids. And me. It'll be good for us."

"You go. Take the girls. See if you can go up to your sister's place."

"Really? You're going to stay?"

"Just to keep an eye on things."

She touched his hand. "Tell me the truth. Did you do this? No, don't look at me like that. Did you or didn't you? If you did, you must have had a good reason for it. Just help me try to understand, okay?"

"You don't trust me anymore, do you," he said.

"After those photos from the bar? And you abandoning a little boy on a raft? Maybe I'm just a little less confident these days."

He'd thought they'd settled that already. The woman in the bar was a complete stranger, and someone had thought it amusing to take photos, even pose a few shots afterward, just to get at him. He knew most of the tabloid journalists in New York and put this kind of stunt beneath none of them. But he also considered that this was all part of some larger plan that was connected to the disappearance of Joey Proctor. And he wondered why whoever was behind it hadn't yet demanded a payout.

He took a deep breath and looked at his wife. "Ash, look… We have a beautiful family, I have a successful business, and if someone's trying to destroy me or what we have, they're not going to succeed. As long as we stick together. Okay?"

She smiled a little wistfully and nodded. "All right, Alex."

"Take the girls up to Old Saybrook after school tomorrow," he said. Ashley's sister Susan and her husband, Ted, had a house on Plum Bank Road, and a few days there by the beach would at least partly make up for the vacation time they'd lost in Captiva over Labor Day weekend. "I've got a stack of pending projects on my desk, and this'll give me a chance to review them outside the office here at home."

He grabbed his coffee and slid off the stool.

"Wait...Alex. These things that've been happening." She took a moment, because it was the most terrifying possibility. "It's that kid, isn't it. The one you left behind."

He turned back and set his coffee mug on the counter, making a mental note to call his attorney.

"Look. It's just not possible. He's probably dead, Ash. Gone."

"If he is dead, then everything that's been happening is on you, Alex. You started it. And you know it."

"I just wish I could undo it."

"So you have a conscience, after all."

"Listen," he said. "Joey wouldn't even remember me."

Ashley began to load the dishwasher. "But he does, doesn't he? You never forget something like that."

She started putting the silverware in the machine. "He knows where we live, he knows where you work. He knows who we are. The pool with the blood. The words he left in it. This song about a dock. *A dock*, for god's sake, do you even get it? Sitting on the dock of the bay? Think that's a coincidence? A dock? On the water? Because now he's in our house. He's in our life." She turned to look at Alex. "He's in our *heads*."

Part Five

32

WORDS NO LONGER MATTERED, CARRIED NO meaning, possessed no weight for two people who had nothing to say to each other. Something had happened, something bad had taken place, and these people who the day before had a son no longer had one in their car or back at their apartment, but instead had one who wandered in the speculative wasteland of his mother's imagination.

After meeting with the Jensens and the counselors, Joey's parents packed up their son's things—his camp T-shirts and shorts his mother had specially ordered for him, the ones conforming to the camp colors and logo. This was the blur that was the day. The other campers in the bunk had been sent off to an activity so she and her husband could pack in private. There were the letters and cards she'd sent Joey every few days, including the funny one with Snoopy on it and the one with Batman on the front, because he was a big fan of the Caped Crusader, as he liked to call him. He'd written his parents almost every day the first week, begging them to take him home. After that, the letters came less frequently. He was busy, he liked arts and crafts, he liked playing tennis, he liked the group sings they had. He liked his counselor, who talked to him a lot, and he liked Friday night dinners, which were always followed by a special dessert.

Diane stuffed the cards and letters she'd sent him into her bag, and then she was done. The mattress was bare. She did everything but fold it over like the one next to it. Joey's father sat on the counselor's bed, hospital corners crisp and intact, just as Steve had shown Joey when he'd first arrived. She looked under Joey's bunk and found one of his camp T-shirts. It was rumpled and dusty, and when she held it up she realized how little he really was. Alone out there someplace. And then she saw the red stain on the side.

"What?" Alan said.

"This is blood."

He took it from her. "It's just paint, Diane." He sounded exasperated.

"Are you sure?"

"Jesus Christ, what are you trying to prove? That something, I don't know, something happened to him, someone hurt him? That there's some, what, some goddamn conspiracy, some cover-up, involving the whole camp? Come on. This is nuts."

He was right; it was paint. Joey liked arts and crafts. He'd gotten paint on his shirt, and somehow it had found its way under the bunk. Unless he had been trying to hide it. She sat beside her husband.

He said, "Let's just get out of here, okay?"

She said nothing.

"Did you even hear me, for Christ's sake?"

Diane said, "You want to have an argument now? So everyone can hear us?"

She picked up the shirt and folded it. *Folded it.* And why, for what, for the day Joey might show up at their door on Park

Avenue? What was it people liked to say—that all they want is closure? She used to mock the expression as belonging to daytime TV shows or bad prime-time dramas or sad families a thousand miles distant from her. But now it made sense to her, now she needed closure more than anything, something definite, even the worst imaginable outcome. Just end this, she thought. Just shut it down forever.

Please god do this for me.

She put her hands to her face, because this is how people in their position were meant to think and act. The distressed parents. The grieving, uncertain people who had to return to a life they both despised. She had already learned to hate her husband; now she was beginning to hate herself.

She took Joey's can of tennis balls and the tennis racquet they'd bought a week before camp began at the big sporting goods store on Third Avenue, and the books he'd brought with him, fantasies about wizards and boys like him who felt too small for the world they lived in. When she looked up, Steve Fenton was standing there, blurred through her tears, and it startled her.

Quietly he said, "I just wanted to see how you were doing. If you needed any help."

"We're all done," Alan said. "But thanks. You said that you and Joey talked a lot. Did he ever mention anything that sticks out?"

Steve was obviously confused by the question.

"Just...something that might lead you to think he'd walk away from camp. Or that he was feeling so unhappy that he might try to hurt himself."

"Not really, no. His concerns were just like those of a lot of other kids. You know, they get homesick, there are sometimes problems with other kids—"

"Was he bullied?" Diane asked. "Was he?"

"At first you find kids teasing the smaller ones. It happened to me when I was his age. It's completely normal."

"But it's hard when you're only eight," she said.

"That's why I paid extra attention to him. And he seemed to do fine." He stopped himself before adding *in the end*. "I just want you to know that I liked Joey very much. He was a very special kid. And I hope he comes back."

"He's not coming back," Joey's father said. "Not ever."

They said nothing to each other for the first hour of the drive. When he pulled off the main road, she said, "What have we done, Alan?" It was the first time in weeks, in months, that she'd called him by his name, in the same way he'd stopped using her name, as though both were engaged in a long rehearsal for the inevitable end of their relationship.

"Where are we?" she asked, looking around, her voice rising in panic. "Where are you taking me?" For a moment, she thought he might drive deep into the country, where the road turned to dirt, and murder her.

"I thought we'd get something to eat. That diner we stopped at is down this way."

"Where we ate with Joey?"

"That's exactly—"

"You're saying you want to go back there, just the two of us. Without Joey. Like it's just another day."

"Everything has to seem normal," he said. "Otherwise we'll never live again."

She looked at him curiously. "What are you saying? 'Seem normal'? What does that even mean?"

He parked next to a pickup truck outside Little Dee's. The truck was filthy, as if it had been driven through mud and hadn't been washed. There was what looked like a smear of dried blood on the edge of the tailgate, and he was glad Diane hadn't noticed it. This was hunting country; people went out and killed things.

"I don't trust that Steve Fenton," he said. "Not for a moment."

"He seemed fine," she said. "Sympathetic."

He turned off the engine. "We'll see."

He noticed that a tear was running down her cheek. He touched the back of her hand, and she turned to look at him.

"There's nothing we can do, Diane." He held his palms apart, weighing air, a substance as empty as his words.

"We can hope."

"Hope."

"We can hope, Alan."

"For what?"

They sat unspeaking in the diner. It was past lunchtime, and only a few other people were there. She recognized a grungy man in a John Deere hat, the same one who'd walked past her when she was on the phone with Eli when they'd driven Joey to camp five weeks earlier. The man had said something lewd, and she'd forgotten exactly what it was. She couldn't recall it because Eli had been telling her on the phone what he couldn't wait to do the next time they were together. Her lover, Eli, and then this dirty man who'd propositioned her: two sides of a coin, she thought.

"Eli's Comin'"... When she'd first gotten to know the sculptor, she'd bought the CD the song was on, the version by Laura Nyro, and listened to it incessantly on her Discman, privately through headphones when she went to the gym. It made her smile. It gave her hope. It pleased her beyond measure, as if it had been written and sung especially for her. *Hide your heart, girl.*

Now she no longer even wanted to see Eli. She never wanted to restore furniture again, not ever. Pleasure belonged to the past, along with passion and climax and the soft minutes afterward. She wanted to divorce her husband, change her name, walk away, get herself good and lost in a place where everything was strange to her—language, customs, expectations—and where one day she might find a bewildered Joey waiting for her.

They ordered something to eat, and Alan went off to the bathroom, not even excusing himself, because these days that's how he was, a man whose life had gone all wrong, a man who blamed everyone but himself. His business was moribund. His debts were growing. He had failed in every possible way.

She looked up at the photo of Teddy Roosevelt. He had been there that first time, he was there still, and because he was dead he knew nothing of Joey, nothing of what might have happened. She remembered how nervous Joey had been sitting across from her. Fidgety, his eyes shifting, as if trying to find something to focus on. She realized they were sitting at the same table as they had the first time. Except now everything was different.

"You the one with the kid?"

She looked up to find the man in the hat looking down on her. He held the check for his meal in his grubby, oil-stained fingers. There was a deep, open scratch on his palm, and the blood looked fresh.

"The one who went missing?"

"Yes." She looked almost expectantly up at him, as if hoping he might have a lead, a clue.

"I lost my daughter when she was five. I lost my wife at the same time. Way long ago."

"That's very sad."

"You're a pretty lady."

"Please leave me alone."

"I'd like to take you home. I want to make you happy."

"Where is my son?"

"You mean you don't know?"

She was still staring at where the man had been standing when Alan returned from the bathroom. He said, "What'd that redneck want?" He glanced out the window as the pickup backed up and drove away.

"Just saying he was sorry about…all of this." She watched the truck pull away, its wheels spinning in the dust of this hot August day.

They arrived back in the heat-bound city at nightfall. The apartment smelled stale, and the stink of death was in the air. Another mouse had expired under the sink where the D-Con was kept. They eat, they thirst, they suffer, they die. At first she felt bad for them. This was no quick death, as though they had to be tortured, punished before they would mercifully expire, their mouths gaping in agony. You spent a fortune on real estate in Manhattan, you lived in the finest neighborhood with the prettiest people, and when you turned your back, the rats and the mice and roaches moved back in, because in truth they owned the property, and when the apocalypse had come and gone and the city was reduced to rubble, they would still be there with their whiskers and their tails and their dead little eyes.

Alan turned on the air conditioning, and she dropped the duffel bag stuffed with Joey's things beside the front door. She walked to his room and, without looking inside, shut his door. It wasn't over. It would never be over.

And once again she thought: *What have we done?*

33

WHEN ALEX WALKED INTO THE OFFICE ON Friday morning, everyone turned to look at him. He realized how tired he must appear. And he knew how lately he'd seemed distracted, not quite there. Now he just looked lost. Adrift.

"Where's Pete?"

"This isn't his project," Sandy said. "He's doing the Brooklyn site, remember?"

"Right, right. I don't know where my head is this morning." He glanced at the agenda his secretary had printed out for him, as she did each day. He said, "He's coming in after you. Okay, so obviously you think Detroit is still worth a visit?"

"Milwaukee Junction is going to be the next hot neighborhood in the city."

"Or," Rob said, "the *first* hot neighborhood," and they laughed.

Sandy said, "There's a lot of rehabilitation and investment going on in the area. Lofts are being developed, and artists in the city have already started making down payments on them. People are actually moving there—from Chicago, Chapel Hill, even New York. Compared to the prices here in the city, these are real bargains. What you pay rent for five hundred square feet in a studio in Park Slope will get you a whole house there.

And three new restaurants are opening within a quarter mile of one another in the area we're proposing."

"Fast food?"

"Not even. There's an upmarket barbecue place... Here are some photos of it."

Actually, it did look pretty decent. Polished wooden bar, modern tables and chairs. An open kitchen. Portraits of famous blues musicians on the walls. The chef even looked like Buddy Guy in his heyday—processed hair and a grin so wide and trusting you'd eat one of his shoes if he served it.

"He's one of the top barbecue guys from New Orleans. He has family in Detroit and wanted to move back up north. The other two restaurants are an Asian fusion place and a steakhouse."

Rob passed Alex a photo of the spot where the hotel would stand, a boarded-up warehouse. Alex looked at it and shook his head a little. "What's the zoning situation?"

"We've looked into it from every angle. There's no problem whatsoever. The neighborhood is hungry for a real face-lift and much-needed tax revenue. And, yes, there are incentives to go along with it. I say we go in now with plans for a hundred and fifty rooms and a restaurant and bar. There's a jazz scene there, and we could even have live entertainment on weekends."

"Why not just open a restaurant?"

"Because in ten years we'll be sorry when someone else puts up a hotel."

Alex laughed. "You talk like a real-estate mogul, Rob." He smiled for the first time that morning. "Okay. We should all fly out there for a day next week. To be honest, I think it's kind of intriguing. I can't imagine any other developers are even thinking about Detroit."

"Mark Pearson is," Sandy said.

He looked at her. "I know Pearson. I ran into him the weekend we were in Captiva. He's a piece of work, isn't he?"

"He's a piece of shit," Rob said. "He grabbed the Sturges out from under us."

"All the more reason for us to get on top of this thing. Let's work out a day when we're all free. We'll fly out on my plane, have a look, and then we'll decide. What's happening with the Mason?"

"The exterminators confirmed the rats and mice didn't get into the building on their own. And the one in the oven? That's an industrial piece of equipment, tight as anything. The only things that get in there are Reg's entrées."

Alex sat back and looked up at the ceiling. "We have no one to pin this on."

"My advice?" Rob said. "After the cleanup, we offer a few weekend and holiday specials. Get the chef to change the menu at the grill. Make it look like we've had a complete makeover. People will forget about what happened. And the Pete Wells review in the *Times* is still online."

"Keep an eye on all that, will you, Rob?" Alex looked around at the others. "Okay, so anything else?"

They shook their heads.

"Great party, by the way," Sandy said. "Thanks. It was fun."

"Send my best to Ashley," Rob said. "It was good seeing her again."

"You bet."

Five minutes later, Carol let Pete into the office. Alex was standing at the window when he saw the young man's reflection coming up alongside him.

"Look at this view," Alex said. "I never get tired of it. Now talk to me about Brooklyn."

"I've put together a comprehensive evaluation of the property, along with inspectors' reports and a preliminary cost analysis. I also took another look at the neighborhood. Walked around, met a few people who live and work in the area. They're definitely open to a hotel at that location. The existing building is an eyesore, and it's becoming a drag on the street's commercial property values. Residential values overall have been more or less level, maybe a little up for the year. Which indicates it's a pretty stable neighborhood."

"You have the paperwork here?"

Pete winced. "I got a late start this morning and left it at my place. I can go back now and pick it up if you—"

"Listen, I have an idea. Why don't you take the train up to my place this weekend, let's say Saturday, and we can go through it. My wife's taking our daughters up to her sister's house in Connecticut this afternoon, so I'll be free to work with you. We can even have an early dinner before you head back."

"Are you sure?"

Alex turned to him. "I wouldn't invite you if I wasn't. I think it's a good idea. We can sit, have a drink or two, hash this thing out. Bring everything—paperwork, photos, anything you've got. Oh, and the inspectors' reports. They'll need to be filed here on Monday."

"I have PDFs."

"Print them out. I like working with paper."

"I can do that. So tomorrow, okay?"

"Perfect. We'll spread everything out on the dining room table and go carefully through it. Sell me on this, and I'll make it your deal to close, your first for Mason House Properties. Food and booze is not optional."

Pete seemed genuinely flattered. New to the company, about to bring in his first account, his first property. He even blushed a little, betraying his youth, though, Alex thought, not necessarily his innocence.

"Email when you know what your train's due in, and I'll pick you up at the station."

After Pete left, Alex picked up the phone and told Carol he wanted no calls for the next fifteen minutes. He opened his drawer and took out the slip of paper with the name Marty Pollock written on it. When he Googled the man's name, the first link that appeared was to an IMDB listing, with a single credit for a TV documentary episode titled *Dark Murmurs: Legends Rural and Urban.* "The Return of John Otis." Alex Googled another link to a faculty web address at NYU's Tisch School of the Arts. When he clicked on it, he saw a photo of a young man with a goatee, a mustache, and an almost shy, thin-lipped smile, along with his university email and office phone number. Alex picked up his cell phone and keyed in the NYU number. It was answered after the first ring.

"Marty Pollock."

"Mr. Pollock. You don't know me, but I happened to read that you made a film—"

"Look. I'm in a meeting with a student, and I've got a lecture in ten minutes. Is this about a particular project, or are you—"

"Actually, it is. Is there any chance we could possibly meet, say sometime next week? My name is Alex Mason, by the way."

There was a pause.

"Mason. From Camp Waukeelo?"

Alex sat straight up in his chair. "You know me?"

"Let me put it this way. I know *of* you."

34

Kurt Garland had been Alex's personal attorney for over ten years, and because few dared bring suit against Alex, they didn't often have the occasion to see each other. But Alex had asked Carol to book them a table at the Bar Room at 21, and they were seated off in a quiet corner while they ate their Dover sole. Being a chip off the old Melvin Belli, Kurt nursed one of several martinis, while Alex stayed with club soda. That afternoon would be devoted to getting the Mason House Hotel in order and ensuring the inspector would be available to look it over the following week. Staying sober was a priority.

Without mentioning Joey Proctor, Alex described what had been happening to him and to his family.

"What are the consequences if I find out who's behind this stuff and I decide to act on my own? I mean, I have every reason to believe my family's in some kind of danger."

"You're asking me what happens if, what, you shoot someone? Are you fucking joking, Alex?"

"Not if my family feels threatened and—"

"Ever hear of the police? They get paid to kill people. They do it all the time. You'd be doing it for free. And if you can't absolutely prove self-defense, you'd go on trial. And don't even ask… We don't have a stand-your-ground defense here. This isn't Florida."

Alex leaned in and lowered his voice even more. "I just want to know the consequences."

"Of you shooting a trespasser?"

Alex rested his hands on the table. "Exactly."

Kurt set down his drink. "Tell me. Are you genuinely feeling threatened? Because if you are, I'll say it again: in cases like this, the cops are your friends."

Alex set down his drink and shook his head. "No police. This is a private matter. I want zero publicity about this."

"In that case, I'd hire round-the-clock security. You can easily afford it."

Alex had certainly considered that, but it wouldn't end his troubles. Bodyguards might scare someone off, but that someone would always be there, out in the world, waiting for his moment. Tormenting Alex with these stunts seemed pointless. Unless someone wanted to drive him over the edge or bring down his business. The only person who could do that would be Alex himself, through negligence or carelessness. And so far he'd proven to be an astute and responsible businessman.

"No bodyguards. No way I'd do that to my family."

Kurt folded his arms. "Just tell me, Alex. What's this really all about?"

"Attorney-client privilege covers lunches at 21?"

Kurt laughed. "Even if we had this conversation at adjoining urinals it would be protected."

Alex still didn't want to say too much. Bringing up what had happened with Joey would open up a whole other avenue of thought, a place best left unvisited for the moment. What was past was past, except that what was past was never past. What was past was now woven into his daily life. What was past, he realized, may well even be his future. Unless he could put an end to it.

"Let me try a different question. What's the statute of limitations for, say, negligence?"

Kurt stared at him for a long moment. "You need to be more specific, Alex."

The waiter appeared at their table. "Another martini?" he asked, and Alex smiled because, of course, Kurt was always happy to have another.

When the waiter left, his attorney asked, "What the hell are we talking about here?"

Alex took a breath. He knew he couldn't avoid mentioning Joey Proctor. "Something happened when I was in college."

"Please don't say you raped someone."

"Come on, Kurt. I was a counselor at a boys' camp and left a kid on a raft."

"Okay, so?"

"I forgot about him."

Kurt sat back as his drink was delivered. He pulled an olive off the little spear and chewed thoughtfully. "That's hardly negligence."

"No one ever saw him again."

Kurt leaned in. "You need to tell me more, Alex."

"When I went back to check on him, he was gone. They never found a body."

"It's got to be somewhere."

"They searched the camp top to bottom. Plus all the surrounding properties. I'm only wondering what happens if, you know, a body eventually turns up."

"What state are we talking about?"

"Let's start with where it happened, in Massachusetts."

"I'll double-check, but I think the statute of limitations there for negligence is something like three years. Here in New York, it's two. You're off the hook, Alex. And unless DNA is involved, connecting someone who disappeared and probably died all those years ago with someone today isn't going to get very far in a court of law. Now, what the hell does this have to do with you being threatened?"

"Because I think the kid I left out there has come back to bring me down. To break up my marriage. To terrorize my family."

The waiter took away their empty plates and left dessert menus. Alex stopped him before he could leave. "Let me have a Macallan. Straight up." To hell with staying sober.

"Eighteen-year all right?"

"Whatever," Alex said.

"You're really in bad shape, aren't you?" Kurt said. "Normally you're pretty armor-plated."

"Yeah, well, this is different."

"Okay, so I see where you're going with this. You think if this guy shows up—if you even recognize him as the kid you left, which is kind of doubtful—and tries something, you could shoot him dead and put it down to self-defense. It's going to have to be a hell of a lot more than him just ringing the doorbell and saying hi. He actually has to threaten you."

"Doesn't him simply getting in touch imply a threat?"

"Only if there's intent—he says he's going to harm you or members of your family. If he just shows his face, it's not intimidation in and of itself." The attorney sat back and fingered the stem of his glass. "You're carrying a lot of guilt around, aren't you?"

"I was stupid, that's all. But I didn't hurt the kid."

"No. You abandoned him. You assumed he'd save himself. And then someone else probably came around and did it for him. Or abducted him. And now the boy is gone. Contributory negligence is probably the worst of it for you. But, as I said, the statute of limitations—"

Alex leaned in. "I just want to know. Tell me what could happen if I took matters into my own hands."

Kurt lowered his voice nearly to a whisper. "Killing him, is that what you're saying?"

Alex nodded once.

"First of all, I don't want to know anything more about what your intentions are. I wasn't privy to this conversation, and I never once encouraged you to break the law, am I correct?"

"Of course you didn't—"

"Because there is no way in hell you can win this if you do away with or even harm him. Unless you can prove that he actually threatened you or that you're not in your right mind. Which right now seems pretty obvious to me. I'll have the rice pudding," he said to the looming shadow of the waiter, and the waiter set down Alex's drink and said, "Very good, sir."

"And another martini."

Part Six

35

ALEX SAT IN THE CAB OF HIS PICKUP AT THE LITTLE red building by the Hudson River that served as the local train station. He'd bought the truck as a contrast to his $200,000 Bentley, because at times he liked to appear more like the people he was not and could never be: those who worked with their hands, who hauled things and spit on the sidewalk, who got into the dirt and the mud and the grit, who wondered where their next dollar would come from, who simply made do—something he'd never experienced in his entire life. He knew these were the very people who could never afford a single night in one of his hotels, or who would balk at the cost of a drink at one of their bars.

After his father died, Alex had inherited his family fortune and his business and learned how to make it grow and, along with it, his name and his reputation. But when he got into his truck, he felt as though his success had been the result of tremendous struggle, as if the vehicle itself had turned him into an ardent Bolshevik, as though life had been a four-wheel drive through tempests and rockfall, blasting obstacles thrown in his way, though in truth the vehicle had mostly lived inside the garage. It hadn't been scratched or dented, the high-end audio system filled the leather-upholstered cab with the music and talk of his choice, and the finish was as bright and pristine as it had been when it rolled off the dealer's lot in Mount Kisco a few years earlier. But the thing he liked best of all was that, when he did drive it, to the liquor store or the post office, people didn't glare at it as they did the Bentley.

A few other cars were parked at the station, their drivers also waiting for the 4:20 out of Grand Central, though Alex recognized none of them. The station belonged to his past, when he and Ash were living in a nearby townhome, an old estate turned into condos, an easy twelve-minute walk from the station. As the property had belonged to a wealthy family back in the twenties, most of the original details had been retained, including the Italian gardens with their elegant columns and massive stone urns, elements in a landscape designed by Frederick Law Olmsted. The pool was an example of 1920s architecture straight out of a John Cheever story, as were most of the people who lived in the area during the Masons' time there, with their pastel trousers and polo shirts, their incipient potbellies and full-blown marital problems only whispered about over bourbon and dirty martinis.

He and Ashley were the outsiders, the attractive young childless couple, blonder than blond, lighter than air. Now Alex was on top of it all; the people he knew back then, his neighbors who could hardly restrain their disdain for these pretty people, were no longer heavenly bodies in his universe and only orbited into view every so often. People had often asked why he and the family didn't live in Manhattan, but he appreciated the privacy of being outside it, and enjoyed driving himself into the city, even when traffic was hell and he was running late. His Bentley was as quiet and well-appointed as the most expensive rooms in his hotels, and in it he could tune out the world.

The train was about to pull into the station. Alex watched as a handful of passengers stepped off. A middle-aged woman got into an old Volvo wagon he'd seen before in town with its peeling Obama and Hillary stickers, and decals from a few too many prep schools and Ivies forever bonded to her rear window, indicative of expulsion or outright failure or the more innocent option of a transfer. A woman speaking on her phone headed up the hill on foot. A young African-American couple loaded up their Audi with their shopping bags. But there was no Pete.

The train pulled away, heading north to Ossining and points beyond. Alex got out and walked down to the deserted platform, hitching up his trousers and looking again at his watch. He wondered if Pete had fallen asleep and would only realize what had happened when he'd awaken to find himself in Peekskill or even at the end of the line in Poughkeepsie. If he'd missed the train, surely he would have called to let Alex know. He waited a minute more before walking back to the pickup. And when he opened the door, Pete was sitting there, already belted into the passenger seat.

Alex felt as if he had been sabotaged by the narrator of someone else's story.

"I got in early to Grand Central and took the 3:20."

"How long have you been here?"

"About an hour. I walked around, strolled along the river. It's a gorgeous day."

"You should have called."

"You're right, I should have."

Alex turned the key. "But you didn't."

"I don't often get to see scenery like this." Pete shrugged. "I mean, I live in a studio apartment in Bushwick."

"How did you know this was my truck?"

Pete smiled as if he harbored a secret he was dying to tell. "The party you threw for the team? Your garage was open, and I remembered your plate."

MASON2. As if he were a man with nothing to hide. Alex put the pickup into gear and backed out of the space.

As soon as they got to the house they sat down to work. As Pete laid out his argument for pursuing the project, Alex thought the man had done an amazingly comprehensive job. Though the inspection reports were mixed—the building was unsound in several critical ways, which almost certainly meant it would have to be taken down, its replacement built from the foundation up—the location was the selling point. Pete's artist friend, a master's candidate at Columbia University's School of Architecture, had come up with a rendering of how the building would look situated on that block. Alex had to admit it was very promising.

They worked for nearly two hours and, as they sat with their drinks on loungers by the pool, talked about Pete's role in the project, should Alex decide to go ahead with it.

Alex said, "You know, I was looking once again at your CV back at the office the other day. I have to say, it's pretty impressive. University of Chicago, then Harvard Business for your graduate degree. You put me to shame," he said.

Pete lifted his beer and nodded in thanks. He said, "Wharton isn't all that shabby, Alex."

"That's true. Where are you originally from, Pete?"

"New York."

"So you grew up in the city." Just as Joey Proctor had, Alex remembered, recalling the boy's parents who'd driven up to camp the morning after he disappeared.

"Riverdale, actually. Went to Collegiate. You know, the whole prep school thing."

"And summers?"

"Camp. Like most kids I knew."

Alex shrugged. "So how'd that go?"

"It was okay."

Alex stared into his drink. Almost time for a refill. "Not a happy camper, I guess."

"Maybe only occasionally amused."

Alex went to the drinks cart, threw some ice in his glass, and poured another few shots of Scotch. "Is that where your swimming thing happened? The one you told me about?"

"Yeah. That sort of ended summer camp for me."

"Here. Let me get you another."

Alex could feel the liquor going quickly to his head. Suddenly off-balance, he covered it with a deft move as he handed Pete another Corona.

"You okay?" Pete said.

"We've had a few issues here at the house, and it's been a bit tense. It's good for me to unwind a little tonight." Alex sipped his drink and set the glass down on a table. "We're being harassed by someone, and we don't know who it is or why it's happening. It's been especially stressful for my daughters."

"God, I'm sorry to hear that. Did you call the police?"

Alex explained that there wasn't much they could do at this stage without anything more specific. "So we're more or less on our own with this one. We only hope it's come to an end."

"You don't think it's a competitor, do you?"

"It's a possibility," Alex said. "Anyway, it's why Ashley's with the kids in Connecticut. To get away from all the stuff that's been happening."

Pete joined him as they waited for the grill to heat up. Alex had bought a few nice cuts of steak and some corn, and had a local deli put together a salad. He picked up his glass and realized he shouldn't have had another. Too much alcohol, and he would lose control of his words. This was what Joey was doing to him, he thought. He wondered when he would decide to stop.

"Before we both get too buzzed, cap off your pitch. I'll put up the water in the kitchen for the corn, and then we'll throw on the steaks."

Pete shaped the air before him with his hands. "It really comes down to the fact that Brooklyn is very hot, and there aren't that many neighborhoods left that haven't turned into another Park Slope or Williamsburg. So time is important here, Alex. I'm thinking we call the hotel Mason Red, for Red Hook. A boutique establishment, but very personalized. We make it a real location. People will want to come back, and often. Create a dynamite restaurant by hiring a Brooklyn-based chef, someone up-and-coming with good word of mouth. First-rate spa, great gym."

"No pool?"

Pete smiled. "No way."

Alex laughed. "Taxis don't like to go to Brooklyn from Manhattan. That could be a problem."

"Not with Uber and Lyft it isn't. That's how most people my age get around these days."

Pete followed Alex into the house and looked around at the spacious kitchen. "This is a beautiful house."

"You didn't get to see it when you came to the party, did you?"

"We were all outside mostly."

Alex turned on the pool lights and switched on a unit on the counter and pressed Play. The music could be heard out by the pool, the same song that had awakened the family.

"*I'm sittin' on the dock of the bay…*"

"Who is this?" Pete said.

"Don't recognize it?"

"Never heard it."

"Otis Redding," Alex said. "An old song, but I kinda like it. You?"

"Yeah, it's mellow. Nice. I like his voice."

Pete followed Alex back to the pool, now all lit up on this warm, still evening. Alex opened the grill and laid on the steaks. They immediately began to sizzle.

Alex said, "I think you did an amazing job with the research on the property, and your pitch is definitely one of the best I've ever heard. But there's another reason why I invited you here, Pete. I just need to know, I just want the air cleared. And be honest with me, okay?"

Pete's smile began to fade. He watched Alex sip what was

left of his drink. When he tried to set it down, he missed the table and it smashed to the ground. Alex didn't even seem aware of it.

He went on, "Before you took this job, did we ever meet?"

Pete looked confused. "I knew who you were, of course, but I don't think we were ever introduced."

"Because I'm beginning to have a feeling you're at the company for a reason."

Alex shifted unsteadily to the point where Pete put a hand out to steady him, even though those few beers had already gone to his own head.

"Just answer me, Pete."

"Isn't it enough that I like working here?"

"Joey. That name sound familiar? Like the name painted on the wall in the Brooklyn property?"

Pete seemed genuinely puzzled. "I don't know what you're getting at, Alex."

"Come on, you know all about it, don't you? Just tell me, and it's no big deal. How about the blood in the pool? And the elevator stunt? And this music? Anything? No? Yes? The photos you took at the Mason House bar?"

"Why would I—"

"Let's say I'm right," Alex slurred. "No, no, no, just hear me out. What do you want…an apology? Money? A better position in the company?"

Pete set down his beer. "Maybe I should just go home."

Alex went to the drinks cart, grabbed a fresh glass, and filled it with more Scotch. He drank half of it and put the glass down. His face was red, and he was sweating heavily. "I saw your file. You wrote in your cover letter that you were only applying to one company for a position. The one with my name on it."

"Because you head one of the most successful businesses in the—"

"I don't think so, Pete. You gave it away when you said you don't swim. That some counselor traumatized you. Yeah, I get it. I know I was wrong. But a lot of time has passed, right? So when did you change your name?"

"Alex, I don't under—"

He jabbed Pete in the chest. "You applied for the job so you could get close to me, didn't you. So you could get into my life. See my house, meet my wife, right, Joey? Those rats and mice in the Mason House... They didn't just get there on their own. So what really happened to you after I left you on the raft?"

Now he had a hand on Pete's shoulder and gripped it hard enough to make the younger man wince. "Someone come by with a boat and take you away? Were you kidnapped? It couldn't have been John Otis. That's just a story counselors have been telling for years."

Pete broke loose from Alex's grip and took a step back, closer to the edge of the pool. "I think I'd better go. I'll walk down to the train. You're in no shape to drive."

"Just say it. Say you did it. And then we can figure out how we can make it right between us." Alex grabbed Pete and began to shake him. "Say it, for fuck's sake! Just fucking admit it!"

"Okay, okay, yes, all right, whatever you want me to say." Pete broke away and held out his hands, looking bewildered.

"I did whatever you think I did, and I'm sorry. Does that make it better?"

"You did it all, didn't you? The blood, the name in the room, the photos, the rats, the—"

"Just let me go home, please?"

Beyond drunk, Alex smiled crookedly and patted Pete's shoulder. "Good boy. It's over now, isn't it. It's finally over."

He gave Pete what he thought was a dismissive nudge: he was finished with the whole matter. Instead, Pete lost his balance and stumbled backward into the deep end of the pool. He began to flail and struggle, churning up the water and getting even further from the edge. The man was drowning, grappling frantically and futilely for a handhold, anything that might save him, and the look of terror on his face mirrored that of Joey's twenty-one years earlier in Echo Lake. Alex leapt into the pool, feeling the weight of his sodden clothes pulling him down, and put his arms tightly around Pete. "Don't fight me... Just let me help you. Let me help you out. Just take it easy. I'm not going to let you drown, I promise. Just relax and trust me."

But Pete kept struggling, pushing him away as his lungs filled with water. For one moment Alex detested Pete as much as he'd hated Joey for being so helpless, so much the victim. But this time there was no choice. He'd save him now, deal with him afterward. Money would change hands. Silence would be bought.

When Alex tried to pull him out of the water, Pete gasped for air and struggled even more, pushing Alex away until he went under one more time and fell limp, his arms outspread, his body no longer responsive. It took a moment for Alex to realize how quickly it had all happened. Alex grabbed hold of Pete and slowly and arduously pulled him up the ladder.

The song continued to play over and over again as he dragged Pete onto the side of the pool. He pumped the man's heart with no result and, his mouth to his, tried to give him breath, crying, "Come on, Pete, don't leave me!" Everything he'd learned in training to be a swimming counselor was failing him.

Pete Kellerman was dead, his eyes wide open, staring blankly into Alex's face.

"Oh Jesus," Alex said, still on his knees. "What the hell have I done?"

It took him most of an hour to get Pete wrapped in a tarp and loaded into the back of the truck, a moment when this young man had become an object of weight and dimension and little else. Alex shut the tailgate, got into the cab, and sat stunned at the end of the driveway. Yet it was the most peace he had felt in weeks, just sitting there. It was finally over. Joey was dead.

Now life could go on.

36

A LONE BLUE HERON FLEW JUST ABOVE THE WATER, its long wings languidly agitating the air, heading toward the first light of morning as something broke the surface with a splash, startling a flock of swallows flying high overhead. The thing bobbed for several seconds, sending ripples out to the edges of the lake. And then everything was quiet once again.

Alex lay on the bed, still in the clothes he'd changed into the night before. He kept trying to convince himself that it had really all come to an end, that the ordeal the family had gone through was finally over. Joey had survived the raft and had devoted a little too much of his time to trying to get revenge, when he could just as easily have confronted Alex, admitted who he actually was, and maybe asked for something in return: money or a better position in the company. In this transactional world, it made perfect sense to Alex: Pete—Joey—had joined the company not only to get closer to Alex but to benefit himself. In his shoes, Alex would probably have done the same thing. And now it was finished. It was an accident. Alex had genuinely tried to save him, and failed. He'd done the best that he could, and what had taken place that night could never stick to him. An accident, he reminded himself. Nothing could touch him now.

It was only when he woke the next morning, sober and exhausted, muscles aching, that he realized he had gone too far. He could have reported what had happened as a simple drowning—Pete had had a few too many drinks, Alex had gone inside to start the corn, and when he came out Pete was dead. *This sort of thing happens all the time*, he thought. *A routine matter for the local police.* Alex would be cleared after an investigation. But now it was too late. Now it was no longer an accident. And no one would ever know what had taken place here.

Where was Pete? It was a question that only he could answer.

Alex got out of bed and came down the stairs and saw that he'd forgotten to set the alarm system the night before. The front door was unlocked, as was the door in the kitchen leading out to the pool and tennis court. Unlocked but not ajar. But everything was where it had always been: the artwork in the living room, the electronics—nothing had been disturbed or taken, no one had come in during the night. And now Joey was no more.

Seeing his truck parked under the portico, Alex grabbed his keys and pulled the truck into one of the four garage bays. He opened the tailgate and saw nothing that could give him away except for a few drops of water. He climbed into the truck bed, pulled off his T-shirt, and only left when every drop was blotted.

As always, the Sunday *Times* was at the bottom of the driveway, flung over the gate in its blue plastic bag. Over coffee and a few Advils, Alex leafed through the business and real estate sections, then showered and made some toast and more coffee. He felt nothing. His mind was clear, as though sleep had cleansed him of any speck of guilt that might come later to trouble his mind. At noon he heard a car pull up, and the voices of his daughters made him smile and be grateful for what he still had. Now it was over. Now they could start anew.

His wife and the girls were refreshed from their weekend away. Becca and Lyndsey barely greeted their father and went up to their rooms as Ashley fetched a vase for the flowers her sister had cut for her. She filled it with water and set it on the counter where the sunlight angled through the kitchen windows.

He asked how their weekend had gone.

"We had a great time. You know Susie's pony, Applejack? Lyndsey had her first ride on it."

"Lyndsey? Really?"

Ashley smiled. "She was scared at first, but then she looked really comfortable. Susie even taught her how to trot. I think she may ask for riding lessons. What's wrong, Alex?"

"What do you mean?"

"I can see it in your face. Something's happened, hasn't it?"

"Everything's okay now."

She took his hand. "You're trembling."

"Too much coffee."

"No, there's something else."

"Like I said. Everything's okay now."

"What do you mean by 'now'? Everything's okay *now*? I mean, what are you saying?"

"Just...don't raise your voice, don't panic." He took a breath. "Let's go outside." They walked out to the pool. He said, "Listen. It's finished. No one's going to bother us again, I promise."

"What did you do, Alex?"

"Don't ask me about it, all right?"

"You need to tell me everything."

He gazed down into the pool. Nothing but water, deep and blue, filled with sunlight, a single leaf floating on the surface.

She followed his gaze. "What is that?" She fished it out with the net. What he had thought was a leaf was a crumpled twenty-dollar bill. "How did that get there?"

He knew there would be something, some gap in the lie, some fissure for others to pry open and explore. She kept looking at the twenty as if it made no sense to her.

"I don't know, Ash. Just forget it, okay? I wanted to tell you that the kid who works for me, Pete Kellerman? It's all come out now. He was the one I left on the raft. He must've changed his name and taken the job so he could, I don't know, get back at me. But it's over now. Nothing more to worry about."

She just stared at him. "You're sure it was him?"

"He admitted to it. He said he was sorry he bothered us. He felt especially bad that you and the kids were so frightened. It's finished, Ashley. We can move on now. He's gone from the company; he's out of our life. Forever."

"And did you apologize for what you did to this guy when he was a kid? I mean, to do all of these things to us, to your business… He's either got to be crazy, or he can't let go of what you made him go through. It must have been so traumatic."

"And now it's over, okay? Done. We're not going to discuss this again."

"So, what, you paid him off?"

"Something like that."

Before she could ask any more questions, their phones simultaneously chimed with messages. Both had been sent from a blocked number, and each launched the same footage: someone walking through their house, step by step. First to Lyndsey's bedroom. She slept on her stomach and her mouth was slightly open, and on either side of her was an array of stuffed animals. The camera swung away and returned to the hallway, and as Ashley watched, she clamped a hand over her mouth, because she couldn't believe what she was seeing.

Becca slept in a tank top and was smiling at something. Beside her was her one-eyed bear, the same one she'd had as a baby. Ashley said "I—" and then fell silent as this person moved down to the master bedroom. The door was ajar, and a hand in a blue surgical glove pushed it open slowly. In the gloom one could just make out two figures in a bed, like the opening moments to a scene that would end with blood splashed on the walls and bodies with their heads blown off.

"What is this? Who is this?" Ashley asked, her voice shaking. "He's going to kill us."

Alex put a hand on her arm, but he had to keep watching as the camera came closer. Alex was wrapped in the covers, while Ashley slept naked, her eyes hidden behind a mask, her mouth open in a half smile. A moment later, the hand pointed at Alex's head, as if about to put a bullet in it. Then the hand recoiled, as though the deed were done.

Ashley grabbed Alex's arm as she staggered and nearly fell.

"No… No, this can't be happening," he said.

"My god," she said. "My god, my god." She and Alex looked at each other with the same shocked expression.

"It's impossible," he said.

"He was *here*, Alex. He was in our daughters' bedrooms." She looked again at her phone. "He was standing over the bed. *Our* bed. He was wandering around the house, and we didn't even know. We didn't hear a thing."

Alex ran the footage on his phone again. He paused the scene in their bedroom. "There's a reflection in the mirror."

He could just make out the dark profile of someone with long, protruding eyes and a mouth with some kind of deformity, tubular and monstrous. It was something inhuman, completely alien, and for Alex the name John Otis came to mind.

Ashley looked up at him and said, "What? What?"

He just kept staring at the phone. Like everything else that had happened, it didn't make any sense. Because Pete was dead; Joey was history.

"Whoever did this, whoever put the…whatever, the blood in the pool and all the other things—it's the same person who sent those photos to you," Alex said. "From the hotel bar. He was trying to set me up."

That meant Pete was alive, sending this stuff to them. But he couldn't have survived, Alex thought, remembering the man's lifeless body by the pool, his dead eyes looking right at Alex.

Unless he did survive.

"I don't want the girls to know about this," he said.

"I don't ever want to sleep in this house again," Ashley said. "It's contaminated, it's not ours anymore, it belongs to this…thing."

Alex grabbed her arm and pulled her back to him. "We

can't do that. This is our home. We'll get a whole new security system. New locks. I'll hire someone to watch the property."

"You think that'll end this? This whatever it is, this *monster*, is in our house, Alex. *Our* house. While we're *asleep*. Tell the police about that piece of shit who works for you. You can pay him whatever you want, but I want him put away, you understand? Get him the fuck out of our lives."

Alex wrapped his arms around her and held her against him. "Just take it easy. We need to think. I need to think. It's going to be okay."

"God knows how long he's been doing this. And how did he get our phone numbers to send this vile stuff? What happens next? He goes after the girls? He rapes me?"

She sat on one of the chairs by the pool and held her head in her hands. He scraped a chair up close to her and took her hands. There were tears running down her cheeks.

"I'm not going to let anyone hurt you or the girls, I promise you, I swear to you."

Ashley pushed him away. "You said it was done, Alex. You said you'd dealt with him, that he'd leave us alone. You're the man who tells the world how he makes things happen. Snap your fingers and everyone jumps. Except it's not working, is it, because we're not dealing with some wacko property developer who competes with you. Now we've got a psycho in our lives, and you don't know how to handle it, do you?"

He had no answer for her, because she was right. She stood and wiped her cheeks with her palms. "You may have paid this guy off, but he's still coming after us. And now we can't get rid of him, can we. It's never going to be over."

37

HIS SECRETARY STEPPED OUT OF HER OFFICE WHEN she saw Alex walking toward it. He looked pale and unrested; the night before, he had sat up in the living room, in the darkness, until one thirty, his gun by his side. But no one came. The house remained quiet. And he slept fitfully there, in his clothes, until just before daybreak.

"You all right?" Carol said.

"Just tired."

Quietly, she said that there was a detective waiting to speak to him. He stared off into the distance.

"Alex? He's in the reception room."

Lieutenant Carver got to his feet as Alex walked in. The cop said, "Can we talk someplace private?"

Alex opened his office door and asked Carol to hold all calls for the next half hour. They both remained standing. "You're Briarcliff police, right? This is Manhattan. What's the problem?"

"I went to your house, but no one was home. I figured you needed to learn this before anyone else. The body of a man identified as"—he referred to his notepad—"Peter James Kellerman was found early this morning floating in the Tarrytown Reservoir. A jogger spotted him and phoned the police. I understand he was one of your employees."

Alex looked out the window at the overpriced view. He felt something tighten inside his chest. He could hardly breathe. After a moment he said, "My god, that's terrible." No. It was worse than that. Even in death, Joey was with him.

"A business card found in his wallet indicated that Mr. Kellerman worked for your company. Tarrytown PD contacted us as they knew you lived in the next town."

"I just can't believe it. Pete was the newest addition to our team. A promising young guy, too." Alex opened his hands in a gesture of helplessness. "How could this happen?"

"There were no signs of struggle or violence. So at the moment we're thinking he may have taken his own life. But it's still inconclusive."

"That's unbelievable. He was about to take on a major project here. It was going to kick-start his career at Mason House Properties."

"Suicide hasn't yet been confirmed by the coroner's office, you understand. It's just an assumption. One of many."

"I can't believe it. Pete was a great kid."

"His driver's license indicated he was twenty-nine. Not really a child."

Carver asked what Alex knew of Kellerman's private life. Only what Pete had told him, he said: that he lived in a studio apartment in Bushwick. He didn't know if he had a girlfriend, a boyfriend, or even what his interests were outside of work. His Facebook profile gave little away. He had friends, he drank beer, he liked football. As far as Alex was concerned, Pete's life was a blank page.

"So you didn't socialize outside of work, then."

"Once a year my wife and I have my people over to the house for a cookout. But apart from that?" Alex shook his head. "I like to keep work separate from my social life."

Carver began looking at the magazine covers and photos on the wall. He turned to Alex and smiled. "I'm impressed. You know everyone. Bill Clinton?"

"It was a charity thing I'm involved with."

"The mayor. *Two* mayors. The governor. Wait a minute..." He stepped closer. "Am I seeing this right? Tony Bennett? Bono?" He smiled and pointed to another photo. "Wait, don't tell me. I have his pants..."

"Ralph Lauren."

"You weren't supposed to tell me."

"I have to get to work, Lieutenant. So—"

"My wife bought me one of his shirts last Christmas. It's pink, so I can't really wear it to work." He smiled.

The detective's cell rang, and he excused himself and stepped out of the office. Alex was about to close the door on him when the lieutenant pushed it back open.

"That was the coroner's office in White Plains. Kellerman had traces of chlorine in his lungs. Possibly from a swimming pool. Yet he was found in a reservoir."

"Meaning what? He drowned twice?"

"I'm just reporting what they told me. The district attorney wants it opened as a homicide case. We may have further questions for you and your staff, so please make everyone available over the next week or so." He got ready to leave, pausing at the door.

"Anything unusual happen to you or your family lately? I mean after the whole thing with the CD player?"

Alex remembered the film sent to him and Ashley, and he winced a little. It was the last thing he'd want this man to see. "No. Nothing."

"You're sure of that."

"Absolutely. It's been fine."

"I'll be in touch."

When Alex came out of his office a short time later, the rest of the team was gathered in the hallway. Sandy held a crumpled tissue, and her eyes were puffy and red.

"You heard, then," he said grimly. The cop must have told them on his way out.

"I just can't believe it," she said. "It doesn't make any sense. Pete killing himself?"

"Did he ever say anything about his life at home, what he did, what interested him?" Alex asked.

Rob said, "I once went out for drinks with him after work. He seemed just like an ordinary guy. He didn't really talk a lot about stuff outside of work. I think he mentioned something about him and his girlfriend going to her sister's wedding in Seattle next month. That was about it." He shrugged. "But he really looked up to you. He told me that. He'd lost his father when he was young. I guess you sort of took his place."

38

WASHINGTON SQUARE PARK WAS BUSY WITH college students, dog walkers, parents pushing strollers. Everyone looked happy: after the rainy, overcast day before, this was a flashback to the summer that was already becoming a memory. Someone in the distance was playing conga drums. A young guy listening to music through earbuds skateboarded by. Alex stood by the arch, where they'd planned to meet, and was looking at his watch when a voice called out, "Mr. Mason?"

Marty Pollock was a short, wiry young man with a goatee and mustache. He wore a blue chambray shirt, a navy blazer, jeans, and Converse sneakers. Over one shoulder was a blue backpack. He introduced himself, and shaking his hand, Alex said he appreciated him taking the time for them to meet.

"Hey. Anything I can learn about this whole thing will be really helpful to what I'm working on, you know? Look, it's a nice day, so let's sit for a little while. Do you have time? I mean, I know you're a really busy guy and—"

Alex smiled. "Like I said on the phone, I'd even be happy to buy you lunch. I read a little about the thing you did for TV, and I just want to hear more about Joey Proctor and this John Otis."

They found an unoccupied bench near the man playing the

congas. Another, older man—deeply tanned, his torso and arms covered in tattoos—joined him with a second instrument as they began trading fours. A few people stopped to watch and drop coins on the blanket they'd laid out. The tattooed man smiled, revealing a mouth full of gold.

Alex asked how Marty had become interested in the Joey Proctor story, and the younger man laughed a little. "Actually, I was there."

That revelation was startling. "When it happened? Do I know you?"

"When were you at Waukeelo exactly?" Marty said.

"Just for one summer. I was eighteen, so it was, what, twenty-one years ago? I was a swimming counselor, working with ages eight through fourteen."

"I was seven, in the younger group. I probably saw you a hundred times a day. Sorry if I didn't register it." He smiled.

"So you had… Let me try to remember—"

"Rich Murray." Marty laughed.

"Right, right. Rich Murray. God, it feels like forever since I was there."

"Yeah, Richie was great."

"So you're a swimmer."

"Whenever I get the opportunity. Anyway, to be honest, it was my first and last year at any camp. Things got a little tight for my family after that."

"But you became interested in what happened to Joey?"

"Everyone knew about him. Even in the days after it happened, it was turning into a legend that became part of the whole John Otis narrative, which was completely understandable. One night we heard the story of Otis, the next day a kid goes missing. Scared the hell out of everyone. I don't know if you're aware of it, but the John Otis thing goes way back, long before Joey went missing. I think counselors were telling that story even as early as the 1950s. Long time ago."

"But it all stayed with you," Alex said.

"I remembered it when I first came here to NYU as a student. I did my concentration in documentary filmmaking and thought I could do something with the Joey Proctor mystery."

"That explains the show you did on John Otis."

"That was my first credited project. I pitched the Otis story to the show's producer, a guy I'd met at a panel in Austin a year earlier. One thing led to another, and he asked for documentation and a treatment. Six months later, we set it up, pulled in some additional financing, and after I brought on a cinematographer I began production. When you called, I recognized your name from my research."

An attractive young woman in pink shorts and a white tank top gracefully rollerbladed past them and out of the park. "What do you mean by research?"

"I got hold of the police reports filed the day after Joey disappeared, plus whatever had been written up afterward. I guess the whole thing went cold after a few weeks, because there was nothing more."

"And my name was in them?" He realized his voice betrayed more panic than surprise.

"Just that you were interviewed, along with some of the other counselors. Steve Fenton was Joey's bunk counselor, and he had a lot to say about the kid. He wasn't a happy little guy.

It seemed to Steve and the camp owners that his parents were barely on speaking terms." Marty shook his head. "I don't know. That's why it's thought he might have just walked away from camp. He was lonely, he had nothing to go home to, really, and maybe he just decided to find some other future."

"At eight years old?"

"Some kids that age have been known to commit suicide. It's rare, but it happens. The whole thing is just really sad."

It struck Alex as being more than sad; had he known about Joey and his parents, he might have treated him more kindly. Not pushed him so hard to be in the deep water. Not left him on the raft.

"And no one's seen him since, I gather."

Marty lifted a finger. "That's not completely resolved. I'll get to that later."

"There's some doubt?"

Marty took a pouch of American Spirit tobacco and a packet of rolling paper from his backpack. "About Joey? Well, that's the thing. Look. All those other names…you know, the kids who were supposed to have vanished before him?" He lit his cigarette and took a long drag. "That was a load of horseshit. I tracked down two of them… They didn't even know their names were being used like that. The counselors were just screwing with us. One of the great lessons in telling a compelling story is to be precise. To give dates, name names, add little details that seem unbelievable. The more unbelievable they are, the more people believe the story."

"I don't get it," Alex said.

"Because when you bring in something from left field,

something a little outrageous and out of the ordinary and surrounded by very specific facts, they say to themselves, 'That's so weird that it's got to be true.' And you're more than halfway to selling them your fiction. Like that one kid they mentioned... Henry Cassidy, I think it was. He was, like, this really blond boy who never tanned, so the counselors said he was an albino. It was just so out there that it was more than credible. You almost expect a kid like that to disappear into thin air. Like a cloud."

Alex remembered the big book of camp photos, and even recalled the pale little boy who seemed somehow doomed even then. "What happened to him?"

"Henry? I found him," Marty said. "I found his grave, rather. Upstate. In Utica. Died when he was fifty. Heart attack. Left a wife and three kids."

"Wow. That's sad."

"But here's the other thing," Marty said. "Years before the summer you and Joey were there, some local kid actually did disappear."

Alex looked at him. "You're serious?"

Marty nodded. "This was before the Jensens bought the camp, a week after the season was over. The kid was nine, I think, maybe ten, and one day he decided to see if he could take one of the rowboats from the waterfront and go out on the lake. All they found was the boat, bobbing up against the shoreline." He lifted his shoulders. "The kid had vanished. I looked into this as much as I could. The police were tight-lipped about the whole thing, which I thought was weird, considering how old the case was. The impression I got from the detective in charge of it was that they suspected one of the guys hired to work at the camp—"

"Counselors?"

"No, just the men who maintained the property. They were all local guys, you know, handymen and landscapers. But nothing really panned out."

Alex asked if the boy had been found.

Marty shrugged. "They're not saying. Which I take to mean that he hasn't been, and they think whoever was responsible is still around. The police keep things quiet, hoping that someone will come forward with information. You know, guys get complacent over time, then one night they get drunk, they talk too much, and it all comes pouring out. People hear it, people call the cops."

"But you chose, what, to do Joey's story instead? Why him?"

"Because I was there. That's something that helps sell a story like this…my own proximity to it. And I decided a whole story could be built around just one little unsolved mystery of an actual missing kid and the legend of John Otis. Put them together, and you've got the beginnings of one hell of a tale. We hear of abducted kids all the time. Sometimes it's a relative, an estranged husband or wife. Other times it's as dark and horrible as you could imagine. You have any?"

"Kids? Two daughters."

"Then it must have crossed your mind at some time. You're a famous guy in town, an established name. You must have thought that you could be the target of something just like that."

Alex's smile faded to a frown. It hadn't occurred to him. All his professional life he'd considered himself invincible, and only over the past few weeks had he realized this bulwark he'd built from the ground up was becoming a ruin, open to the world.

"Yeah, well, I don't like to think about it," he said.

"But you *have* thought about it, because everyone who has kids does."

"You have none, I'm guessing."

"I'm in a relationship," Marty said. "Actually, she's an actress, and maybe because our careers keep us busy, we haven't really worked out the future for us as a couple." He smiled. "We'll get around to it one of these days."

He flicked an ash away, took a long puff, then rubbed the cigarette out on the ground and tossed it in a nearby pail. "But what happened to Joey Proctor might have been as simple as that he drowned, and for some reason his body couldn't be found. Which means it's still somewhere in the lake, as some still think."

"Is that possible?"

"Honestly? I don't think so. They did a few more underwater searches—I think four more dives—and found nothing."

Alex considered it. "So Joey really could still be alive."

Marty looked at him for a long moment. "Alive and somewhere out there… Yeah, definitely."

Alex took it in and said nothing.

"You okay?" Marty said.

"Yeah, I'm fine."

"And who knows what kind of a man he'd be now? I mean, anything's possible, right? Without a body, it may mean that something else happened to Joey, something a whole lot weirder. This story of John Otis… It's a legend that somehow"—he spread his hands wide—"amplifies and deepens the tragic story of an eight-year-old who vanished. Can a legend kidnap an actual child? Can a rumor come to life and wreak havoc? If you have time, I'll show you what I've got. My place is only a few blocks away."

Marty lived in a faculty apartment on Bleecker Street, in a soulless tower owned by the university. A woman on her way out greeted him by name and looked curiously at Alex, as though she either recognized him for who he was or suspected him for what he might do.

They rode the elevator up to the nineteenth floor. Marty unlocked a door halfway down the hall. They stepped into a living room that also served as his workplace. Corkboards crowded with documents, photos, and maps, some tacked over others, ran the length of one wall, while beneath them were three long folding tables covered with an array of electronic equipment: an iMac, two laptops, cameras, recording gear, coils, tangles of cables, and various devices Alex didn't recognize. Boxes of blank DVDs were stacked in a corner of the room. On the walls were framed classic movie posters: *Blow-Up*, *Rear Window*, *Don't Look Now*.

Alex recognized the same camp photo tacked to the corkboard that he had in the box in his basement. Around it were pinned enlargements of some of the kids' faces, as well as snapshots of the waterfront and several newspaper clippings, some photocopied, others yellow with age. Alex bent over to get a better look. He said, "It's funny, but all these years later I still recognize some of the kids."

"Still remember their names?"

"Let's see. This one was…Jonathan something… Frasier or Grazer?"

"Grazer. Jon died on 9/11. He'd just been hired by Cantor Fitzgerald."

"I'm sorry to hear that. I remember he was always the clown of the bunch, always cracking jokes."

Marty came up alongside him. "How about this one?"

"Yes. Definitely. Great swimmer. I worked with him a lot."

"Remember his name?"

"Matt something. Matt Hall? Something like that?" He shrugged.

"That's pretty good for so many years later. Matt Healy. I interviewed him about four years ago when I first started researching this project. He's an attorney here in the city."

The name seemed vaguely familiar to Alex. He wondered if at some time in the past they'd crossed paths.

Marty pointed to one of the men in the back row with all the counselors, the one standing in the middle of the row. "How about him? He look familiar?"

"He was the owner, right?"

"Right. Dave Jensen. But that's a whole other story."

"You have no more pictures of Joey here, though."

"Of course not," Marty said as he switched on his iMac. "He disappeared, didn't he?"

39

AS THE COMPUTER BOOTED UP, MARTY SAID, "When I began teaching documentary filmmaking, I started with a statement that was meant to send my students on a journey into their own projects. Basically, at the heart of every story there's an empty space. That's why a person makes a documentary in the first place. Not necessarily to chronicle an event or an era or a decade or a whatever—which is fine in its own way—but to provide an answer to a question. It doesn't matter what it is, or how big or small it is. If there's a mystery, it'll draw us in."

The screen saver was a slide show consisting of close-ups, like a series of mug shots, of the counselors and kids at Waukeelo the year Joey disappeared. When Alex's face appeared, he said, "Guess I was young once, huh?" and Marty laughed. Alex had had more hair then, it was lighter and redder than it was now, and whenever he'd been out in the sun, he'd ended up with freckles, which he'd hated all his life. The smile on his face in the photo was the kind of smile you wanted to punch out of existence. He had been a cocky young guy then, a dedicated frat boy, captain of the swimming team three years running, and, at best, only a B student, which mattered little, as his father had donated considerable sums to the university. He dated at least two of the university cheerleaders and joined campus organizations for the sole purpose of meeting girls—even a children's charitable group, the mission of which had always been unclear to him.

For years, ever since leaving grad school, he'd been running from this version of himself, and now felt he'd reinvented himself completely. Would someone who'd known him then still recognize the arrogant young undergraduate he'd once been? He had virtually no contact with any of his friends from those days. He didn't attend college reunions, and if, as sometimes happened at conferences he'd attended, he thought he recognized someone from his fraternity, he went out of his way to avoid him. Once, in a SoHo restaurant where he was dining with Ashley, a guy in a suit who'd been shooting looks at him from his own table walked up and asked if he was Alex Mason.

"I think you've got the wrong person," Alex said. "Sorry."

But after he'd returned to his table, the man kept looking over at Alex.

"Do you know him?" Ashley said.

"Yeah. A long time ago. I don't want to know him anymore."

"Why? What did you do to him?"

Alex shook his head. "It's all in the past. It's long gone."

He'd been a fraternity pledge whom Alex had tormented to the point where the guy left both the fraternity and, a few weeks later, the university.

Marty noticed Alex's distraction and said, "You need to be somewhere, don't you?"

Alex checked his watch. "I have a meeting at one of my hotels in an hour. But I'd like to hear more about this."

"So before you go, let me cut to the chase," Marty said. "This mystery I talk about with my students, this empty space… It's like the eye of a hurricane. The storm roars in with the wind and the thunder and the rain, and then, *bang*, it's clear and calm. Sunlight and balmy breezes. And you think, 'Oh great, it's all over, peace at last.'"

"Before the storm kicks in again."

"And we always remember the eye as being something weird and wonderful and just so way out there. That's why we're all interested in stuff like this. We try to fill it with all kinds of theories and crazy notions. John Otis took Joey. Joey wandered off and was kidnapped. Joey drowned. Joey this, Joey that, but we still don't know what happened to the kid."

"Did you ever meet him?"

"Of course. They used to put the seven- and eight-year-olds together for arts and crafts. Remember the cottage they used for that on the way to the big field? The husband-and-wife team that ran the activity?"

"Sort of."

"So sometimes we'd be working on the same thing at the same table. Mosaics or painting, whatever."

"What was Joey like?"

"Quiet. He could really concentrate on things, really dig down deep when he was involved in one of the projects. He didn't joke around a lot. He was small like I was, and when you're a kid and you're little you tend to keep to yourself, I guess. Make yourself inconspicuous. Because there's always the danger of the older kids beating up on you. Sometimes you want to become invisible."

"Interesting."

"But at the same time, you want to be recognized for who you are."

Alex had been a small kid before high school, so he knew what it was like to be picked on. And he knew that some would settle for being the victim for the rest of their lives. But he'd intended early on to show everyone what he was really capable of doing. That was Alex: self-made man, a millionaire several times over, a beautiful wife, beautiful children, beautiful house, beautiful car. But that was all over now, because his past had left a door open and someone had walked into the family. The poison had already begun to do its work; the ugliness had started to show its face.

"A documentary is like a jigsaw puzzle," Marty was saying. "Only one piece will fit in the end to make the picture complete. What can only be the truth. Check this out."

The screen saver gave way to an old black-and-white photo of a gaunt, grizzled, angry-looking man in his late twenties, wearing overalls and not looking into the camera.

"John Otis?" Alex guessed.

"You might think so. It's rumored that Otis was the product of an incestuous relationship between his father and his older sister, Annabel, who disappeared soon after John was born. She stopped coming to school and was never seen again in town, and of course the rumor went around that her father, the man who impregnated her, had murdered her and buried her body either in the woods or in the dirt cellar in the house. But it was never conclusively determined."

"Conclusively."

"Skeletal remains were found, but there was no way to match DNA, as there's no living relative of the Otis family. Unless John is still out there. If he's still alive, he'd be nearly a hundred now."

"So there really was a John Otis."

Marty clicked to another photo, this one of a group of men with pickaxes and shovels. "A lot of the local men were hired to clear the land that first was a Boy Scout camp before it eventually became Camp Waukeelo." He put his finger on the screen. "That's believed to be John Otis."

This time, a cigarette hanging from the corner of his mouth, Otis was smiling as he leaned on a shovel.

"The money was probably pretty good, and Otis liked working with his hands. But in the late 1930s, he was still living in his father's house. The family name back in the early eighteenth century was Oates. Over generations it got changed to Otis."

"This whole thing sounds like something from Appalachia."

"The Berkshires may have become an attraction for the wealthy—the writer Edith Wharton lived there, for instance, and now we have Tanglewood and Canyon Ranch—but there was also a really poor segment of the population, though it's less obvious today."

"Have you seen Otis's house?"

"It burned down about ten years ago."

Marty clicked on a file, and a wrinkled snapshot of a big, black house appeared on the monitor. It had small windows and gothic details, as though it had been designed for a Hollywood horror film. "The picture was taken in 1934 by a local police officer who'd come to see what had happened to John. The kid just stopped coming to school."

"So what happened when the cop arrived?"

"John's father came out with his shotgun and threatened to kill the officer. He didn't give a shit what the law thought about him, and he probably passed that attitude down to his son."

The next photo showed only a stone fireplace and chimney still standing. "I took this just before I did the TV episode. No human remains were found on the property."

"So John escaped."

"So it seems, if he was alive when it happened."

Alex looked at his watch. "I really do have a meeting to go to."

"Are you still interested in this?"

"I am. Very much."

"May I ask why?"

Alex took a breath. "Well. To begin with, I was Joey's swimming counselor. It was terrible how he just disappeared, and I guess I just want to know as much as I can about it. I remember his parents and just feel really sorry for them, really sad."

Because if Joey was still alive and turned out not to have been Pete Kellerman, then it would require a whole new strategy on Alex's part. He began to think that this Marty Pollock might give him the lead he needed.

"Then let's set a day and a time that work for you."

"And let me take you out to lunch afterward, okay?"

"I never turn down a free meal," Marty said, and they both smiled.

Alex needed to hear everything this guy knew. Because there was the truth, and then there was the legend, as Marty put it.

"Next time you come, I'll show you the good stuff."

"So there's more?" Alex said.

"Oh. You ain't seen nothing yet."

40

IT WAS A TWO-HOUR DRIVE TO CAMP WAUKEELO from the house. Alex wasn't sure what he was looking for or even why he was going, but something was drawing him back. Maybe it was all this talk of Joey; maybe he just wanted one more look at the raft. Maybe this time he'd come down to the waterfront and find the boy still on the raft, and everything that had happened since—college, grad school, Ashley, the girls, the hotels—was nothing but a dream.

Rob and Sandy were flying to Detroit with him on Friday, and they needed a few more days to prepare all the documents—regarding tax structures in the city, zoning regulations, and population breakdown by income—for review before they left. Alex had requested the Gulfstream be checked over and fueled up the day before the Detroit trip.

He'd told Ashley that he'd be leaving early the next morning, though he'd be back in time for dinner. "I have a site I have to look at up near Albany," he lied.

She looked at him. "That's the first I've heard of it."

"It was one of Pete Kellerman's ideas. I just want to have a look for myself."

"A Mason hotel near Albany? With all the Motel 6s and Days Inns to choose from up there?"

He laughed and gave her a kiss. "It's not a long drive. Straight shot up the Taconic. I'll be out of here before breakfast. I'll grab something on the road. And, who knows. Maybe I'll conclude that you're right. I just have to see for myself."

The day broke sunny but cool, and as he got closer to the Massachusetts border, it become grayer and darker, looking as though it might rain at any minute. Up ahead, he saw a gas station and a diner, Little Dee's. He hadn't bothered to get breakfast earlier, so he took a seat at the counter.

The waitress handed him a laminated menu. "Coffee?"

"Please."

She looked at him, then looked again. "I know you, don't I? You been in here before?"

"Actually, no. Never."

"I know I've seen you someplace."

He nodded. "Maybe in a magazine or on TV?"

Her eyes lit up in recognition. "You're the guy with the hotels."

He smiled and ordered scrambled eggs, bacon, and wheat toast. An elderly man sitting in one of the booths got up to pay his check. He wore a John Deere hat that had seen better days, its brim a little chewed and sprouting loose threads. He looked as if he'd been sleeping rough for a good part of his life. He saw Alex looking at him.

"I know you, too," the man said. His voice was not much more than a raspy whisper.

"Okay."

The waitress brought Alex his breakfast.

"I seen you up here. Once, maybe. Maybe more."

"I haven't been here for over twenty years."

"That's what I mean," the man said, pocketing his change. "That summer the kid disappeared. You were there, weren't you."

"How would you know that?" Alex's voice was sharp.

"I worked at the camp. Odd jobs. Cleanups. Tree trimming, that sort of thing. I used to see you down by the lake." His smile was a sparse array of stained and rotting teeth. He took a toothpick from a dispenser beside the cash register and slid it into the corner of his mouth as he perched on the stool next to Alex. He smelled of stale tobacco and unwashed clothes.

"Look," Alex said. "I just want to eat my meal and then be on my way, okay?"

"I also seen what you did. The way you throwed that little boy into the water and then left him on the raft. You didn't see me, though. You didn't see me for one second, because I was clearing some brush farther on up along the edge of the lake. But I saw you. And then you swum back and walked away, just like that."

He smiled and let his mouth work the toothpick to the other side.

"Are you going to leave me alone?"

"That your fancy car out there?"

Alex swiveled around to face the man directly. "What do you want from me?"

"Just a little friendly chitchat."

"Not now."

"I know you."

"Look—"

"I know what you did." The man reached over and took

a strip of bacon from Alex's plate with his dirty fingers. Alex couldn't believe what was happening. Here was a man who had seen him bring Joey to the raft and who was now eating his breakfast.

"Take your hands off my meal."

The guy smiled and touched the brim of his cap. "I'm an old man now," he said. "Not much time left. A lot of unfinished business to take care of. I keep thinking about that little boy and this great big rich man in New York City who builds hotels and who's always in magazines and on TV, like you said to Tina here."

Quietly, Alex said, "Are you threatening me?"

"I play it as I see it," the man said. He slid off the stool, walked out, and climbed into his pickup.

Alex said to the waitress, "Who is that guy?"

"Ed Unis. Been around like forever. Eats here most days. He used to cut lawns, trim shrubs, that kind of thing. People hired him to do odd jobs. Still do, sometimes. Sometimes he even shows up to do them. Sometimes he doesn't. Disappears for weeks, then he's back in here, taking up space."

The man was sitting in his truck, lighting a cigarette and watching Alex through the window. Watching and waiting.

She poured him some more coffee. "Don't worry about Ed. He's all talk and no action." She glanced out the window. The pickup was no longer there. "Anyway, he's gone now."

41

BECAUSE THE SEASON HAD BEEN OVER FOR NEARLY a month, the camp was closed but still accessible by the narrow road that led to it, its cracks and fissures tarred over so often after so many brutal winters that it looked like a complicated road map to nowhere.

Alex brought the Bentley to a gentle halt to look down toward the Camp Waukeelo sign with its image of a boy paddling a canoe into the sunset. Or sunrise. Because the wind had picked up, the sign swung a little on its hooks. He wondered if he should just turn back, as though were he to proceed, get out of his car, and walk past those familiar landmarks—the bunks, the social hall, the dining hall, the owners' cabin—all the way down to the dock and the water and raft, he might somehow let loose something dark and vengeful, something much stronger than Joey Proctor, that for all of these years had been waiting for him to return. Or maybe it was a kind of voodoo, and this visit would rid his family of whatever curse had grown comfortable in their home.

According to the sign, it was now a coed camp, and when he walked down the hill that led to the dining hall and the lakefront, he saw a new computer center near the owners' cottage, as well as several additional bunkhouses that hadn't been there in his time. The door to the social hall was unlocked. The stage was just as he remembered it, except now a single folding chair stood open on it. Dust hung in the air, catching the sunlight, immobile. A few posters remained tacked up on the big bulletin board by the door. That past summer they'd put on *Rent*, as well as an evening devoted to the results of a filmmaking activity. This really was a whole new camp, undoubtedly with new owners, and there would be no place for John Otis or stories of horror in this enlightened atmosphere.

As before, the big leather albums could be found on their shelves on the left side of the room. He ran his finger along the spines until he found the volume containing the summer he'd been there and opened it to the big camp photo he had at home. A musty smell rose from it, as if it hadn't been opened in decades. The photo was the same one Marty Pollock had pinned to his corkboard, the one Alex had in the cellar at home. But this one was different; where Joey Proctor had been sitting, his face blurred, was an empty space. Someone had cut him out of the photograph, precisely following the lines of his body. As if he'd never existed.

"Knew I'd find you here."

Alex looked around to find Ed Unis smiling in the doorway. He was a larger man than he had initially appeared, taller and more broad-shouldered. There was something about him that resisted all the usual prejudices. He wasn't quite a homeless man, not nearly an outlaw. Just someone who seemed to come out of nowhere. A chill fell over Alex.

"Did you follow me?" he asked.

"Uh-uh. Didn't need to."

"Meaning what?"

Ed laughed. "Meaning that I know your mind. In the end, they all come back to the scene of the crime. I seen it all my life."

Alex shut the book and shoved it back on the shelf. "There was no crime."

"Sometimes you don't have to do something to make it wrong. Sometimes you just have to *not* do something. What's that called? Sin of omission?"

Ed walked into the room and looked around. "Things've changed, as I guess you've noticed. Now they have girls here. Pretty girls. Sometimes they bring me on to do little jobs, repairing porches and bunkhouses. Sometimes I come down at night and watch the girls in the showers through this little tiny hole in the wall. Not the real little ones, I mean the teenagers, the ones who have stuff to admire."

"What do you want from me? Money?"

Ed Unis shook his head. "I'm doing just fine without a penny of what you own. I have something a lot more valuable. I have your reputation. I have your name." He opened his hand as if holding something precious. "I have your life."

"So call the police. There's nothing they can do. I was a college kid who simply forgot about a boy on the raft. That's not a crime, and I can't be prosecuted."

"That kind of thing, it gets in the newspapers, it could leave people with a bad taste in their mouths whenever they say your name. People you do business with. People you love." He smiled. "People who already hate you for what you are, for the money you have, that fancy chariot you drive around in."

Alex came closer to him. He would play the man's little game. "So where does that leave you? What's your plan?"

Ed lit a cigarette. "Come on, take a walk with me, have a look at the place. Don't worry, I'm not gonna hurt you."

They walked down to the waterfront and looked out over the lake. The raft bobbed a little in the water, just as it had the night Alex had shone a light on it and found it empty.

"This dock here? I rebuilt a good bit of it the summer before last. Same with that boathouse there."

"That wasn't there when I worked here."

"Back then they'd just pull the boats onto the beach and upend them so's the rain wouldn't get in. Then the boys would turn them over and all the spiders who'd moved in would come racing out." He laughed. "Now they keep them in that glorified shed. And charge the parents a shitload more than when you were here. Food's better, too, I hear. Bunks are pretty much the same. Every September I'd be called in to replace screens or fix the doors to the toilets. Kids can be pretty hard on this place."

He turned his attention to the raft. "For a kid who can't swim, that's kind of scary, sitting there and wondering how he's going to get back."

"Just leave it, will you?"

"I picture him waiting. Waiting for you to come back and save him. The sun goes down, and he's still waiting. Nightfall, and he's still there. He doesn't dare move, 'cause he could fall in the water and drown."

He lit a Camel and coughed into his fist. "But you wanted him to swim. And he can't do it, because when you're that afraid of something, nothing's going to cure you of it. You'd rather die than give it a try, as the poet once said."

"And you did nothing to help him?" Alex said.

The man smiled. "Wasn't me that left him there, was it."

"That's your excuse?" Alex said.

"Probably not nearly as bad as the one you came up with. Anyway, someone had to take care of him."

Alex took a moment to absorb this, the implication of the words landing hard in his stomach. "Where the hell is he?"

The man smiled. "I didn't say I had nothing to do with it. I'm just saying someone might have. Who that might be is none of my concern."

"So you took him," Alex said. "Maybe I'll contact the police when I get home. Okay? Are we finished here?"

Ed smiled. "Fine and dandy with me, chief. Call the police. And then I'll tell 'em how you abandoned the little boy on the raft just like he was halfway to nothing. Then see what those newspapers and magazines have to say about you."

The man is bluffing, Alex assured himself. He was an ignorant local just trying to make trouble.

"Are you finished?" Alex said, turning to walk away.

"And then it gets dark, and you come down here and shine your light on it, and no one's there. Yup, that's right, I seen that, too."

He smiled a little too smugly, and Alex quickly changed his mind. The man knew. He knew too much.

"I also met the boy's mother. Pretty lady, she was. I invited her to spend a little time with me, you know, just so we could get to know one another, but I guess she wasn't interested. And then I saw her when she and that husband of hers come back the day after her boy vanished. She wasn't so pretty then."

Alex said, "I need to be going."

"Not until I'm done with you."

"What does that mean?"

"Just that. Someone's got to stand up for that little kid."

"What are you intending to do?"

"Make a point, that's all."

It occurred to Alex that this man knew where Joey was. "If you don't want money, then what is it? Do you want me to turn myself in for something that's borderline negligence and nothing more? I mean, it's been over twenty years. I know the statute of limitations has come and gone on this thing."

"You must've been feeling pretty guilty to go look that one up."

Ed kept smiling in his strange, unsettling way. When Alex began to walk back up to his car, Ed just stayed where he was, down by the lake, smoking his cigarette, watching him.

By then it had begun to drizzle, and after Alex turned on the engine, the wipers automatically activated. The radio came on a little too loudly, and he turned it off. It would be a relief to return home in silence, in the quiet of a dark, rainy afternoon. As he backed the Bentley out and headed down the road, he turned his mind to the Detroit project, letting his thoughts take him out of the past, away from this place. He had a feeling that once he saw the area for himself, he might change his mind. One building alone doesn't necessarily improve a neighborhood; it needed a whole-scale revival, and only developers with real faith in the future of the city would commit to it. And then he thought: he could start things moving; he'd be a leader, a hero to the city, and others just might follow and work on improving the neighborhood.

Anything to put a shine on the brand.

He crested a hill and came to an abrupt stop when he saw Ed Unis's pickup blocking the road out of camp. He'd parked it sideways across both narrow lanes, leaving no room to drive around it. Now Alex was trapped; this had been Ed's plan all along. And now, Alex realized, he was going to die. He was about to call 911 when he saw Ed in his rearview mirror lumbering toward him. He locked the doors and waited. Ed stopped by his door and twisted the air with his hand. Alex lowered the window a crack.

"I seen your phone there. I know what you're thinking. You're forgetting one thing, though… What I seen that day and then that night. And after I tell them that, little man, you'll be sorry you ever came back here."

Ed was right. There was nothing Alex could do but wait for this man to move his truck and let him drive away. When Ed opened the door of his truck and leaned in to get something, possibly a shotgun or a pistol, Alex pressed the accelerator to the floor and drove as fast as he could. Zero to sixty in four seconds flat, just as advertised.

He backed the Bentley away, and Ed Unis's body crumpled to the ground. Alex pulled it by the man's work boots into the woods as far as he could go before they became impenetrable, made all the more difficult because the man's stomach had been torn open, his intestines spilling out, foot after foot of them, dragging along beside him. He left the body under a pine tree, making it seem as though the man had been attacked by a wolf or a coyote, as undoubtedly it would be in the coming days. The ground was boggy, and he could only hope that over time Ed Unis would sink deep enough so that no one would spot him. And he suspected that right now no one would ever miss the man.

Alex pulled the Bentley off to the side of the road and climbed into Unis's pickup. On the floor of the passenger side were a naked Barbie doll, a coil of insulated cable, and a few crushed Bud Light cans. The incongruity of it seemed malign. As far as Alex was concerned, everything about this man was corrupt. His death would mean nothing but one less monster in the world.

He drove the pickup a hundred yards until he reached the dirt road with the sign *KEEP AWAY!!! ENTRUDERS WILL BE SHOT!!!* He unhooked the chain and eased the truck slowly down the road in first gear, stopping when he saw a pond off to his left. He pulled up to the edge of it, wiped his prints off the steering wheel and door handle, and put the truck in neutral. After that, it was easy enough to push the truck into the water until only the roof was visible. It would be months before anyone would find Ed's body or his pickup. And there was nothing on it that would lead the police back to Alex. Ed Unis was as insignificant a person to him as a stranger on the street. And the camp, revisited, now more than ever belonged to the past.

On Alex's drive home, the rain had grown steadier and heavier, and he was happy for it, because by the time he pulled into his driveway, all the blood and viscera had been washed from the front of the car. There wasn't a dent or a scratch. His Bentley looked as good as new.

42

"YOU WERE RIGHT," ALEX SAID AS HE JOINED ASHLEY and the girls at the dinner table. "It's a lousy location."

Ashley smiled. "Should've listened to me in the first place. Then you wouldn't have killed a day driving up and back in the rain."

There had been no witnesses. There was never much traffic on the road during the off-season, and with rain threatening, no one was about to drive up to look at the camp.

"Tell Daddy what happened at school today, Becca," Ashley said.

"It's not that big a deal."

"Just tell me."

Without looking at her father, she said, "I got accepted into the honors English program."

"That's great. Congratulations."

He reached over and squeezed her hand. Becca shrugged, as if what she had achieved was worth very little in the scheme of things. She knew that his interest in his daughters' school activities was mostly limited to sporting achievements, not academics. Becca was by far the better student and would almost certainly get into her first-choice college. Lyndsey was an average student who only displayed interest when it came to drama and art. She reluctantly played soccer and volleyball, preferring the periods when she was confined to the bench, while Becca was an eager participant in all athletics. Because of her advanced skills, she'd been chosen for the junior varsity swimming team and had begun to show some prowess at field hockey. Becca would grow up to look like her mother, while Lyndsey was the child Ashley really cherished, as though she saw more of herself in this sensitive little girl than in the thirteen-year-old overachiever sitting beside her.

"Everything okay otherwise?" Alex asked, and Ashley said everything was fine. When he looked at her, he saw something else there. Something dark and anxious, as though she could read his thoughts and see Ed Unis's face as the life was crushed out of his old body.

After dinner, when the girls had gone up to their rooms, he said, "What's bothering you?"

"Nothing."

"Come on, Ash. I can see it."

"It's just that it's kind of agonizing, wondering what's going to happen to us next."

"Everything's going to be fine from now on."

"Except that nothing that's already happened could have been predicted by either of us. Which means it could happen again. It just comes out of nowhere. I mean, what if he gets in the house again?"

"We have new locks, an upgraded security system."

"The last system was supposed to be the best. But someone was able to get in and film us. That's the scary thing, Alex. He was walking around, and no one heard a thing."

"It won't happen again."

His idea of keeping his gun under his side of the bed was hardly going to deter an intruder. And by the time Alex would have shot the man, he could have already murdered their children.

"And you still haven't found someone to watch the place."

"I don't think we need someone sitting in a car every night doing nothing but waiting. It'll just attract attention. Right now we're as secure as we'll ever be."

Alex wasn't sure what had woken him at half past two the next morning, but he lay there, wide awake and staring into the darkness. No, he knew exactly what it was. He remembered the diner, Little Dee's, and how the waitress had recognized him. She'd also witnessed Ed Unis confronting Alex at the counter. When Ed's body was found, she would know who was responsible for his death. Alex could only hope that she would be glad to be rid of the man, no matter who had done it.

For the next hour or two, he wondered how he could silence her, until he fell into a heavy sleep and forgot he'd ever thought about it.

43

MARTY WAS WAITING IN THE DOORWAY OF HIS apartment as Alex stepped off the elevator. "Thanks for taking the time to meet with me," he said.

"No problem. I don't have to teach until late this afternoon."

Marty poured Alex a mug of coffee. "So. Everything going well?"

It was not a question Alex was accustomed to hearing. It implied that things hadn't been going well, that he'd been under siege, or that his business was in trouble, and the only way to answer it was to be factually vague, as though his life were full of secrets that could only be revealed at the most auspicious and profitable of moments.

"We're busy looking at new locations," Alex said, "trying to increase our visibility in different regions of the country."

"I would say you're doing amazingly well so far. You're a big name, Mr. Mason."

"It's Alex, okay?"

Marty smiled. "Someone like you… You're on top of your game, from everything I've read."

"You follow me, then."

"I read magazines. You know, I've seen the pieces on you. The *New Yorker*. *Vanity Fair*. The usual places."

"Sometimes they're not so kind."

"It's all part of the gig, though, isn't it? You make money, you build buildings, and people turn you from being a living, breathing person into some two-dimensional character in a B movie. Rags to riches. Pennies to millions. And, as we all know, everyone's a critic."

Alex laughed. He knew the feeling well. Though there never had been rags, he let people assume that his journey to the top had been an arduous one, that he'd struggled and fought to get where he was. While, in truth, it had all been handed to him once both his parents were dead. As he always liked to say, the legend is so much more compelling than the truth.

"I've actually been to the Mason House," Marty said.

"You stayed there?"

"It's way beyond my means. I just went to the bar one night when I was in the area with a friend. It's a really nice hotel. One day maybe I'll make enough money to spend a night there."

"I'd be happy to set you up with a special rate if you ever want to make that happen."

"But I'm here, aren't I? I'm lucky to have this place."

Alex glanced around. "It's nice."

"No. It's *perfect*," Marty said.

The screen saver was running its usual slide show. Faces of counselors. Faces of campers. There was Alex. There was Dave Jensen. There was Steve Fenton. It seemed so long ago, Alex thought, and yet Joey was still out there. No, that was wrong. Joey wasn't anywhere. He wasn't miles and miles away; he was closer than Alex could ever imagine. As though he were hiding in the man's shadow.

"We were talking about John Otis," Marty said. He clicked open a folder on his computer's desktop with Otis's name. "I told you about the family background. How their name changed over the years and all that stuff, right?"

Alex nodded.

"So. This is where things really get weird."

"What do you mean?"

"The whole John Otis thing. It's why I'm making this movie. You'll understand why when you hear the rest of it."

Marty clicked on a file, and what appeared to be a scan of a newspaper article appeared on the screen.

"This was when John Otis was arrested for being a Peeping Tom in his neighborhood. This was...June 1949. He was probably twenty-six, twenty-seven. Some campers also claimed they saw him watching them from the woods behind the bunkhouses. He was still living at home, though by then both his parents were dead. People steered clear of his house, especially kids. Witnesses said he got just as aggressive as his father had if anyone came near the place."

"And the camp stories about him?"

"Counselors started telling the kids about him sometime in the fifties. I'd spoken to a guy who'd been there in 1959 and for...let me see"—he sifted through some papers on the desk until he found what he was looking for—"three years after that. Charlie Schulberg. He's retired, lives in Arizona now. He'd heard the stories, and from what he said, they really weren't all that different from what we were told when we there. Joey and I, I mean."

"Just to scare the campers," Alex said.

"That's half of what my movie's about."

"But Otis may have been completely innocent."

"Or even dead by then. But in and of itself, a legend told well can terrify people, even if the threat is no longer alive. It's what hearing it does to your brain. It sparks all the old, deep fears you'd thought you'd long ago forgotten. It's kind of a primal thing, like how people used to talk about dragons. It's why the best horror movies can really catch fire. They make you think you see what's only being suggested. Listen to this."

He opened another file, footage of an interview with a man in his late sixties. "This is Mike Farrelli, who was a detective at the time Joey disappeared. It's from an interview I did with him about six weeks ago. Even after he retired, Mike kept researching the case." He looked at Alex. "And he's still at it."

The detective was sitting in a chair in a living room. Behind him, slightly out of focus, was a bookshelf, a few framed pictures on the wall. A golden retriever trotted into the room, and the man smiled and bent to pat him. The dog circled a few times before settling at the man's feet.

Farrelli had a full head of very white hair. But his eyes were what lent him a sense of gravity, as though he were focusing on something not in the room. Long off the police force, he was still caught up in the mystery of Joey Proctor. The footage opened in the middle of a sentence: "…and one of the theories we tossed around was that, assuming Joey had remained by the…whatever it's called: the swimming place, the swimming area—"

"The lakefront," an off-screen Marty prompted.

"—he might have been picked up by someone who lived nearby. Because we learned that no one ever saw him again after the swimming activity. Which suggests he was left at the waterfront or decided on his own to stay there, which is strange in itself, as he was known to be scared of the water. Anyway, they may have seen him, boated over to check if he was okay, brought him to their home. Maybe to one of the cottages across the lake from the camp belonging to the summer people."

Marty said, "Instead of taking him to the camp?"

"Whoever took him in might have felt he'd be safer with them, especially if something had spooked the kid." The detective's dog yawned, and Farrelli smiled at him.

Marty paused the footage. "You hear that? That something might have spooked Joey?" He looked at Alex. "What could that have been?"

Alex seemed a little stunned by the question. That was another way into his life, he knew, and he was instantly on his guard. "Like I said, I dismissed the kids, and they went back to their bunks."

"All except for Joey. And that's what Mike Farrelli's getting at."

"Really," Alex said. "So this detective doesn't think Joey was kidnapped or even, I don't know, drowned?"

"You would know best, wouldn't you? You were probably the last to see him at the swimming activity."

Alex thought of Ed Unis, who'd witnessed the entire thing. It had taken less than fifteen minutes, and like a pebble thrown into a pond, the ripples were still making their way through the years. Because apparently Joey was still alive and inside Alex's life.

"Mike told me that one theory they'd been considering was that whoever took Joey called his parents from wherever he was brought. Let's say that something frightened him, maybe one of the kids who had been picking on him, and he told them this. They called his parents, and the Proctors drove up to the cottage and saw the perfect way to make some serious money. They had been really well off, with an apartment on Park Avenue they obviously didn't want to give up. But it was understood that Mr. Proctor's business had suffered some major losses around that time. There was a risk they would lose it all."

"So they'd, what, pretend that they never saw Joey again, claim negligence on the owners' part, and sue the owners of the camp?"

"Which in fact they did. I mean, there was no one else who could be held accountable at the time. The Proctors settled for just under eight million. The Jensens didn't even have a fraction of that amount. The suit destroyed them, and they never recovered from it. They had to sell their home and the camp, and had nothing left. You remember Dave Jensen, right? The owner?"

"Very decent guy, I liked him. His wife was really nice, too."

"He killed himself a year later."

Alex felt as though he'd touched a live wire. "God, no."

"He had rented a little bungalow just outside Lenox, and two days after signing the lease, pulled his car into the garage, closed it up, left the engine running. His son found him an hour later. The kid was eight years old when it happened."

Alex exhaled at length. "Jesus, this is a real tragedy." He vaguely remembered the little boy walking into the Jensens' cabin.

"It gets worse," Marty said. "They say the son never really got over it. That he never really was the same."

"That must have been brutal."

"David's wife...remember her? Nancy? She had nothing

to live on. After Dave's death, she moved with her son to an apartment over a laundromat in Pittsfield. She worked a couple of days a week cleaning other people's houses, but it was never enough. They were destitute. She knew what was coming. She had no choice but to give her son up for adoption, and once he was with his foster family in Philadelphia, she did what her husband had done. Except she used alcohol and pills. It was weeks before they found her body. I'm told the son took the foster family's name."

44

Alex sat back, overwhelmed by the enormity of the thing. One small, careless act had led to such a string of tragedies.

"Everyone was affected by what happened," Marty went on. "There were consequences all over the place. Like bodies on a battlefield."

Alex nodded. "So it is possible that Joey's still alive," he said.

"The other theory is that someone took him in and kept him captive."

"Someone meaning John Otis?"

"I mean truly kept him prisoner. Abused him and maybe even murdered him. Beyond all that stuff they told us at camp, the other part of the John Otis legend is his reputation as a child molester. Just makes him more of a monster, doesn't it?"

"And Joey's parents?"

Marty looked through some papers on his desk and found his notes. "Alan Proctor died of a massive coronary five years after Joey's disappearance. Did you know...? No, probably not. But, among other things, Alan Proctor was a real-estate investor here in the city."

"Really." Alex had never heard of him during the years he was in the business.

"They say he was involved in some pretty shady dealings. I mean, I don't know, I don't understand any of this. Hey...maybe you and he had crossed paths at some time, when you were on your way up in the world." He smiled. "Small world, huh?"

"And Joey's mother…?"

"Diane Proctor was institutionalized with late-stage Alzheimer's this past year. Now she doesn't even remember that she ever had a son. Maybe that's a blessing, I don't know."

"You're still in touch with this detective?"

"Mike? Now and again we toss theories back and forth to each other. I'm actually scheduled to fly down to talk to him again next month. He thinks he's getting close to a solution."

Alex took it in for a moment. "And then what?"

"He'll break the case wide open. Maybe even write a book about it. We're even discussing working together on it."

Alex looked at him. "Do you think it's possible he'll find out what really happened?"

"It has to be over sometime, doesn't it? Once you've discarded all the possible explanations, all that'll be left is the one true answer. He actually feels he may know who was responsible."

"And there would be some legal ramifications to all this?"

"If whoever was responsible is still alive, well, yeah." Marty smiled. "Don't trust me on that. I'm obviously not a lawyer."

Alex sat back and took a breath. "Is this detective still up north, in wherever, Massachusetts?"

Having Joey in his life was one thing; having a detective on the verge of investigating him was quite another. Alex felt his mouth go dry and asked Marty for a glass of water. The filmmaker returned with a bottle of Evian, and Alex drank half of it straight off.

"Mike lives in Florida now," Marty said. "His wife died a few years ago. He's like me. He's obsessed with this case. Like everyone involved, he wants closure before he dies. But he's been playing with another hypothesis that I find kind of interesting."

Marty fast-forwarded through the interview with Mike Farrelli as a date and time stamp sped by on the bottom of the footage, resuming it at normal speed.

Farrelli was saying, "Just after I retired all those years ago, my wife and I spent a week in St. Petersburg. It'd been a rough winter, and we both needed a break. She had to replace a suitcase that had broken, the zipper, you know, so we went to this Walmart in town, and while she was shopping—me, I hate to shop—I waited in the kind of foyer they have where they keep the shopping carts. Know what I mean? That…space, that, I don't know, that area. Anyway, the wall was covered with these posters of missing children. Forty or fifty of them. Photos of kids and renderings of what they'd look like now. Some of them had been gone for ten, fifteen years. Others for only a few months. There was even a girl who'd been missing for twenty years. And then I realized something. Joey's parents had never put together one of these. He'd never been listed on any of the databases or lists of missing and exploited children. I thought that was the key to this whole thing. That there might have been a whole other story here."

In the interview Marty said, "Do you have any idea what it could be?"

Farrelli lifted his shoulders. "Not a clue. But someone out

there probably does. That's one part of the mystery. The other is what happened to Joey once the group was finished with their swimming activity. Because he just sort of seemed to drop out of time. You know what I mean?"

Marty closed the file, and the monitor went black before the screen saver came on. He rolled himself another cigarette and cracked open a window. "My plan is to make a full-length feature based on the story. Take a kind of *Blair Witch* approach to it. Lots of handheld, you know, some sequences that look like found footage. I'm going to have a lot of scenes of this stuff...you know, creepy things found in the woods, skeletons, strange markings on the trees. Cops walking through the woods and finding these weird things. Here. Look at this. I just finishing editing it."

He opened another film file. Two men, one older than the other, both wearing orange hunters' vests, held hunting rifles as they walked through snowy woods. The point of view was from behind them as they stamped through the freshly fallen snow.

"Hell of a morning, isn't it," the older one said.

"I'd forgotten how pretty it is up here."

"You just realize that? We've been coming up here since you were nine years old. That's twenty years by my counting."

"Now watch," Marty said, moving quickly ahead in the footage.

The hunters stopped. The younger one looked up at a branch of a birch tree. Hanging from it was what looked like a boy with a noose around his neck. The boy was naked, and his penis and testicles had been cut off. Marty paused the film.

"Did that actually happen?" Alex said.

"Does it matter? I mean, what counts is that stuff like this makes audiences' flesh creep. The big difference is that, at its heart, this is a true story: a kid disappears and gets lost in the narrative, as if it were a black hole in the universe. And the approach will only look like a documentary. But sometimes there'll be more fiction than fact. Kind of blurring the genres. Interviews with real people mixed with acted scenes. Just like what the counselors used to tell around the campfires...use real names and put them in the tale. Mike Farrelli's going to be part of the film."

"So he's the real thing."

"The dogged detective who won't give up. A good procedural always needs one. I just want to make sure it ends with the truth." He sat back. "I want my movie not just to make money but at least hint at who might have been responsible for this kid's disappearance."

"What if you never find out what happened to him?"

"I don't think we ever will. But at least we might discover what took place in those hours after the group was sent back to their bunks. Or it might jar someone's memory. There were probably nine or ten or more kids at the dock that afternoon. One of them might eventually recall the events of that day."

Feeling overwhelmed by this story in which he had played a pivotal role, Alex sat back and shook his head. "This really is a big deal."

Marty shut down the computer. "But I also want to make sure it's a hit. Scaring people is half the game. It's what opens movies. And I mean that in both senses of the term. Ideally, I'd like to set everything in motion with a website full of all this stuff...the newspaper clippings, bits of Mike's interviews. I'm hiring an actor to do voice-over narration. Roll the whole thing out over a month or so until people get drawn into it. Then if I can launch the film at Sundance at, say, a midnight showing…? Hey, I may just have a hit."

He rolled his chair back and opened his hands as if forming a screen for the images he was about to describe. "We'd fade in on an open field on a dark summer night. Picture campfires with boys sitting around them. We've seen that scene hundreds of times before in movies. It's a cliché, yeah, but it works."

"That's how the movie begins?"

"We see the glow of campfires on the faces of the boys. Now it's time to tell the story."

"John Otis."

He nodded. "After this, the boys will never be the same: that's what they always say, summer after summer as they unravel the tale of a crazy man who steals a boy every seven years. Except this summer, in fact the next day, one of their own will go missing. The campfires die down and the boys walk through the darkness back to their bunks, led by counselors and their flashlights. It's a dark night, and the kids are probably wondering who's watching them from the woods. In less than twenty-four hours the legend will become reality, and, for some of these campers, life will never be the same."

Marty clapped his hands and spread his arms as though to break the spell. "The idea is to make audiences think it's going to be a horror flick with all the usual scares."

"But it isn't."

"Frankly? I think it's much, much worse. Because what's real always is. It's all in the details, isn't it?" He smiled. "So. Still interested in buying a starving college lecturer lunch?"

45

IT SOUNDED RIDICULOUS, IF SHE THOUGHT ABOUT IT too much, but it was the spinning that would save her. Three days a week for a solid hour while music she would never normally listen to blasted as a heavy-thighed woman with a booming voice so horrible to hear that it made you pedal all the faster, as though you might be able to escape this monster, put them through their paces, telling them to go faster, harder, to *pump pump pump* those legs. Ashley would walk away from it weak-kneed and wobbly, soaked in sweat, but feeling more herself than she did at home, as if here she could shed her roles as wife and mother and simply be reduced to what she really was, strong-willed and independent, the person she had lost sight of so long ago.

Instead of showering at the gym, she drove home where she could clean up in private. She'd had enough of the older women eyeing her body by the lockers, reminding her with their looks that one day she would be like them, all droop and hang and regret.

She parked under the portico and locked the door. Once inside, she went to enter the security code and saw the system was already off. She had been the last to leave, after Alex had headed into the city and the kids were in school, and out of habit she would have armed the system. Yet now it was off.

She looked up the main staircase as if expecting to find an intruder, but the house was quiet. It took her several moments to realize she had probably forgotten to set it. It was careless of her, and she would be sure not to mention it to Alex. She had a quick shower, then, as was her custom, filled the tub and watched the bubbles form while she lay back and shut her eyes. *Me time*, she thought. And now she had the entire house to herself. After this she'd have a salad, then run to the supermarket and pick up the girls from school on the way back. She felt herself drift into sleep, and then something abruptly woke her.

She blinked her eyes a few times and looked again at the light fixture in the ceiling. There was something there that she'd never seen before, what looked like a small, round glass button. She rose from the water and belted on a terrycloth robe. She took a closer look.

She knew just what it was.

She went into the master bedroom and checked the ceiling light, but there was nothing. Because here it was wedged between the corner of the mirror and its frame. She touched it with her finger, then went into the girls' bedrooms. When she scanned Lyndsey's room in all its kid chaos, she saw another button catch the light. One of the eyes on her daughter's American Girl doll had been replaced with a lens. Someone had been watching them.

Someone still was.

46

WHEN THE DOORBELL RANG, SHE LOOKED OUT the window, recognizing Lieutenant Carver, the detective who'd been there before.

She opened the door and apologized. She was still in her robe, and her hair was wet and uncombed. "I just got back from the gym, and I was in the bath."

"Sorry for catching you at a bad time, Mrs. Mason. Is Mr. Mason in?"

Beyond Carver, leaning against the Crown Vic, Detective Ettinger was giving his fingernails a close inspection.

"Is this about what's been happening here? Did you find out who it was?"

"When do you expect your husband to be home?"

Carver must have known that he could just as easily have gone into the city to speak to Alex in person, but sometimes being in the right place at the wrong time was the smarter move.

"Probably no later than seven," she said.

Her face must have given her away, because he said, "Is something wrong, Mrs. Mason?"

"It's a private matter. Just something I need to speak to my husband about. And I have to get dressed and pick up my daughters at school."

"We'll come back later. Again, sorry to have disturbed you."

She shut and locked the door and made sure the system was armed. She called Alex's cell and left him a message to expect the police there when he returned home. Then she went into the kitchen and dug an ice pick out of a drawer. She went from room to room, finding a lens hidden in each, obvious to anyone who took the time to look, which meant whoever had planted them was expecting to be caught. She knew she was being watched as she moved through the house, breaking the glass in each lens with the pick, ending up at the last one in her bedroom mirror.

"I don't know who you are, I don't know what the hell you want from me and my family, and I don't expect you just wanted to see this since you'd already had a good look when I was sleeping."

She unbelted her robe and exposed herself to the lens. Then she closed it and flipped him off.

"Now get the hell out of our lives!"

She worked so vigorously to break up the last lens that she shattered her own reflection.

47

FOR ONCE, ON A SCHOOL NIGHT, ASHLEY LET THE girls eat in front of the television in the family room, while she sipped wine and waited outside in the twilight for Alex to pull up. As she saw the headlights appear, she checked her watch: ten past seven. The days were getting shorter; all that remained of this one was a thin glow on the horizon. If whoever was behind these things wasn't caught soon—if he only suspended his activities for a time—the winter was going to be a long and difficult one. For all of them.

There were pills, out-of-date antidepressants sitting in her nightstand drawer, prescribed by a psychiatrist she saw for a few months after Alex's affair. She hadn't dipped into her stash since then, or rather she had once or twice, but she sensed that soon she'd need to rely on them more regularly. As though all those years ago she had seen this moment coming, when her world was beginning to fall apart all over again.

Alex saw her expression as he got out of the Bentley. "What's happened?"

"I don't want the girls to know about this."

He followed her up to the bedroom. She switched on the light and showed him the broken lens in the frame of the mirror.

He extracted what remained of it. "It's just glass," he said.

"Nothing didn't come out of nowhere," she said quietly. "Someone came in and did this. All over the house. Someone's spying on us, Alex. What the hell is he looking for?"

"It's only a lens. See? There's no transmitter, no wires. No one can see anything."

They went into Lyndsey's room. He pried the one from her doll. "Nothing there. It's just glued on."

"What it means is that someone hacked into our new security system and got in. There's nothing we can do to stop this guy."

He finished removing what remained of the dummy lenses. "You were home alone?"

"After spinning class. I thought I'd armed the system, but I must have forgotten." She looked at him. "What?"

"Nothing. I was just thinking."

"What, that *I* did this? Just like I filmed myself sleeping? This makes as much sense as if you were behind all of this."

"That's crazy, Ash."

"Whoever it is is still here. While we sleep, while we're out. I mean, I thought it was all over, the whole Joey business. Because you told me it was. You promised me. You said you'd paid him off."

Alex let his hands drop to his sides. "It wasn't Pete. He was found dead in the reservoir. The cops think he killed himself."

"The reservoir up here?"

He nodded.

Ashley looked shocked. "And you don't think this has anything to do with your paying him off, or whatever you did?"

"Look. I offered to write him a solid reference and told him that if he ever talked about what happened in camp all those years ago, I would fight him in court."

"And then he killed himself. Jesus, Alex. So this means what, that this Joey is still alive? That Pete wasn't him?"

He nodded. "I don't know what else to say."

"Then I'm taking the girls and moving to my parents' place until this thing is finally over. If you want to stay here, fine. Deal with it on your own."

Becca shouted from downstairs that a car had pulled up. "That's the police," Ashley said. "I told you that detective came here to speak to you."

Alex went downstairs just as the doorbell rang. The lieutenant held up his ID, even though Alex knew very well who he was.

"Can we talk someplace in private, Mr. Mason?"

The three of them went into his home office and shut the door. "What's this about?"

"As I mentioned before, Mr. Kellerman had chlorinated water in his lungs. The reservoir, of course, is just fresh water."

"So?"

"You have a pool."

"He never swam in it. Pete told me he couldn't swim."

"How was he as an employee?" Carver said.

"Fine. Great. You know, really ambitious, very detail-oriented."

"Did you know him, Mrs. Mason?"

She thought for a moment. "I met him briefly at the staff party we throw every year for Alex's people."

"How did he strike you?"

"He was young, but my husband has employed a number of people in their twenties. You need to start early in this business."

The lieutenant looked around the room, at the photos lining the walls. "Just like your office in the city," he said. "Lots of you and famous people. Ever thought of doing anything more? Like politics, maybe?"

Alex laughed. "Nobody would ever consider me seriously for anything but what I do. I'm successful, and to pretend to be something else would be fraudulent."

"And you're happy with where you are in life, I guess."

"Perfectly content."

"Do you have any reason to believe anyone in your company envied Mr. Kellerman for his success, or for the attention you paid him?"

"Not that I know of. He'd only been with us for maybe seven or eight weeks."

"We're only asking because Mr. Kellerman had a return ticket from the station nearest your home in his wallet. Less than a mile from here. It suggests that maybe he'd come up to see you, or you'd invited him…?"

"I didn't see him at all," Alex said. "He'd been here once, for the party I told you about, but not since, no."

"Tell him about the lenses," Ashley said.

"It's nothing—"

"I have time," said Carver.

"Somebody got into the house today while we were all out and left these, I don't know what you'd call them, fake lenses. To make it look like we're being spied on."

"Somebody got into your house. Is that what you're saying? I remember that you have one of the best alarm systems money can buy. And that you were intending to upgrade it."

"Like that last time," Alex said. "You know, when we woke up with the music playing and the door open—"

"And he filmed us," Ashley interrupted. "While we were sleeping. Our daughters and us. He wandered all over the house. Like he owned it."

Carver looked at Alex. He seemed bewildered. "And you never told us this?"

Alex jangled some coins in his pocket. "The footage was sent to both our phones at the same time. And it was…intimate, let's just say."

Carver took a long few moments before his next question. "May I ask an indelicate question? Were you and Mrs. Mason engaged in some sort of sexual—"

"We were asleep," she said. "That's intimate enough, don't you think?"

The lieutenant closed his notebook. "All of this is starting to make me think that someone at your office could be holding a grudge against you. Maybe a former employee who felt unfairly let go?"

Alex pretended to consider it for a moment. "The last time that happened was, I think, twelve years ago. And he got out of the business. Now he runs a private equity firm in the city. Sometimes I run into him. We get on very well. Especially as he makes a lot more money than he did working for me."

"People who work for Alex like him," Ashley said. "He treats them like equals."

"But they're not equals, are they," the cop said. "When you say hop, they hop."

"Not in my office. We work as a team."

"But there's outside competition."

Alex smiled. "Of course. But other developers wouldn't stoop to these kinds of things." He waved his arm in the air.

Carver checked his watch. "Then who would?" But no one had an answer. He wished them a good night and walked out to his car as Alex stood in the doorway, silhouetted against the lights in the house. Ettinger was behind the wheel, texting on his phone. He pressed Send and slipped it into his pocket. "I thought you'd be longer."

"Didn't need to be."

"How did it go?"

Carver latched his seat belt. "Pretty much as I thought it would."

"So what do you think?"

"I think he's lying," Carver said. "But then again, everyone is, right?"

Part Seven

48

IT WAS ALMOST A YEAR TO THE DAY AFTER JOEY disappeared when Diane Proctor spotted her son on the platform at the Astor Place subway station, a few blocks from her studio. She had just come down the stairs to catch the uptown 6 train, when, through the crowd of people edging to board it, she caught sight of Joey and an older man stepping into the car. Too stunned to push her way through to follow him, she watched through the window as they sat together, an older, well-dressed man and her son, his hair longer than the last time she saw him, in a T-shirt with an abstract drawing of a skull on it. He looked more like a teenager, wise in all the worst ways, than the nine-year-old he would have then been. For a brief moment, his eyes met hers, and when the train pulled away, she cried his name out loud and ran to the edge of the platform, and everyone there assumed she was just another crazy New Yorker attempting to kill herself. Someone grabbed her shirt before she went over onto the tracks, and she just collapsed onto the platform, wailing into her hands.

When Alan walked through the door at seven, she said, "He's alive. I saw him." She hadn't changed her clothes or showered, and looked as if she'd been rummaging through garbage pails. Her hair was all over the place, and her shirt was torn, and she smelled of stale sweat. Her face was red and blotchy, as though she were running a high fever.

She told him exactly how it happened, what Joey looked like, the T-shirt he wore, the person who was with him. "This was the man who took him from the camp, Alan. Our son's here, he's in the city, we can find him if we just keep looking."

He threw up his hands. "You imagined it, Diane. Joey's not here. He's not anywhere."

"But I saw him. I know my own son."

"And this man took him." It was neither a question nor a statement of truth. He tried hard not to sound condescending. Lately he'd begun to replace whatever love he'd felt for her during the better years of their marriage with something very like pity, until it inevitably tipped into loathing.

Driven mad by her child's disappearance: in more objective moments, it was how he thought about it. Like something out of a Greek tragedy. By then she'd become a kind of stranger to him. He foresaw it all: separation, divorce, then death. There was nothing to look forward to, no son to watch grow and go out into the world; no more children, no pride, no laughter. You left the world with nothing of you but someone else's memory: a woman in the corps de ballet, the lover of another man, the mother of a phantom.

Her hands became fists, and the skin on her face grew tight as she told him again about how Joey was sitting with this man and how he was dressed, and when Alan asked what the man was like, she said, "He was wearing a suit. Maybe forty, maybe a little younger."

A man in a suit. One out of eight million people in the city.

It wasn't the first time something like this had happened. There'd been the phone call in the middle of the night two weeks after Joey vanished. Her cell phone had vibrated and vibrated, and when she answered it, the caller said nothing. She could hear someone breathing, she could sense another's presence, and when she said, "Joey?" the person made a noise, definitely a gasp, and then hung up. That was what she told her husband. The breathing. The gasp. The silence.

The number was blocked. There was no way to know who it was, but already she'd begun to spin it into a story. It was Joey. She was sure of it. He'd managed to get to a phone and call because he was in trouble. He couldn't speak because someone was nearby, someone who would hurt him.

Then there was the time she thought she saw him when they were watching the news on TV, in a crowd at the scene of a crane accident on Madison Avenue. She pointed and nearly screamed, "There...look! It's Joey! Do you see him?"

But by the time Alan looked, it was just a collapsed crane and the flashing lights of emergency vehicles.

This was what was called hope. *Hopeless hope*, Alan thought. But a part of him also believed Joey was alive. And that one day he, too, would start seeing him. And he wondered if going mad was the only solution, the one path to salvation for both of them.

49

THE DOOR TO THE LECTURE HALL WAS FLUNG OPEN and some thirty students filed out, followed by Marty Pollock and a pretty young woman with dreads. Pollock laughed at something she said, and she laughed in turn, and he said good luck, bye-bye, and then he looked up and saw Alex. Marty seemed genuinely surprised. Shocked, almost, and he took a step back, as though he expected the man to strike him.

"How did you find me?"

"It wasn't hard. I called and asked where your class was. I didn't want to bother you at home. You free for a little while?"

"I'm done for the day."

"Good. I'll buy you a drink."

They went to a bar on Waverly Place, which, at this hour, was nearly empty, and took a table toward the back. Marty ordered one of the craft beers featured on a blackboard over the bar, and Alex said he'd have the same. He said nothing until the waitress had delivered their order.

"I believe Joey Proctor is still alive," Alex told him.

Marty just stared at him.

"I'm serious," Alex said. "My family and I have been subjected to some very strange and threatening things. Someone filled our pool with animal blood, and there were words cut into the bottom of it." He told Marty what they were, and about the room at the Brooklyn location, and Joey's name on the wall. And the home invasion, and the video that had been sent to them.

He scrolled through the footage on his phone until he found the one showing the silhouette in the mirror, this thing with protruding eyes and tubes coming from its mouth. Marty looked at it for a few seconds. He said, "This is really fucked up."

"I know."

He passed the phone back to Alex. "You know what this is?"

"Guy's wearing some sort of goggles or a mask?"

"Night-vision, it looks like. And a kind of breathing device, something to muffle the sound of his breath. Whoever this is really planned it out. He's geared up for an expedition. Or an invasion."

Alex set his phone on the table. "That's what scares us. That whoever this is—Joey, maybe someone else—is going to do something a lot worse than this."

"Did you call the police?"

"Of course," Alex said.

Marty sat back and crossed his arms. "Well, this changes the narrative."

"What do you mean?"

"My film. It adds a whole new dimension. A whole other mystery. Maybe even a shot at a sequel."

"I need solutions, not more mysteries."

Marty smiled and leaned in. "You're missing the point, Alex. For some reason, *you're* in it now. Not like before, when you were at camp and you last saw Joey. Your whole life since then has been part of it because, if Joey's alive, that's what he's been thinking about all these years. Why? That's something only you would know. Maybe he's been watching you all this time. You went back to college, you got married, you started a business. And all along he's been there, in the background." He put two fingers beneath his eyes and turned them toward Alex. "Don't you see? You've just become a character in the story. *His* story."

50

ALEX POINTED A FINGER AT MARTY. "IF MY NAME IS used in this movie of yours, I will get my lawyers after you, and this project will go absolutely nowhere. I promise you that."

Marty held up a hand. "Hey. Understood, Alex. But can you tell me this, at least? If everything you just told me is true, then what did you do to deserve all this stuff? Unless, of course, something really, really bad took place that day. Something that would've marked Joey for life."

He sat back and waited.

"We had swimming, I sent them back to their bunks," Alex said.

"Really. That's all?"

Alex nodded.

"Then why you?" Marty said. "Why now?"

"I can't figure it out. I don't know what he wants from me."

"Has he asked for money?"

"He hasn't asked for anything. He's just been...doing these things to me. To my wife, my children."

"What's in it for him?"

Alex took a breath to consider the question. It was one he'd been asking himself over and over. There'd been no demands for money, no legal actions, nothing but different forms of harassment. Unless Joey was building up to something big, some climactic event that would take Alex down. That was something he didn't want to think about. "I wish I knew," he said.

Marty shrugged. "It sounds more like a stunt than a threat."

Alex leaned close. "For Christ's sake, he's broken into my house, Marty. That's not a stunt, that's a crime."

"Fair enough. How long has it been?" Marty asked.

"Since camp? I was eighteen when I was a counselor, I'm thirty-nine now."

"Twenty-one years. Every seven years is how the John Otis legend goes, right? Three times seven. Bingo," he almost shouted, and the bartender turned to look, as though the filmmaker had cried out for another beer.

Very quietly, Alex said, "Are you fucking with me, Pollock?"

"Hey. I own some of this, too, you know. It's not just your story. It's mine, it's Joey's parents', it's the memory of the camp's owners, the people who were ruined from what happened that day."

The waitress came over and Marty ordered another beer. Alex asked, "Do you have any decent Scotch in the house?" and the young woman laughed, as if it were a lowlife gin mill instead of a respectable establishment for the purveyance of overpriced alcoholic beverages.

"Name your poison," she said.

"Johnnie Walker Black."

"We even have Platinum and Blue, if you want to spend that kind of money."

"How about Balvenie PortWood 21 Year?"

"Straight up?"

Dumb question, he almost said.

"Of course."

When she left, Alex said, "I need to hear your honest opinion on this. Do you think it's at all possible that Joey Proctor is still alive? Or is this something else altogether?"

"Honestly? Anything's possible, I suppose. That he's doing this stuff to you?" He shrugged. "You were just the swimming counselor. Doesn't make a lot of sense."

The waitress brought Alex his drink, and he said, "Sorry. Can you make it a double?"

She whipped the glass away, and he waited for her to return. She also brought a little bowl of mixed nuts that she pointedly placed in front of Marty. She asked if they wanted to run a tab, and Marty jumped in. "We'd love that." She gave Alex a withering look as she left.

Quietly, Alex said, "Look. It was the last week or so of camp. I was trying to get the kids into the deep water. You know, kind of a graduation thing. Let them see how far they'd come that summer. Joey wouldn't go, and I pushed him in. I thought he would swim. But he couldn't, and he started to drown. So I jumped in and grabbed him and swam him out to the raft and left him there."

"And you did this why?"

"So he'd swim back."

"Except—you just said it—Joey couldn't swim."

"This is how you learn, Marty. You take the plunge and just do it. It's how you get rid of your fears."

"And what happened then?"

Alex took a breath. "I forgot about him."

Marty let the moment accumulate a little weight, leaving it hanging between them. "You're saying, what, he slipped your mind?"

Alex paused. He nodded.

"Feel bad?"

"Well, yeah, of course."

"Because after that he was gone." Marty seized his glass and finished the rest in one swallow. He lifted it and caught the bartender's eye. The waitress brought him another beer, along with an interested smile.

"That's why I think he's come back," Alex said. "To get his revenge. But I didn't hurt him, I swear to you."

"Had you spoken to the police about this?"

Alex's eyes shifted away from Marty's face. "I just said that when swimming was over he left with the others."

"So you lied."

"I was *eighteen*, Marty. A teenager. Like the kids you teach."

"So you were covering your ass. Because otherwise you might not be the Alex Mason everybody knows these days. Successful people don't do stuff like that. But you probably already know this."

Alex leaned closer. "Don't lecture me, okay? I get it, I know what I did, what I didn't do. Because isn't that what we do at that age? I lost it for a minute, did a stupid thing, and completely forgot about him."

"And that's why Joey now *is* the legend, the kid who really did disappear. You can start with John Otis, but you always end up with Joey Proctor, the unseen one. Apart from you, who knew you'd left him on a raft? No one, right?"

Except for Ed Unis, Alex thought, and now he was gone.

"That's how Joey enters the realm of legend," Marty said. "Like I was saying the other day, in that world there's no single correct answer. Who was the Blair Witch? Fuck if I know. What made the walking dead walk? Fuck if I care. The point is that sometimes there is no answer. Just mysteries. And when you're just another person—like you or me or that bartender there—who finds himself caught in one, you lose all sense of perspective, you lose sight of your own role in it. Only an outside observer could see the whole geometry of the thing, that one point where you stand in relation to everything else. Am I losing you?"

Alex smiled thinly. "You're doing a helluva good job of it, Marty."

Marty divided the table with his hands. "This is the movie, you see, and then here, this is the audience. One moment it feels lost, the next it thinks it has a fix on how it's going to proceed, where it's going to go."

"Because of this, whatever you called it, geometry?"

"Except that my job as the filmmaker is to pull the rug out from under you. To upend all your expectations from one moment to the next. It's my responsibility to introduce twists and turns so that the story keeps pulling you in."

"Until—?"

He leaned forward and looked at Alex. "Until you realize that all along you've been sucked into the narrative and made part of it. You've been played." He sat back and smiled.

Alex sipped his drink and felt the warmth slip over his tongue and down his throat. It even tasted like too much money. Setting down his glass, he said, "Explain all of this to me, please. I'm not getting it."

"You're a rich man. A successful man. You build things you can see, you can touch, that people pay for, that people enjoy. It's all three-dimensional. Steel. Concrete. Glass. Even the money you earn has weight and value. You can look at it, you can feel it, you can see the number up in the corner. I'm guessing this is a comfortable place for you, a world of certainties. A predictable kind of life. But beyond that—man, there's a whole other world. There's a flow, there's a structure, that you're only now becoming aware of." He rippled his hand in the air. "You think Facebook is anything more than an elaborate work of fiction?" He sputtered out a laugh. "That's as imaginary a world as has ever been conceived. Two billion versions of the truth competing for approval. And beyond that? There's always the Matrix, right?" And with a laugh, he splashed open his fingers like fireworks.

Alex smiled broadly. "You've got to be on some kind of drug."

"You forget what I do. I play with reality. I bend it, I speculate, I make what you think is real into something completely incredible, just as I make the unbelievable into something you take as the honest truth. Look...color movies and black-and-white movies, right? Which is more real to us?"

"Color, I guess."

"Wrong. Black-and-white. Because that looks like *truth*. It's old photographs from the Civil War, it's footage from when the concentration camps were liberated, it's documentary, right? Karloff with bolts in his neck raging through the countryside in color would look like a joke. But in black and white? It looks like horror. It feels like truth. It haunts us. It's like a ghost that takes up a few hours of our time in a darkened theater. Sitting around the campfire, we bought the whole John Otis thing completely. Was it real?" He shrugged. "Maybe. Maybe not. But it scared the hell out of us. Monsters and zombies and vampires are one thing: comic book stuff. But twenty years ago, crazy guys who steal kids? That was getting a little too close to reality. And it still is today. Because you see people in the street, on the subway, and part of you wonders what they're capable of doing." He sipped his beer. "But someone is responsible for Joey's disappearance, and I'm hoping to shed some light on that."

"Have you begun shooting this thing?"

"Absolutely. I've got lots of footage so far. Just need to edit it."

"So how much is left to do?"

"I have the ending, at least."

"Is it good?"

Marty smiled. "Wait till you see it."

Alex sat back and looked at him with something close to envy. Knowing that it was going to be done and out of the way was all he wanted with this matter.

"You say Joey has returned, right?" Marty said.

"I'm saying *maybe* he's back."

Marty briskly rapped his knuckle twice on the table. "Joey's dead."

"You don't know that."

"That's right," Marty said, sitting back. "And neither do you."

51

THEY WERE ABOUT TO HAVE DESSERT AS ALEX walked through the door. Ashley took one look at him and excused herself from the table. "Can I talk to you for a moment?" she asked, and they went into the kitchen.

They argued in whispers. "You're drunk."

"I had one beer and a couple of Scotches. I'm not even buzzed."

"Then what's going on? Another woman I'll be hearing about tomorrow?"

"I met with Marty Pollock, that film guy I told you about. We went to a bar in the Village and talked for an hour, that's all."

"Oh, yeah, sure."

He grabbed her arm a little too roughly. "What are you trying to say, Ash?"

She stepped back and looked at him as if he were a stranger. "Don't you ever lay a hand on me like that again."

He shook his head. "Sorry. Sorry. I didn't mean to."

She softened. "All right. Get yourself some dinner. Try to pretend we're a happy family."

When they returned to the table, Becca said, "Who's Joey Proctor?"

Alex just looked at her. Already he was on edge, and just

hearing the name pushed him even closer. "What?" It came out as something hard and aggressive, and Becca shot him the kind of look she would have aimed at one of the other alpha girls in her class.

"Because a guy named Joey Proctor just asked to friend me on Facebook. He says he was a friend of yours."

Alex shared a look with Ashley. He said to Becca, "Where's your phone?" She covered it with her hand. He clutched the air. "Give it to me." She looked away in a semblance of *No way*. "Give me the fucking phone!"

Becca flinched. Alex never spoke that way in front of the girls. Ashley patted Alex's arm. *Calm down*, it implied. *Get a grip*.

"Dad's not going to search through it," she said. "He just wants to see what this guy's Facebook page looks like."

Reluctantly Becca handed the phone to him. He glanced at the screen and slid it back to her. "I'll be right back," he said.

He went into his office, shut the door, and entered Facebook. He ran a search for "Joey Proctor," and the first suggested profile displayed its photo as an empty raft in a lake, exactly what was on Becca's phone, the same raft Alex remembered from the camp. There was nothing about where Joey Proctor lived or what he did. Just an age: eight. Alex couldn't get any deeper into the account because he wasn't his friend, not like Becca said the guy claimed he was.

"Son of a bitch," Alex said to himself. "He's still fucking with us."

He rested his finger on the track pad and waited. And waited. Finally, he clicked for a friend request. A moment later it was accepted.

Alex typed in a PM:

Do I know you?

Oh yes. Very well.

Where are you?

You know exactly where I am.

Are you near my house?

Maybe I'm even in it.

I can call the police.

They'll never find me.

Why did you try to friend my daughter?

So that you would friend me. And now we're friends. Unfriend me all you like, but I'll always be with you. Until the day you die.

Ashley said, "Alex? Please come back in here."

Becca looked up at him as he returned to the dining room.

"Tell him, Becca. Show him your phone again."

Alex held out his hand. "Show it to me."

"*No*."

"Now! Hand it to me, goddamn it!"

Lyndsey flinched while Becca looked stone-faced at him. He could stand there all night, he thought, but eventually he'd get his way. She rolled her eyes and handed him the phone.

It was too late. Now Becca and Joey were friends.

52

WHEN THE PHONE RANG, ALEX PICKED IT UP IN the kitchen. It was Ellen Siegel from the office. He could hear she was in a busy place: music, chatter, laughter, glasses—

She said, "Let me go outside. It's noisy in here."

Ashley looked expectantly at Alex. "Ellen from the office," he said.

"I just got word that Mark Pearson put in the winning bid on the Brooklyn property," Ellen said. "Milt Golub's over the moon about it."

"Milt was supposed to wait for our offer."

"Looks like someone told him we were no longer interested," she said.

Alex held up a hand. "Wait... How the hell would Pearson even know about the property? We had the whole project under lockdown. No leaks. Nothing public."

As a siren passed, Ellen waited for it to round the corner. She said, "I'm also told that Pearson's got his eye on building a hotel on the same block in Detroit we were considering."

Alex asked her to hold while he took the call in his office.

Once inside, he said, "Who told you this?"

"Rob just called me. He heard it from a guy he knows who works at Pearson's company."

Alex remembered how Mark Pearson had confronted him at the Captiva resort. How ugly it had begun to turn. *On a dime*, Alex thought.

That must have been the moment he decided to go directly after Alex.

He waited a few moments to let it settle in. He said, "Did this guy at Pearson's office say where he'd heard about our plans?"

"That's why I called you," Ellen said. "It was Pete."

He sat down and rubbed his brow. "Pete. You're certain?"

"Absolutely. Now that Pete's dead, he was free to confirm it to Rob. By name. Pete leaked everything to them. Every project we were planning, all the documentation. Now there's a hole a mile wide in our operations."

When Alex opened the door, Ashley was waiting for him in the hallway. He started telling her what he'd just heard and then ran out of words.

"But it doesn't matter anymore," she said. "Because Pete's gone, isn't he?"

"Think about it, Ash. He was leaking information about the company, and now he's dead. The police are going to be looking at everyone in Mason House Properties, but most of all they'll be looking at me."

"Listen." She put her hands on his shoulders. "After the party, he was never here. So you're okay, you're in the clear. Right?"

"He never came here afterward."

"And that boy you left to swim back, the one who disappeared…?"

"Joey Proctor, yeah."

"Now he's really inside Becca's life."

"What are you talking about?"

"She just got a PM from him."

Say goodbye to 13, little girl.

53

USUALLY THE DRIVE FROM THE OFFICE TO THE Mason House Hotel took barely fifteen minutes, even in the worst of traffic. They seemed to have been sitting and going nowhere for at least that long. What Alex had heard the night before felt like a blow to the chest, taking all the wind out of him. If Pete had been a mole in the company, then his dying spared him the punishment he would certainly have earned. Had he lived—had Alex been able to save him from drowning in the pool, had he found out what his employee had been up to—no one would ever have hired him again. He would have been banned from every property development company in town.

Except for Mark Pearson's. Alex wondered if Pearson had already been using Pete when they ran into each other in Florida. He'd never known the man to be so sure of himself before that. Until then, they'd had a cool but cordial relationship, as Alex had with most of the developers in town, save for one or two whose simple existence offended him. He should have read Pearson more easily. One too many drinks, Alex thought, and he was off his game.

He said to their driver, "Jimmy, what's going on?"

"I think there's a moving van double-parked on Fifty-Ninth."

Now that he was paying attention, Alex could hear the bad

jazz of horns uselessly blaring. He checked his phone: nothing. Not another word from Joey Proctor. Becca had unfriended him and hadn't received an additional request from him after that. When he checked Facebook to see if Joey had posted, there wasn't a single entry. The guy had either blocked even his friends from seeing anything or had signed up just to get deeper into Alex's life. One day, Alex thought, Joey would slip up on Facebook and open a window into his life. And then Alex would deal with him.

Finally, the traffic opened up, and Alex and his team were dropped at the hotel only five minutes late for the grand reopening. The entire hotel staff—among them the chef, Reg Dwyer, his sous chef, and prep cooks—was already assembled in the lobby as waiters filled champagne flutes from bottles of Moët. They were intending to open to the public at noon, and the hotel was already two-thirds booked for the weekend. It would take a few weeks before they could claim they were back on their feet. The manager, Chris Harper, knew someone who worked at the Styles section at the *Times* and was trying to see if he could get an item in the paper before too long.

Alex had decided that they needed to own the story, that admitting to what had happened without knowing how it happened was the best strategy. Then the reopening, with the new menu and all-new Italian bed linens, would be something of an event. Because appearance is everything, Alex had worked with his usual designer to make over the lobby. You walked in, saw something new, and assumed the Mason House had completely reinvented itself. Before, the lobby had been shades of red, from wine to carnelian; now it was a mixture of greens and yellows, all subdued shades, easy on the eye. It suggested someplace clean and welcoming. It *embraced* you, as his designer said.

"Smile," Ellen said to him as they approached the entrance. "We need to make this work."

He turned on his trademark Alex Mason grin, broad and white-toothed, as the doorman let them in. The staff clapped as Alex and the team took their places. The photographer hired for the event took a series of shots.

Alex waited for the applause to die down. "Please—everyone—take a glass, even if it is only ten in the morning. And, team, please remember we have a full day's work ahead of us, so take it easy on the bubbly stuff."

Everyone laughed.

"Let me begin by saying how very proud I am of each and every one of you, first, for sticking with the Mason name and not running off to less lucrative jobs under much less honest bosses." He thought of Pearson, whom he intended, one way or another, to bring to ruin in the near future.

There was more laughter, but already his mind was several steps ahead. If he could arrange to have rats and mice smuggled into the man's Red Hook hotel the day it opened—as had happened here at the Mason House—then he would succeed. At least for a time.

And there was always arson to fall back on.

"I'm especially thankful—no, grateful—for how well the crew did in getting us back up and running according to all the stringent health and safety requirements in the city and the hotel industry. So let's raise a glass to you, and to ten more amazing years."

He took a sip and set his glass down. After a few more photos, with Reg, Chris, and the entire staff behind him, he headed back to the limo. His cell phone went off as he was about to reach the car. It was Ashley.

Something very bad was happening.

54

THE POLICE WERE ALREADY THERE WHEN HE PULLED up to the house.

"What do we know?" Alex said.

"The text on Mrs. Mason's phone came from a blocked number," Carver said. Alex looked at the message. The author of it claimed to have taken Lyndsey when she was outside for recess.

"There's no way we could investigate further, not in the time we need to do this."

"Please tell me it is possible."

"Only if we send it out to technicians in the city. And that could take a few days, especially if there's a backlog."

It seemed absurd when a young girl's life was at stake. "They won't make an exception?"

"We don't have a lot of time. When a child goes missing, there's a corridor of forty-eight hours. But with someone as young as your daughter, the first three hours are the most critical. And right now we're halfway there since the text came through."

"No mention of a ransom yet?"

"Not a word."

"Jesus. Jesus."

Ashley's eyes were red, and she clutched a tissue.

He put his arm around her. "Becca doesn't know, does she?"

She shook her head. "She's still at school."

"We're going to find Lyndsey. I promise you, babe."

"Actually," the lieutenant said, "as we told Mrs. Mason, at this stage we're optimistic we'll find her safe and sound." He seemed to be taking the whole matter a little too casually. "Think, Mr. Mason. Any possible reason why someone might want to take revenge on you or your family? Anything you think of may help us find your daughter."

Alex had no words left. This was the worst thing in the world, the unimaginable. The kind of thing that makes you want to undo everything you've ever achieved, everything you've ever coveted, all you've put in the bank, the entirety of your whole miserable life. Anything to get her back.

He thought of Lyndsey by the pool in Captiva, terrified of him because he had scared her, nearly threatened her. He'd never truly made it up to her after that. And now she was gone. At that moment he felt like the most insignificant person in the world. Nothing that had come to define him mattered anymore, not his achievements or his money. Not even his name. And, for the first time in years, tears came to his eyes.

Carver looked at Ashley. He said, "I wonder if you could leave us for a few minutes so we can speak to your husband alone?"

"No, this is our daughter we're talking about—"

"It's about a separate matter, Mrs. Mason."

Alex suggested they go into his office. Ettinger shut the door and joined his partner. Carver said, "We're thinking this may have some connection to the death of Mr. Kellerman."

Alex opened his hands. "That makes no sense."

"To be honest, we believe you were in some way responsible for what happened to your employee."

"That's crazy. Why would I even want to go near something like that? I have a reputation, I run a business—"

Carver went calmly on. "He apparently had no relatives or friends who lived in this town or anywhere else in the county. The train station is near your home. You have a pool, and you're less than fifteen minutes from the reservoir where he was found. Mr. Kellerman was your employee, yes, but we also learned in the past twenty-four hours that you had something of a motive."

Alex shook his head vehemently and looked as if he was about to walk out of the room. "You can't prove any of this."

The detectives shared a brief look. "So you're not asking what that motive might be?"

"I don't need to, because it has nothing to do with me."

"Actually, we can prove all of what I just told you. What we can't prove is that you were directly connected to Mr. Kellerman's death and the disposal of his body. That's the one piece of evidence we're missing."

"And you're wasting time talking to me about this while my daughter's missing? Just get out there and find her. Do your jobs, for Christ's sake."

"All right, Mr. Mason. We'll call you the moment we learn anything."

They watched the detectives' car disappear down the driveway. Alex shut the door and armed the security system. As the morning waned and a cloudless sky gave way to a milky haze, the house seemed especially empty. As though something more than Lyndsey had disappeared. But that wasn't true, because they both knew that something had been added to the household, just as it had with Alan and Diane Proctor: a great, palpable emptiness that could only be filled with speculation and nightmare.

Alex went into his office and opened his laptop. He clicked on Facebook to see if Joey had posted anything new. His timeline was still blank. There was just the picture of an empty raft in Echo Lake.

This was what Alex's life would be from this point on: like a photographic negative, suspended between the present and the past.

Just a ghost of himself, haunted by another.

55

AFTER GOING UPSTAIRS TO LIE DOWN FOR A FEW minutes, Alex must have fallen into a deep, dreamless sleep. When he opened his eyes, Ashley was standing at the foot of the bed, holding her phone out for him to see. Her mouth was moving but he could hear nothing, because she was without speech, and all the color in her face was absent.

It was a photo of a little girl, fully dressed, sitting on a raft in a lake, taken from so far away that it could be anyone. Yet it had to be Lyndsey. Alex's phone chimed a new text message from a blocked number.

HOW DO YOU LIKE IT WHEN IT HAPPENS TO YOU?

He sat up and demanded that Ashley give him her phone. "I'm going to the police with these."

"What if he sends another text?"

"I need the cops to see these."

The police station was twenty minutes from the house, sharing an anonymous brick building with the fire department. Alex asked for Lieutenant Carver and was told he was on his lunch break.

"No. Now," Alex said. "This is urgent."

"He's not going to like this, you know."

"Just say Alex Mason needs to speak to him."

The duty sergeant picked up her phone and keyed in an extension. "I have a Mr. Alex Mason here, Lieutenant Carver."

She listened for a moment and looked up at Alex. "Down the hall, second right."

The lieutenant looked up as Alex filled the doorway. "Mr. Mason. How can I help you today?" He wiped his mouth with a napkin and tossed it in the pail.

Alex placed the two phones on the man's desk beside a half-eaten Italian sub and a copy of the *Daily News*. Carver looked at the sent photo and the text displayed on the second device.

"What am I missing here, Mr. Mason? 'How do you like it when it happens to you?' What does this have to do with the disappearance of your daughter?"

"Look. Something happened just over twenty years ago. I was a swimming counselor and left a kid on a raft."

"Like this photo on the other phone?"

"Something like that, yeah."

Carver shrugged. "Okay. So?"

"He couldn't swim."

"Go on."

"I thought he'd make his way back."

"Even though he couldn't swim?"

"And when I came back to find him later, he wasn't there."

Carver stood and stretched and, taking both phones, excused himself and left the room, returning a minute or two later without the devices.

He said, "And you think, what, this stuff, all these things

that've been happening to you are because of this little boy you left on a raft? That somehow he's come back into your life?"

In all his dealings up until then, Alex's presence would steal all the air out of a room. He was someone people read about and saw on TV, a man whose success seemed to know no bounds. Now he looked like a ruined man. His hair was unwashed, his clothes were rumpled, and there was a smell about him that Carver recognized from visiting his father in the retirement home in White Plains, the sour reek of indifference and neglect.

"Because frankly, Mr. Mason, I don't agree. Yeah, people get angry, they want revenge, but you know, unless the victim is totally insane, it all really does wear off after a while. Twenty years? I don't think so. People forget, people move on. What I do think is what I said before, that this is about Mr. Kellerman's death, and I'll take it a step further: I believe you're trying to divert our attention from what is very likely your responsibility for it. You planned it, you executed it, and now you're trying to convince us that you and your family are victims of, what, someone trying to get revenge for something that happened twenty years ago?"

Alex was suddenly drained of energy and will. He said, "They never found the boy. They think he may have been kidnapped or drowned. But I know he's somewhere out there, and it looks like he's just taken my daughter."

"So you're being tormented by a dead person? This is a little out of our jurisdiction," the lieutenant said with a hint of a smile.

"You find this funny? With my daughter out there with this guy?"

Carver's smile flattened. "Actually, I find it tragic. Here's this young guy working for you, and he's dead. And I think you killed him."

Alex could feel his temper rising. "You have absolutely no proof of that."

"Not yet, anyway."

"And you never will, because I never did it."

"And if you did?" Carver said. "And it came out? What would happen then?"

"You know very well what would happen. I'd be ruined."

The detective looked longingly at the remains of his sandwich. "No, Mr. Mason. You'd be in prison for a very long time."

"My family would be disgraced."

"Only if they let themselves be, Mr. Mason."

"And my daughter? What the hell are you doing about it apart from eating a sandwich and reading the headlines?"

"Oh, we'll find her. Trust me."

Alex couldn't believe that the man simply picked up his lunch and completely ignored him. There was a tap at the door before another officer brought in Ashley's phone, along with a USB cable.

"I want you to look at something," he said to both men. "Matt Decker, Alex Mason."

Alex merely nodded. Carver said, "Matt is our sort-of technical guy. Sort-of, because this is the kind of stuff he does at home, and we can rely on him to do things for us now and again." He smiled. "When he's up to it."

Decker plugged one end of the cable into Ashley's phone and the other into a port on Carver's computer. He turned the monitor so that both men could see it. It was the photo of Lyndsey on a raft. He enlarged it, then pulled in on the girl. Her expression was fixed: a big smile, two wide-open eyes, and light-brown hair instead of blond hanging down in two braids.

"What's happened to her?" Alex said.

"Let's go in a little bit more." Decker focused it the best he could.

"That's not Lyndsey," Alex said a little too loudly.

"It's not anybody," Decker said. "It's a doll on a miniature raft, probably in a bathtub. Nice bit of special effects going on there."

"But it's not your daughter, Mr. Mason," the lieutenant said. "Something we already knew."

—

By then, Ashley had blown through the second of two red lights, having already sped past three stop signs, and because it was lunchtime and the town was busy with traffic, she began weaving around other cars, pushing seventy, until she was in the countryside, her tires squealing as she sped around the empty curves. She heard the sirens before she saw the cruisers, flashers ablaze, rising up behind her, and she cut sharply in at the sign that read *Long Hill Country Day School, K–12.*

She pulled up hard before the main building as the police blocked her car with theirs. Ignoring them, she threw open the door and stopped at Lyndsey's classroom.

The two teachers and all the students looked at her.

"Where's Lyndsey? What's happened to my daughter?"

"She's not here, Mrs. Mason." The woman spoke quietly, hoping to prompt Ashley to do likewise.

"What? Then where is she?"

The teacher came to the door and lowered her voice even more. "In her remedial reading group. They should be just finishing up now in the library." She looked over Ashley's shoulder at the two cops. "Is there a problem I can help you with, officers?"

"So she's here, she's at school?" Ashley nearly shouted.

"Of course she is. Otherwise we would have called you."

56

"You've been duped, Mr. Mason," Carver said. "We knew your daughter was okay, because the first thing we did was call her school. But we didn't say anything to you or your wife because we wanted to figure out what this was all about."

"Are you out of your mind?"

"This elaborate...whatever you want to call it... I'm guessing it's a way to get publicity, attention from the press?"

Alex didn't need to rely on stunts to attract attention. He had a brand. He had a name. He had a face that everyone knew, a voice that was instantly recognizable. He was a major player in the New York City property market. Once he'd branched out even more, he'd have an international standing rivaling any other in his business. And when you're successful, you make few real friends, followed by those who want something from you, and finally enough adversaries to last you a lifetime.

The detective waited for his response. Alex privately wondered if he needed to contact his attorney. "And you think I'd frighten the hell out of my wife just for publicity?"

"Around twenty years ago, a very wealthy and successful man living in the city arranged what looked like the kidnapping of his own son. It came at a time when his business was beginning to fail. He'd planned it as a way to gain sympathy, especially from those who were suing him for his business practices. The whole story fell apart, he was tried on a number of charges, and his business went under. His wife divorced him. Ten years later, his son hanged himself. If this is what you're doing, my recommendation is that you admit to it now and cut your losses. But as far as we're concerned, you've been behind it all—the pool thing with the blood and the words, easy enough to do when it's on your own property, the CD coming on in, may I remind you, your own house, the movies that you said were taken of you and your kids in bed. And now this. A doll on a raft in a bathtub." He shook his head. "Kind of sad, really."

Alex looked him in the eye. "I swear to you, I had nothing to do with any of it."

Carver had the temerity to smile. "But it always circles around to Mr. Kellerman's death, doesn't it. Your company's taken a few serious hits lately. From what we understand, you lost out on a deal in Brooklyn, you've been shouldered out of another potential property in Detroit—"

"Who told you all this?"

"We questioned a number of your employees. Through them, we learned that Mr. Kellerman was reporting back to another developer. Which in and of itself is motive enough. Now, if you want to confess, that's fine. This is the place to do it."

"Let me have my phone back, please."

"Before you make that all-important call to your lawyer, may I remind you that by staging all these stunts and involving the police, you can be facing a number of other charges."

Now Alex knew who was behind it. One name came to mind.

57

UNLIKE EVERY OTHER PERSON WHO'D EVER ENTERED the restaurant, spent a moment with the maître d', caught the friendly eye of a waiter they'd known from earlier visits, even shared a wave with diners they'd eaten with before, Alex pushed his way into the dining room and only stopped when the maître d' took hold of his arm and brought him to a halt. This was not the type of establishment where anyone moved at speed or displayed any form of aggression, apart from the whispered item of gossip or a devastating look across the room at someone whose choice of outfit or spouse was considered in any way improper or offensive to the eye.

"Monsieur Mason has a reservation?"

"Monsieur Mason doesn't want a fucking table," he bellowed, and the waiters, en route with diners' meals, backed away toward the walls.

Alex scanned the dining room, which had already fallen silent at the spectacle unfolding before them. "I want *him*," he said when he saw Mark Pearson sitting with his wife and another couple.

They had just been served their entrées, and with one swift motion, Alex swept everything onto the floor, two $149 rib eyes, both medium rare, the turbot with Château Chalon sauce, the crispy confit of suckling pig, the $2,600 bottle of Grands-Échezeaux 2010, the $734 bottle of Montée de Tonerre, as well four wineglasses, a basket of artisanal bread baked on the premises, and all the silverware save for two teaspoons and a butter knife. It took Pearson a moment to comprehend what was happening, but it was the other man at the table who stood and confronted Alex. The front of his tan trousers were stained red with wine, suggesting a urinary tract infection of monstrous proportions.

"What is this?" Pearson's friend said. "Who are you?"

Alex leaned over Mark just as he was getting to his feet, put his hand on Mark's shoulder, and pressed him to his chair. Now Alex was right in his face. The other diners on this busy night recognized Alex and began to photograph and videotape him on their phones. The waiters stood frozen in place. The maître d' got off the phone with the police, while a columnist for the *Daily News*, dining with his wife and two other couples several tables away, had alerted his paper about what was happening. He already had three possible headlines for his item, and within two minutes his editor texted his approval.

Loudly enough for everyone to hear, Alex said, "I know what you're doing. And if you don't fucking stop—if you don't leave me and my family alone—I swear I will kill you, you son of a bitch."

Two uniformed cops were crossing the room to get to Alex when Pearson said to them, "This is a personal matter. Just let it go, officers."

One of the cops asked if he was sure about that. After all, a threat was a threat. "Yeah," Pearson said. "It's fine. I'll deal with him."

"We're not leaving until he vacates the premises," the cop said.

"Before this, I was happy to be competing with you," Pearson said to Alex. "That's business, it's how it works. But now I intend to ruin you. I will bring you down, Mason, I swear to you, and you will never do business in this town again. Now pay for the damages and our meals and get the hell out of here before I change my mind and decide to press charges."

The house was completely dark when Alex returned home just before midnight. He assumed Ashley and the girls were already asleep. What had happened at the restaurant seemed as though it had taken place in a dream. Before he'd left for the city, he'd called Pearson's home number and was told where he could be found. Alex had come to the restaurant with the sole intention to blindside the man, to speak quietly to him, to let him know Alex was aware of everything he'd done, but then things had begun to escalate, as though what had been happening to him and his family over the past month had finally found its release.

Now there was no going back, no chance for an apology. He could never again go to that restaurant, a favorite of his and Ashley's, and he knew that word would get out to other restaurants in the city. And this metropolis where he had established his name and his brand, where he conducted business every day, was already starting to shut down on him.

Now he was about to lose everything else.

58

WHAT HAVE YOU DONE TO US, ALEX?"

The sound of Ashley's voice startled him as it came out of the darkness. He could see her almost as an outline, a disturbance in the night, sitting in an armchair, her legs crossed, a drink by her side.

When he reached to turn on a lamp, she said quietly, "Leave it off."

He went to the bar cart and poured himself a Scotch and sat across from her. He said, "So you heard."

"So has everyone else," she said. "It was on the news. There were photos. Some footage people recorded in the restaurant. I can't tell you how many texts I've had from friends. Emails. Phone calls. People telling me how sorry they feel for us. For me. For Becca and Lyndsey. Your name is becoming a very ugly joke, Alex. I guess that's something else we get to share with you."

He sipped his drink and set it down. "Girls okay?"

"They're at my parents' place in Bedford. I didn't want them here in case the press showed up."

"Have they already been here?"

"At the gate, yeah, a few. The *Post*. The *Daily News*. Two TV channels. I told them to go away, or I'd call the police."

He nodded, though she couldn't see his response. "I'm tired," he said.

"So am I."

"I was stupid."

"Lyndsey knows nothing about that whole thing with the doll on the raft. Let's keep it that way, okay?"

"And Becca?"

"She's thirteen years old. She's not interested in anything we do."

"But she knows what happened tonight?"

"They both do, Alex. Just like the rest of the world."

Ashley's voice was cold and flat in a way he hadn't heard since the time he'd had the affair. Intimacy had returned over the years, and her voice had reflected it. It had become as warm and honeyed as her smile, her hair, and her body. And now it was gone.

"I'm asking you again, Alex. What have you done to us?"

"I didn't do anything. We're as much the victims as—"

"So you'll keep blaming who, some kid you left to die on a raft? It's not that I don't believe any of it, Alex, because I do. I've come to know you better than anyone else in the world. But what happened tonight had nothing to do with a camper all those years ago when you were a counselor. This was only about you. You are your own worst enemy. And people like that always end up their own victims."

He held up his palm to interrupt, but she said, "I'm talking. You're listening."

When he got up to get another drink, she recoiled slightly, as though he might assault her. Now he knew that everything had changed. The dynamics, something he'd always prided himself on controlling, whether in business dealings or family issues, had tilted out of his favor. His voice meant nothing now; all he could do was find his way back in.

He said, "You want that refilled?"

"It's just water. I need to keep a clear head."

He couldn't see her expression in the darkness. She had chosen the setting well.

"What is that supposed to mean?" he said.

"I've been thinking, Alex. Not just about tonight, but ever since these things began to happen—the pool, the photos, the break-ins. It's as if I walked into a storm and can't find my way out of it. It just keeps getting worse, and I don't think it's going to end soon. And I've been thinking that I really have no idea who you are. I don't even know why I married you."

"You married me," he said, "because I have enough money to let you live the way you do. Your Mercedes. This house. Our summer place, your clothes. The trips we take all over the world. The school the girls go to. You don't have to do a damned thing. Just live. Enjoy every minute of it."

"You think I'm so shallow that I'd marry you simply for *things*? That they bring me all this joy you're talking about? What's been happening has really made me see it all very clearly." He opened his mouth to speak, and she said, "I'm talking, remember? Now you will listen to me."

He sat back and sighed and finished his second drink. He would humor her and sit quietly. He got up and, instead of pouring himself another, took the bottle back to his chair. He'd been in this kind of argument—*discussion*, as she liked to call it—before, and it usually ended up in the bedroom, or at least with both of them being civil to each other over a last drink. By morning it would have been forgotten, just another blip in the timeline. But now he could feel it lurching out of control. He would have to apologize to Pearson, probably in a more public manner than he'd prefer, though his ace in the hole was that he could counter with the knowledge that his competitor had been spying on his business all along. One man's sin matches the other's. And the thought of it, the idea that Pete Kellerman had been working for this despicable man, made him even angrier.

Ashley was saying, "I know what you're capable of when you're at your best, Alex. You're kind and trusting to your employees, you give a lot of money to charity, and yes, you keep us comfortable, never wanting anything. But I also know what you're like when you're at your worst, the side your people at work probably never see. And now I'm seeing it again, because clearly you have no idea who I am. You think I'm just an accessory, like your fancy car—"

"Which you—"

"You never ask what I think, how I feel, what I want to do with my life. You'd be better off with a dog, as far as I'm concerned. Make it roll over. Beat it when it doesn't obey. Throw it a bone now and again. Make it fetch, make it come."

"You—"

"You can be cruel, thoughtless, and just a little too unforgiving for my tastes. And if it really did happen, if you did leave a little boy to die on a raft because he couldn't be like you, because he couldn't be a man, then I'm not sure I want to live with someone like that. Someone with no conscience, no heart or soul. And I'm certain I don't want my daughters around that kind of person."

He realized that she hadn't moved, hadn't changed her position, hadn't even lifted her glass to drink. He wondered if she'd been preparing this speech for a long time. Probably the sentiment had always been there, but the words had needed to be found. And now she had a voice that reduced him to silence.

She paused, and he said, "May I say something?"

"Now it's your turn, Alex." Amazing how her voice barely modulated. She was calm and confident. She'd come into the deep water and taken to it with ease.

He said, "If you're thinking of taking my children from me, it's definitely not going to happen."

"You may not have that choice."

"I'll fight you."

"I know you will. You'd leave us all to drown in the end. Wouldn't you?"

She rose from the chair and walked out of the room. He barely heard the front door opening, but when her Mercedes backed out of the garage, he knew it was over. She must have packed her bags hours before, loaded them into the car, brought them to her parents' place along with Becca and Lyndsey.

She'd even left the front door wide open.

59

ALEX HAD ALWAYS HATED GOING TO BED. WHEN he was a boy, he'd keep the radio on all night just to give himself the sensation of not being alone, although his room was just down the hall from the vast space his parents occupied at the other end of the penthouse, with its own bar, TV, and stereo system, and the king-size bed that, as the years went on, would be replaced by two queens, keeping his father and mother reasonably distanced one from the other, ensconced in their own private world of liquor and late-night television and whatever passed for love between them.

His father, he discovered much later, had been unfaithful to his wife since early in their marriage. He even had a son he'd secretly supported, the product of a liaison with a woman in London, who, now in his late thirties, lived in Switzerland and taught skiing at Davos to forgotten actresses and fallen members of the nobility. When his mother was dying, she had smiled at Alex from her bed in Mount Sinai Hospital and told him how happy she'd been in her life, how much she'd loved her husband and her son, and even then Alex knew she was lying.

Her life had been an ordeal, something she survived thanks to twice-a-day reliance on pills of various colors and strengths, which always left her dreamily detached from a world she detested, floating through her surroundings with a kind of supernatural lightness, abandoning young Alex to his room, where he ate sandwiches off a tray while he watched situation comedies and old Mickey Rooney movies on TV. And when his parents took cruises to Europe or flew off to India for weeks at a time, Alex had only their housekeeper to rely on, a sturdy woman from Georgia named Virginia, who, after she herself had had a few drinks, would often let young Alex play with her heavy bare breasts, watching the boy bounce them on his open palms while she sat on the edge of his bed.

In his memory, the apartment seemed as large and imposing as the house he was in now, alone in his bed as the television played some talk show with guest stars and a band. It didn't matter who was on the screen: they were his company, people in his room making him feel as if a celebration were taking place on the edge of his life. One step in the right direction, and he'd be part of it. He reached for his drink—by now he'd lost count how many had come before it—and saw that it was empty. Too drunk to find his way down the stairs, he sat up, took off everything but his underpants, and inspected the damage to the house.

Ashley had taken most of her clothes from the closet and her dresser, along with her jewelry box, implying that the contents might one day have to be sold, should he leave her bereft. Which was unlikely. She would hire a lawyer to match Kurt Garland, and there was every chance she would end up ahead of the game. He might have to sell the house and move into the Mason House Hotel. Or vacate the house and leave it to Ashley and the girls. One way or another, it wouldn't look good. In the eyes of the public, he'd be damaged goods. It would take years to earn back his status.

The girls' rooms seemed especially empty, in a way they didn't when they went to sleepovers. Their beds were unmade, implying Ashley had roused them from sleep when the first calls and texts came about what had happened in the city. And though they had seen far worse together over the past weeks, though Alex considered the family the victims of someone's idea of payback, what he did to Mark Pearson was humiliating to his name, to his brand, and to his wife and children. Ashley knew what would be on the cover page of tomorrow's tabloids: the ugly side of Alex Mason as he assaulted a competitor in one of Manhattan's most prestigious restaurants.

He returned to bed, watched a few more minutes of television, then fell into a heavy sleep.

When he abruptly woke at seven thirty, the television was still on and the anchor for a morning news show was cutting away to a commercial. A man with a full head of white hair and a benign smile patted his sheepdog as they set out for a walk. The man smiled and nodded to passersby, the older African-American couple on the park bench, the Asian woman doing tai chi, the bearded hipster in his hoodie, his ears full of music.

The voice-over began, "I'm a father, a grandfather, and now, well, yep, about to become a great-grandfather. But I also suffer from type 2 diabetes. So when your doctor has that all-important conversation with you about maintaining..."

Alex didn't hear the rest of it. Because the man in the ad, walking his dog, greeting his neighbors, was Mike Farrelli, the detective in Marty Pollock's interview. Alex sat up and looked closely. He couldn't believe it. It was definitely the same man, the one with the theories about Joey Proctor.

And he read the caption on the bottom of the screen.

Actor Portrayal

60

ALEX REACHED A SERGEANT BANKS AT THE LENOX Police, who informed him that their conversation would be recorded. "I'm calling to ask if you ever had a detective in your department named Mike or Michael Farrelli?"

"This is current, sir? Because the name isn't familiar to me."

"I think he retired some years ago."

"I can check on that for you. Can you hold a minute, please?"

Alex was sitting at the desk in his home office, dressed only in his underpants, a substantial flop of belly overwhelming the waistband. He could feel a sharp throb behind his left eye, which meant he'd be hungover for the rest of the day. While he waited, he checked the websites for New York's tabloids. He'd made the front pages of both, each running a similarly unflattering photo of him lunging at Pearson, his mouth distended, his thinning hair in disarray.

"Sir? According to our files, Detective Farrelli retired from the force fourteen years ago."

"I understand that, but is there a number on file where I can possibly reach him? I'm told he's living somewhere in Florida."

There was a pause. "I'm afraid that Detective Farrelli died just after his retirement."

"Died."

"Yes, sir. Fourteen years ago. Heart attack. Is there anything else I can help you with?"

Died? Yet Marty said he'd spoken to the man only weeks ago and was planning to see him again next month.

"Are you sure of that?" Alex asked.

"Just a moment, sir."

Another voice came on the line. "This is Detective Casey. I understand you're trying to reach Mike Farrelli?"

"Yes, that's right."

"I worked with Detective Farrelli. He was on vacation with his wife in Florida a few weeks after he officially retired. Earlier that day he'd called me, and then later that night Eleanor—his wife—phoned to tell me what had happened. They had been out shopping, and on the way back, he seemed excited about something dealing with the Proctor case, and he'd told her that he just needed to let me know what he'd come up with."

He paused. Alex shut his eyes. *What now*, he thought.

"They got back to their hotel room, they closed the door… And that's when he collapsed."

Alex couldn't grasp what was happening. In the interview with Marty, wasn't Farrelli speaking about something that had happened years earlier after going with his wife to replace a broken suitcase? That he thought Joey's parents might have been involved? Then there was that man in the commercial, the same one in Marty's documentary. And now this. None of it was making any sense to him.

"Do you remember what this Farrelli looked like?"

The detective laughed a little to himself. "Long tall Mike, we used to call him. Skinny and bald before his time." And he laughed again. But the man in Marty's footage was white haired and a little on the stocky side.

Alex took a breath. It was as if his whole world had turned upside down. "Let me ask you one other thing," he said. "There was a man named John Otis who'd been arrested once or twice... This was, I don't know, sixty, maybe seventy years ago?"

He distinctly heard the laughter in the man's voice. The detective said, "That again. Oh boy."

"What is that supposed to mean?"

"The old John Otis legend."

"But I've seen photos of him."

"You may have seen photos, but they weren't of any John Otis that we've ever known about. Not by face, not by name, not even by reputation."

"What are you telling me?"

"There's no John Otis. Never was."

"But didn't he live in a house his father built above Echo Lake? The one that burned down? I mean, I saw the newspaper clippings and the photos and—"

Again the cop laughed before ending the call. "Yeah, and I'm the Tooth Fairy."

He'd been played. Made the fool. The footage Marty had shown him of the father and son hunters, the interviews with Mike Farrelli—it was all fiction. A setup. What Pollock had said came back to him: *I make what you think is real into something completely incredible, just as I make the unbelievable into something you take as the honest truth.*

Alex knew exactly what he had to do. He quickly showered and dressed and drove the Bentley into Manhattan. As it was early on a Saturday morning, the traffic was sparse, and there were plenty of spots on Bleecker Street. He pressed the buzzer for Marty's apartment. There was no response. As a couple was just leaving, they held the door for him.

He remembered that Pollock lived on the nineteenth floor. He knocked on the filmmaker's door. No answer. Then he hammered on it with his fist, until one of the neighbors opened his door across the hall. He wore jeans and an NYU T-shirt and a pair of scuffed moccasins. He carried several days' worth of stubble, salt and pepper, and he wore his hair close to the scalp. A dog began to rush out, and he grabbed it by the collar and patted it until it sat quietly beside him.

He said, "Can I help you with something?"

"I need to see Marty Pollock."

"Marty? He's gone."

"What?"

The man opened his hands. "He left. He's finished here. He only had an adjunct position filling in for a professor on sabbatical, and it ended a few days ago when the other guy returned. We both teach at Tisch. Taught, anyway, for him."

"Did you know him?"

"Sort of. I mean, we were neighbors. You know, hello and goodbye and all the usual forms of address."

"Did he say where he was going?"

"Probably back to Los Angeles."

Alex just looked at him. "You're joking."

"He shipped all his stuff out this past week."

"Do you know his address out there?"

"I don't, actually."

"His phone number...?"

The man shook his head.

"So there's nothing?" Alex pointed at the door.

The man was about to go back into his apartment with his dog. "It's empty. Everything's gone."

There was no John Otis. No Mike Farrelli. And right now there wasn't even a Marty Pollock.

And Alex remembered what Marty had also said over lunch the week before: *Don't you see? You've just become a character in the story.*

61

MARTY HAD BEEN BACK IN LOS ANGELES FOR three days, in the Silver Lake bungalow he'd been occupying ever since he'd left the East Coast four years earlier. His girlfriend had a small role in a movie shooting in Vancouver, playing a wealthy divorcée from South Carolina, and they planned on getting together a week later, when she was done and back in town. The owners of his bungalow, an elderly couple, lived in the main house in front, and he was happy to be there where it was quiet and secluded, where he could work without distraction. Sometimes the couple would ask him to do an errand for them, pick up something at the supermarket, or a prescription at the pharmacy, and because his rent was so reasonable, he was happy to comply.

In the days since he'd been back in LA, he had aired out the house and set up his studio in much the same way as he'd had it in New York. There were trestle tables and a corkboard and his iMac, which he'd had professionally packed and shipped. Now there were two photos above his computer: a selfie he and his girlfriend had taken when she'd come to visit him in New York, smiling, his arm around her in Central Park, and a portrait of Camp Waukeelo's owners and their son taken by a photographer based in Lenox. David and Nancy Jensen sit against a blue background, his hand around his wife's shoulders, while their seven-year-old son sits alongside them, his arms crossed, a big grin on his face. A happy family.

And then a family no more.

The time had come to finish his project. He pulled a plastic DVD case off the shelf. It was labeled: *FINAL SCENE/"THE DROWNING."*

This was where the legend could finally end. This was when it all got real.

He slid the disk into the drive and watched the image fizz onto his monitor: handheld footage, slightly grainy, of Alex and Pete Kellerman by the Masons' pool. It's nighttime, and the person with the camera is just distant enough not to be seen by them. But the scene is perfectly lit by the lamps installed around the area.

Pete gestures and says, *"Okay, okay, yes, all right, whatever you want me to say. I did whatever you think I did, and I'm sorry. Does that make it better?"*

Marty turned up the volume as Alex began to talk.

"You did it all, didn't you? The blood, the name in the room, the photos, the rats, the—"

"Just let me go home, please?"

Alex pats Pete's shoulder. *"Good boy. It's over now, isn't it. It's finally over."*

Though he'd viewed this several times since he'd uploaded it from his camera, Marty had to sit back and admire his work once more. He'd been kind of amazing when he'd done the thing with the pool and then when he'd scared Mason in Brooklyn, and stupendous when he'd gotten into the house and filmed them all asleep. As for the whole business with the doll on the raft, well, he did have to take a bow for that as well. It takes a certain kind of mind to work out the strategies, to plan each moment, to have the nerve to act them out. After all, as he would often tell his students back in New York, making a movie is knowing how to manipulate your audience from fade in to fade out, first image to last.

By now Joey Proctor lived inside Alex's head, this boy who now seemed to have always been there, scratching away at his conscience, creating chaos where there once was certainty in a life filled with beautiful things and expensive properties and all the accountants and attorneys he could ever need to help maintain order.

But Joey isn't really dead: now *he's* the legend they talk about at Camp Waukeelo around campfires on warm August nights. His name is spoken every summer, as it will be for years to come. One day he was there, and the next he wasn't. Joey Proctor now had a story all his own, and as long as it was told, he would still be with the living, forever eight years old.

Marty resumed the video just as Pete fell away from Alex's hand and toppled into the pool, a scene that ends when Alex pulls the body out, wraps it in a tarp, and loads it onto his truck. He drives away, his rear lights swallowed up by distance and dark night. And the camera catches every moment of it.

Marty took a padded mailer he'd bought that morning at the Staples on Santa Monica Boulevard, and with a black Sharpie wrote: *Briarcliff Manor Police Department*. Then he added the address displayed on the department website and slid the DVD case inside the mailer.

And he smiled, revealing the same gap between his front teeth as in the photo on the corkboard: David and Nancy Jensen and their young son, Martin. The parents he'd lost. The father and mother he'd never really come to know, who had fallen into poverty and ruin and suicide, all because a counselor had let a child slip his memory.

It's over now, isn't it, Alex had asked Pete Kellerman before he'd drowned. *It's finally over.*

It is now.

Read on for an excerpt from J. P. Smith's next novel, *If She Were Dead*

THE INTERVIEW HAD BEEN ARRANGED FOR FOUR o'clock, less than an hour away, and the moment she got in the car, she remembered it.

She tightened her lips, said "Oh shit," and drove out of the parking area and onto the highway. She was sorry she hadn't arranged it for the next morning, or even canceled it altogether. She tried to recall the voice on the phone, the way the interviewer asked for directions. She lived in the city, the woman from the newspaper said. "I'll take the highway up."

Amelie had described her home: an old farmhouse set on a rise off the road, the low stone pillars that stood on either side of the entrance, a red mailbox that, like her, had seen better days. She said her car would be in the driveway, a dark-blue Volvo. This was the house she and Richard had taken so much trouble to find, to renovate, to enjoy. She wondered if it needed to be cleaned, if she should haul out the vacuum and run it over the wide pine floors, or if she should give a quick dusting to the tables and lamps, even though the cleaning woman had been there two days earlier. She knew it didn't matter, that no interviewer had ever passed judgment on how she lived, the imagined squalor of her living room.

She turned on the radio and opened the window. A driver

in the next lane turned to look at her. His little mustache rose in a smile, and she looked at him through dark glasses and eased her foot slightly off the accelerator. She watched as he pulled ahead, his head tilting to catch her image in the narrow slit of his rearview mirror. She turned up the volume: a woman was singing in German while an oboe twisted its melody into hers, and it was obviously something by Bach, from a cantata probably, a piece her mother would certainly have been able to identify. She tapped her fingers lightly against the steering wheel, for there was something comforting in the rhythm, the mathematical regularity of the pizzicato behind the woman's yearning voice, as though each beat were a step higher on some celestial staircase.

It was three thirty when she arrived home. Amelie opened the refrigerator and put her finger to her lips. She would have to offer the interviewer something, and because it was warm and they could sit out on the deck under the umbrella, she wondered if she should make a pitcher of instant iced tea. She would have preferred a dry martini herself, but that could wait. The last time she made drinks for an interview, the writer had mentioned in the article her subject's evident lust for alcohol, and both her agent and publicist had called her, gently suggesting she stick to a more neutral beverage in future.

She walked quickly upstairs and changed into a skirt and blouse. She stood before her mirror and pulled a brush through her hair. She put on a different pair of earrings. She took her sandals from the closet and slipped them on. She went into the bathroom and brushed her teeth and then took some mouthwash directly from the bottle and spit it into the sink. She smoothed the covers on her bed and banged at her pillow until it no longer showed the imprint of her head.

She wondered if she would have to give the interviewer a tour of the house, or if when she excused herself to use the toilet, the journalist would bolt up the stairs and take a look for herself, rifling through her medicine cabinet, discovering her vivid-pink vibrator in a drawer by her bed.

On her bedside table were stacked a biography, a novel, and the latest *New Yorker*, as well as a lamp and clock radio. The drawer was slightly open and she nudged it shut. Over the bed was nothing but the shadow of what had once been there, a framed exhibition poster so beloved by her ex-husband that when he left, she insisted he take it with him. She still hadn't found something to replace it. She wondered if it now hung over his and his new wife's bed.

On the dresser stood a framed photograph of her daughter, Nina, taken in September when she'd started college at Wellesley. Her eyes glowed simultaneously with pride and excitement and terror. Behind her were other students with their families, arms around shoulders, scenes of farewell. She and Richard had driven her there together, and she remembered the day as having passed without incident.

Without incident. It was in just those terms that she recalled it, as if she were referring to some zone of mayhem in the Middle East, a place of terror and spiritual malaise, where peace, when it came, shimmered into uneasy stalemate. Afterward, after they'd seen Nina into her room at the college and made small talk with her roommate's parents, after they'd fussed with her and kissed and hugged her, the two of them stopped for lunch at a restaurant in town, instantly ordering drinks, saying nothing of substance for the entire hour, as if, were they to trespass on a subject of depth, small wars or skirmishes might break out.

Since she and Richard had split up, she'd added little to the house. It was difficult enough when her mother had died and she'd emptied her Scarsdale home of china and chipped candy dishes and paintings. They still remained in boxes in Amelie's cellar, and they would stay there for years, decades, centuries; it didn't matter because she would never unpack them to reconstruct the suburban Westchester house in which she had been raised. Every time she descended to the bowels of her home, she would see them jutting out of their chardonnay and merlot boxes, brief reminders of the dead and gone, silent reproaches for her having overlooked them. The pity of it was that none of it represented what her mother had been—once a respected concert pianist, in later years a beloved teacher and lecturer at Juilliard. Nothing that defined her remained: the filing cabinets full of sheet music now long gone, a baby grand Steinway sold a few weeks after her death to a private school in Connecticut.

At rare moments, the thought of her mother's death would return to her in unexpected ways. She thought of the half-light of the landing as her mother walked up the stairs, her knuckles white against the dark wood of the banister as she stopped to catch her breath three steps from the top.

Amelie walked into the living room and looked at her watch and then out the window. Now it was ten past four. She hoped it wouldn't last long. Not that she minded being interviewed; in fact, she adored publicity. It was like being bathed in the glances of others or caught in the intersection of a thousand conversations. She enjoyed being photographed; she liked the *snick* of the camera, the intrusion of the lens into her wistful smile, her blue eyes. She thought ahead three hours, projecting herself into the future, shutting her eyes and trying to see herself at that moment: lifting the phone, pressing the numbers, letting it ring once. Then she would hang up. She would wait. Then she would pick up the phone and try the number again. He would pick it up. This is how it went.

A routine that had so far lasted two years.

Reading Group Guide

1. The story opens with the John Otis urban legend, a campfire story passed down at Camp Waukeelo over generations. Did you grow up with any urban legends? How would you feel if you discovered today that they were real?

2. Describe Joey Proctor. Why do you think he latches on to Steve, his counselor? Did you ever have a role model like that growing up?

3. Why do you think Alex Mason leaves Joey on the raft? Do you think Alex is completely at fault for Joey's disappearance?

4. We jump forward twenty-one years from the opening of the novel and meet Alex as a grown man. What kind of person is he? Do you think he has matured since we last saw him at eighteen?

5. Alex pays for his teenage mistakes in a big way. Do you think it's fair that he is punished for what he did at eighteen? Do you think he feels guilty?

6. Did you ever make a mistake that you somehow got away with? If you could go back in time, what would you do differently? If someone found out today, should you be held accountable?

7. Compare and contrast Joey Proctor and Lyndsey Mason. Do you see any similarities between these two young characters? Why do you think Alex tries to force Lyndsey to swim in the deep end, something he did to Joey years before?

8. Many horrible things happen to Alex and his family over the course of several weeks. Which incident would you find the most terrifying? If you were Ashley, would you stay with Alex during this time? How would you protect yourself?

9. Describe Marty Pollock. Why do you think Alex turns to him for help in the first place? What does Alex learn from Marty?

10. What do you make of Ed Unis? Why do you think Ed never tells anyone what he saw the day Joey Proctor went missing? Why does Alex kill him?

11. Marty blurs the lines between what is real and what is fake in his documentary. Why do you think he does this? What is his end goal? Does he achieve it?

12. At the end of the story, we realize that Joey Proctor has now become his own urban legend—a story passed down over decades. What do you think actually happened to Joey Proctor that day on the raft?

A Conversation with the Author

What inspired you to write *The Drowning*? Did you grow up with any urban legends like the ones told at Camp Waukeelo?

When I was eight years old, I was at a summer camp in upstate New York, and what happened to Joey happened to me. I was left on a raft and told by a counselor that I'd either swim back—though I couldn't swim to save my life and was profoundly afraid of deep water—or stay there and die. Because for a long few minutes I thought I would have to try to swim back, for the first time in my life, I was certain I was going to die. The memory of looking into that water remains with me to this day.

All these many years later, I took it a step further, with an idea that suddenly came to me one summer afternoon: What if the swimming counselor forgot about me, came back hours later, and saw that I wasn't there? Nor was I anywhere else. And then, twenty-one years later, it seemed I'd come back into his life. That thought spurred me to write the novel.

As for urban legends, the first I heard was at my next camp, in the Berkshires, located in Otis, Massachusetts. It was the John Otis legend, as related in the novel.

There are so many twists throughout *The Drowning*. What does your writing process look like when plotting such an intricate novel?

When I write a novel, I almost always begin with a particular character in mind and have only a vague idea of what lies ahead—something that comes into much sharper focus later in the process. The journey to the final pages is what makes up the novel itself.

But I treated *The Drowning* in a very different way: I worked out the ending in advance (as one must, say, with a screenplay) and planned out the twists and turns that led up to it. Once I had that inciting incident—that the counselor had forgotten Joey—the plot unfurled like origami, fold upon fold.

Alex comes across as the golden boy who has it all. What is his biggest flaw?

Pride. And when that is a character's flaw, it can become fatal when someone smart in a wholly different way makes that very flaw the target of his revenge. And let's not forget that powerful people, inebriated by their own real or exaggerated success, are their own worst enemies. Their downfall is built into their personal infrastructure.

Do you think Alex deserves his comeuppance?

I leave that up to the individual reader!

In the end, the mystery surrounding Joey Proctor is still intact and the legend lives on. What do you think happened to Joey that day on the raft?

I think it's best that each reader comes up with the answer that's most satisfactory to him or her. What was more interesting to me was not what happened to him, but the fact that he remains a mystery—part of an urban legend, if you will. I kept it as true to life as possible, because not every mystery can be solved. "That's why Joey now *is* the legend," Marty tells Alex late in the book, "the kid who really did disappear. You can start with John Otis, but you always end up with Joey Proctor, the unseen one."

Which character did you enjoy writing the most?

Alex, of course! (Though Marty runs a close second.)

Which character was the most challenging to write?

Alex. The challenge was to make him simultaneously volatile, self-centered, and yet not completely unsympathetic. Not too much of a prince of the city, but a player nonetheless, with his name and business acumen, not to mention his family integrity, on the line. Complex characters are never one-dimensional, so we feel ambivalent toward him. We sense that he's grown out of the eighteen-year-old who abandoned Joey, but we also discern that the young Alex still resides within the older one.

Like most successful businessmen, he's a man who loves control, and this is key to understanding his character: he needs to know that his business and his private life hum along in predictable ways. And at this stage in his life, at least he's trying.

Then his past catches up with him—one event, more or less forgotten, that upends his entire life.

Though Alex himself is manipulated until he loses the ability to control matters, the reader, too, at some point realizes that the blur between reality and fiction has entered the reading experience so that Alex learns only at the end that this story has now become someone else's narrative. In fact, this is a novel that begins with a story being told around a campfire and ends with a different kind of story in which Alex is the main character. And by then, even he doesn't know what's real and what isn't.

What genre do you most often read? Any authors we should check out?

I rarely read a particular genre on a regular basis. Mostly, I do a great deal of rereading of both fiction and nonfiction and don't turn to a large number of contemporary authors unless I've been following their work for some time. Although up until *The Drowning* my novels have been thought of as literary fiction, they all contain elements of the detective story or the thriller. This is something I learned from being influenced early on by certain French authors who mingle genres, among them the 2014 Nobel laureate in literature, Patrick Modiano, whom I've been reading (and rereading) since the 1970s, and René Belletto.

I'm not alone in thinking that more interesting work is being produced in certain genres than in literary fiction these days. There is still much to do with the thriller and detective story, and I intend to explore these further.

A writer I've been reading with admiration recently is the Northern Irish novelist Eoin McNamee, who breathes new life into true-life murder cases. In *12:23*, he relates in what he calls an "almanac of the dire" a plausible conspiracy leading up to the death of Princess Diana. In his *Blue* trilogy (*Blue Tango*, *Orchid Blue*, *Blue Is the Night*), he deals with three famous murders—with dubious convictions—that took place decades ago in Northern Ireland. What makes his work outstanding is the style; it brings to mind that of Don DeLillo, and McNamee's voice in these haunted and haunting books—novels that on the surface are procedurals, but which have undercurrents that hint at a much more sinister world—strikes me as wholly unique. He has been longlisted for the Man Booker Prize, for which any genre books are rarely nominated.

If you had some advice for aspiring authors, what would it be?

First of all, read, read, read before you ever put your fingers on the keyboard or pick up a pen. Read the classics (including those of the twentieth century) to see how the novel evolved. Try to understand how certain effects can be achieved, how character is built up over an entire novel, how such matters as tension and suspense are handled by writers whose works have lasted for years, decades, even centuries. If you wonder why some novels have endured for so long, there's a good reason for it: they speak to the human condition, and they're compellingly readable.

Don't just read in your chosen genre; by unconsciously absorbing the material, you'll lose whatever originality you've been nurturing. I think the only novel I've read featuring a missing child was Ian McEwan's *The Child in Time*, and that was a long, long time ago.

And then persevere, persevere, persevere. Write one book, then another and another. Iris Murdoch once said that the day after she sends off her latest novel, she begins another. There's no lingering over the fate of what you'd just completed. You keep moving ahead and think only of what's to come.

I had to write twelve novels before my first was published. (I also had to move to England, but that's another story.) While for those first twelve I spent the better part of a year writing each of them, my thirteenth was written in a quick five weeks. That did the trick. I sent it to my agent in London, and two weeks later, I was signing a contract in a Mayfair publisher's office.

Rejection is part of the writing life. It's not easy, and it's certainly not pleasant, but even the most seasoned authors are rejected at times. Some of Vladimir Nabokov's short stories were declined by the *New Yorker* long after his reputation was solidified.

Writing is solitary, not collaborative, work. If you're keen on taking a writing course, be careful that you don't end up trying to please the instructor, whether she's a published author with glowing reviews and healthy sales, or a professor who's seen a handful of short stories into print. If you belong to a writers' group, be watchful that your work doesn't become diluted with the opinions of others. The first and last person you must please is yourself—your best audience. Write what you love to read, what you're drawn to at a bookstore, not what you think others might want.

Finally, as my late mentor once told me early on: "One day you'll fall to your knees and thank the powers that be that those early works were never published." Man, was he right.

About the Author

J. P. Smith was born in New York City and began his writing career in England, where he lived for several years with his wife and daughter and where his first novel was published. As a screenwriter, he was an Academy Nicholl Fellowship semifinalist in 2014. He currently lives on the North Shore of Massachusetts. *The Drowning* is his seventh novel.

He still doesn't go near deep water.